Praise for
#1 *New York Times* and *USA TODAY* bestselling author

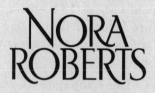

NORA ROBERTS

"The publishing world might be hard-pressed to find an author
with a more diverse style or fertile imagination than Roberts."
—*Publishers Weekly*

"Nora Roberts is among the best."
—*The Washington Post Book World*

"With clear-eyed, concise vision and a sure pen,
Roberts nails her characters and settings with awesome precision,
drawing readers into a vividly rendered world of
family-centered warmth and unquestionable magic."
—*Library Journal*

"Roberts has a warm feel for her characters
and an eye for the evocative detail."
—*Chicago Tribune*

"Romance will never die as long as
the megaselling Roberts keeps writing it."
—*Kirkus Reviews*

"A superb author...Ms. Roberts is an enormously gifted writer
whose incredible range and intensity guarantee
the very best of reading."
—*Rave Reviews*

"Roberts' bestselling novels are some of the best in the romance
genre. They are thoughtfully plotted, well-written stories
featuring fascinating characters."
—*USA TODAY*

Dear Reader,

It is indeed true that home is where the heart is—and sometimes it is more of a who than a where. In these two classic romances, the incomparable Nora Roberts tells the tale of four people who find home where they didn't think to look, and with someone they didn't want to love....

In "Island of Flowers," Laine Simmons has traveled halfway across the world to reconcile with her long-estranged father—and she isn't about to explain herself to his arrogant, judgmental and *very* handsome business partner! Yet from their first infuriating confrontation, Dillon O'Brian causes something magical to stir within Laine. As she works hard to deal with her past, Laine begins to wonder if she's ready yet to embrace her future...in the arms of a very special man.

In "Less of a Stranger," Megan Miller is outraged when the colossally arrogant David Katcherton offers to buy Joyland Amusement Park from her grandfather. Joyland has been her grandfather's entire life—and Megan's, too, since putting her own dreams on hold. So she isn't about to let David get his way without a fight...because it seems the park isn't all he's after!

Where we find home can change throughout our lives, but what it evokes—our need for the feelings of love, comfort and happiness, and someone to share it all with—never goes away!

The Editors

Silhouette Books

NORA ROBERTS

And Then There Was You

Silhouette Books

Published by Silhouette Books
America's Publisher of Contemporary Romance

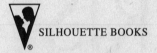 SILHOUETTE BOOKS

Recycling programs for this product may not exist in your area.

AND THEN THERE WAS YOU

ISBN-13: 978-0-373-28593-8

Copyright © 2010 by Harlequin Books S.A.

The publisher acknowledges the copyright holder of the individual works as follows:

ISLAND OF FLOWERS
Copyright © 1982 by Nora Roberts

LESS OF A STRANGER
Copyright © 1984 by Nora Roberts

Printed in U.S.A.

CONTENTS

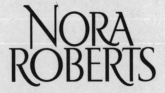

Island of Flowers

For my mother and father

chapter one

Laine's arrival at Honolulu International Airport was traditional. She would have preferred to melt through the crowd, but it appeared traveling tourist class categorized her as just that. Golden-skinned girls with ivory smiles and vivid sarongs bestowed brilliant colored leis. Accepting both kiss and floral necklace, Laine wove through the milling crowd and searched for an information desk. The girth of a fellow passenger hampered her journey. His yellow and orange flowered shirt and the twin cameras which joined the lei around his neck attested to his determination to enjoy his vacation. Under different circumstances, his appearance would have nudged at her humor, but the tension in Laine's stomach stifled any amusement. She had not stood on American soil in fifteen years. The ripe land with cliffs and beaches which she had seen as the plane descended brought no sense of homecoming.

The America Laine pictured came in sporadic patches of memory and through the perspective of a child of seven. America was a gnarled elm tree guarding her bedroom window. It was a spread of green grass where buttercups scattered gold. It was a mailbox at the end of a long, winding lane. But most of all, America was the man who had taken her to imaginary African jungles and desert islands. However, there were orchids instead of daisies. The graceful palms and spreading ferns of Honolulu were as foreign to Laine as the father she had traveled half the world to find. It seemed a lifetime ago that divorce had pulled her away from her roots.

Laine felt a quiet desperation that the address she had found among her mother's papers would lead to emptiness. The age of the small, creased piece of paper was unknown to her. Neither did she know if Captain James Simmons still lived on the island of Kauai. There had only been the address tossed in among her mother's bills. There had been no correspondence, nothing to indicate the address was still a vital one. To write to her father was the practical thing to do, and Laine had struggled with indecision for nearly a week. Ultimately, she had rejected a letter in favor of a personal meeting. Her hoard of money would barely see her through a week of food and lodging, and though she knew the trip was impetuous, she had not been able to prevent herself. Threading through her doubts was the shimmering strand of fear that rejection waited for her at the end of her journey.

There was no reason to expect anything else, she lectured herself. *Why should the man who had left her fatherless during her growing-up years care about the woman she had become?* Relaxing the grip on the handle of her handbag, Laine reasserted her vow to accept whatever waited at her journey's end. She had learned long ago to adjust to whatever life offered. She concealed her feelings with the habit developed during her adolescence.

Quickly, she adjusted the white, soft-brimmed hat over a halo of flaxen curls. She lifted her chin. No one would have guessed her underlying anxiety as she moved with unconscious grace through the crowds. She looked elegantly aloof in her inherited traveling suit of ice blue silk, altered to fit her slight figure rather than her mother's ample curves.

The girl at the information desk was deep in an enjoyable conversation with a man. Standing to one side, Laine watched the encounter with detached interest. The man was dark and intimidatingly tall. Her pupils would undoubtedly have called him *séduisant*. His rugged features were surrounded by black hair in curling disorder, while his bronzed skin proved him no stranger to the Hawaiian sun. There was something rakish in his profile, some basic sensuality which Laine recognized but did not fully comprehend. She thought perhaps his nose had been broken at one time, but rather than spoiling the appeal of the profile, the lack of symmetry added to it. His dress was casual, the jeans well worn and frayed at the cuffs, and a denim work shirt exposed a hard chest and corded arms.

Vaguely irritated, Laine studied him. She observed the easy flow of charm, the indolent stance at the counter, the tease of a smile on his mouth. *I've seen his type before,* she thought with a surge of resentment, *hovering around Vanessa like a crow around carrion.* She remembered, too, that when her mother's beauty had become only a shadow, the flock had left for younger prey. At that moment, Laine could feel only gratitude that her contacts with men had been limited.

He turned and encountered Laine's stare. One dark brow rose as he lingered over his survey of her. She was too unreasonably angry with him to look away. The simplicity of her suit shouted its exclusiveness, revealing the tender elegance of young curves. The hat half shaded a fragile, faintly aristocratic face with well-defined planes, straight nose, unsmiling mouth and morning-sky eyes. Her lashes were thick and gold, and he took them as too long for authenticity. He assessed her as a cool, self-possessed woman, recognizing only the borrowed varnish.

Slowly, and with deliberate insolence, he smiled. Laine kept her gaze steady and struggled to defeat a blush. The clerk, seeing her companion's transfer of attention, shifted her eyes in Laine's direction and banished a scowl.

"May I help you?" Dutifully, she affixed her occupational smile. Ignoring the hovering male, Laine stepped up to the counter.

"Thank you. I need transportation to Kauai. Could you tell me how to arrange it?" A whisper of France lingered in her voice.

"Of course, there's a charter leaving for Kauai in…" The clerk glanced at her watch and smiled again. "Twenty minutes."

"I'm leaving right now." Laine glanced over and gave the loitering man a brief stare. She noted that his eyes were as green as Chinese jade. "No use hanging around the airport, and," he continued as his smile became a grin, "my Cub's not as crowded or expensive as the charter."

Laine's disdainful lift of brow and dismissing survey had

been successful before, but did not work this time. "Do you have a plane?" she asked coldly.

"Yeah, I've got a plane." His hands were thrust in his pockets, and in his slouch against the counter, he still managed to tower over her. "I can always use the loose change from picking up island hoppers."

"Dillon," the clerk began, but he interrupted her with another grin and a jerk of his head.

"Rose'll vouch for me. I run for Canyon Airlines on Kauai." He presented Rose with a wide smile. She shuffled papers.

"Dillon…Mr. O'Brian is a fine pilot." Rose cleared her throat and sent Dillon a telling glance. "If you'd rather not wait for the scheduled charter, I can guarantee that your flight will be equally enjoyable with him."

Studying his irreverent smile and amused eyes, Laine was of the opinion that the trip would be something less than enjoyable. However, her funds were low and she knew she must conserve what she had.

"Very well, Mr. O'Brian, I will engage your services." He held out his hand, palm up, and Laine dropped her eyes to it. Infuriated by his rudeness, she brought her eyes back to his. "If you will tell me your rate, Mr. O'Brian, I shall be happy to pay you when we land."

"Your baggage check," he countered, smiling. "Just part of the service, lady."

Bending her head to conceal her blush, Laine fumbled through her purse for the ticket.

"O.K., let's go." He took both the stub and her arm, propelling her away as he called over his shoulder in farewell to the information clerk, "See you next time, Rose."

"Welcome to Hawaii," Rose stated out of habit, then, with a sigh, pouted after Dillon's back.

Unused to being so firmly guided, and hampered by a stride a fraction of his, Laine struggled to maintain her composure while she trotted beside him. "Mr. O'Brian, I hope I don't have to jog to Kauai." He stopped and grinned at her. She tried, and failed, not to pant. His grin, she discovered, was a strange and powerful weapon, and one for which she had not yet developed a defense.

"Thought you were in a hurry, Miss…" He glanced at her ticket, and she watched the grin vanish. When his eyes lifted, all remnants of humor had fled. His mouth was grim. She would have retreated from the waves of hostility had not his grip on her arm prevented her. "Laine Simmons?" It was more accusation than question.

"Yes, you've read it correctly," she said.

Dillon's eyes narrowed. She found her cool façade melting with disconcerting speed. "You're going to see James Simmons?"

Her eyes widened. For an instant, a flash of hope flickered on her face. But his expression remained set and hostile. She smothered the impulse to ask hundreds of questions as she felt his tightening fingers bruise her arm.

"I don't know how that concerns you, Mr. O'Brian," she began, "but yes. Do you know my father?" She faltered over the final word, finding the novelty of its use bittersweet.

"Yes, I know him…a great deal better than you do. Well,

Duchess—" he released her as if the contact was offensive "—I doubt if fifteen years late is better than never, but we'll see. Canyon Airlines is at your disposal." He inclined his head and gave Laine a half bow. "The trip's on the house. I can hardly charge the owner's prodigal daughter." Dillon retrieved her luggage and stalked from the terminal in thunderous silence. In the wake of the storm, Laine followed, stunned by his hostility and by his information.

Her father owned an airline. She remembered James Simmons only as a pilot, with the dream of his own planes a distant fantasy. When had the dream become reality? Why did this man, who was currently tossing her mother's elegant luggage like so many duffel bags into a small, streamlined plane, turn such hostility on her at the discovery of her name? How did he know fifteen years had spanned her separation from her father? She opened her mouth to question Dillon as he rounded the nose of the plane. She shut it again as he turned and captured her with his angry stare.

"Up you go, Duchess. We've got twenty-eight minutes to endure each other's company." His hands went to her waist, and he hoisted her as if she were no more burden than a feather pillow. He eased his long frame into the seat beside her. She became uncomfortably aware of his virility and attempted to ignore him by giving intense concentration to the buckling of her safety belt. Beneath her lashes, she watched as he flicked at the controls before the engine roared to life.

The sea opened beneath them. Beaches lay white against its verge, dotted with sun worshipers. Mountains rose, jagged and primitive, the eternal rulers of the islands. As they gained height, the colors in the scene below became so intense that they seemed artificial. Soon the shades blended. Browns, greens and blues softened with distance. Flashes of scarlet and yellow merged before fading. The plane soared with a surge of power, then its wings tilted as it made a curving arch and hurtled into the sky.

"Kauai is a natural paradise," Dillon began in the tone of a tour guide. He leaned back in his seat and lit a cigarette. "It offers, on the North Shore, the Wailua River which ends at Fern Grotto. The foliage is exceptional. There are miles of beaches, fields of cane and pineapple. Opeakea Falls, Hanalei Bay and Na Pali Coast are also worth seeing. On the South Shore," he continued, while Laine adopted the air of attentive listener, "we have Kokie State Park and Waimea Canyon. There are tropical trees and flowers at Olopia and Mene-hune Gardens. Water sports are exceptional almost anywhere around the island. Why the devil did you come?"

The question, so abrupt on the tail of his mechanical re-cital, caused Laine to jolt in her seat and stare. "To...to see my father."

"Took your own sweet time about it," Dillon muttered and drew hard on his cigarette. He turned again and gave her a slow, intimate survey. "I guess you were pretty busy attending that elegant finishing school."

Laine frowned, thinking of the boarding school which had been both home and refuge for nearly fifteen years. She decided Dillon O'Brian was crazed. There was no use con-tradicting a lunatic. "I'm glad you approve," she returned coolly. "A pity you missed the experience. It's amazing what can be done with rough edges."

"No thanks, Duchess." He blew out a stream of smoke. "I prefer a bit of honest crudeness."

"You appear to have an adequate supply."

"I get by. Island life can be a bit uncivilized at times." His smile was thin. "I doubt if it's going to suit your tastes."

"I can be very adaptable, Mr. O'Brian." She moved her shoulders with gentle elegance. "I can also overlook a certain amount of discourtesy for short periods of time. Twenty-eight minutes is just under my limit."

"Terrific. Tell me, Miss Simmons," he continued with exaggerated respect, "how is life on the Continent?"

"Marvelous." Deliberately, she tilted her head and looked at him from under the brim of her hat. "The French are so cosmopolitan, so urbane. One feels so…" Attempting to copy her mother's easy polish, she gestured and gave the next word the French expression. "*Chez soi* with people of one's own inclinations."

"Very true." The tone was ironic. Dillon kept his eyes on the open sky as he spoke. "I doubt if you'll find many people of your own inclinations on Kauai."

"Perhaps not." Laine pushed the thought of her father aside and tossed her head. "Then again, I may find the island as agreeable as I find Paris."

"I'm sure you found the men agreeable." Dillon crushed out his cigarette with one quick thrust. Laine found his fresh anger rewarding. The memory of the pitifully few men with whom she had had close contact caused her to force back a laugh. Only a small smile escaped.

"The men of my acquaintance——" she apologized mentally to elderly Father Rennier "——are men of elegance and culture and breeding. They are men of high intellect and discerning tastes who possess the manners and sensitivity which I currently find lacking in their American counterparts."

"Is that so?" Dillon questioned softly.

"That, Mr. O'Brian," said Laine firmly, "is quite so."

"Well, we wouldn't want to spoil our record." Switching over to automatic pilot, he turned in his seat and captured her. Mouth bruised mouth before she realized his intent.

She was locked in his arms, her struggles prevented by his strength and by her own dazed senses. She was overwhelmed by the scent and taste and feel of him. He increased the intimacy, parting her lips with his tongue. To escape from sensations more acute than she had thought possible, she clutched at his shirt.

Dillon lifted his face, and his brows drew straight at her look of stunned, young vulnerability. She could only stare, her eyes filled with confused new knowledge. Pulling away, he switched back to manual control and gave his attention to the sky. "It seems your French lovers haven't prepared you for American technique."

Stung, and furious with the weakness she had just discovered, Laine turned in her seat and faced him. "Your technique, Mr. O'Brian, is as crude as the rest of you."

He grinned and shrugged. "Be grateful, Duchess, that I

didn't simply shove you out the door. I've been fighting the inclination for twenty minutes."

"You would be wise to suppress such inclinations," Laine snapped, feeling her temper bubbling at an alarming speed. *I will not lose it,* she told herself. She would not give this detestable man the satisfaction of seeing how thoroughly he had unnerved her.

The plane dipped into an abrupt nosedive. The sea hurtled toward them at a terrifying rate as the small steel bird performed a series of somersaults. The sky and sea were a mass of interchangeable blues with the white of clouds and the white of breakers no longer separate. Laine clutched at her seat, squeezing her eyes shut as the sea and sky whirled in her brain. Protest was impossible. She had lost both her voice and her heart at the first circle. She clung and prayed for her stomach to remain stationary. The plane leveled, then cruised right side up, but inside her head the world still revolved. Laine heard her companion laugh wholeheartedly.

"You can open your eyes now, Miss Simmons. We'll be landing in a minute."

Turning to him, Laine erupted with a long, detailed analysis of his character. At length, she realized she was stating her opinion in French. She took a deep breath. "You, Mr. O'Brian," she finished in frigid English, "are the most detestable man I have ever met."

"Thank you, Duchess." Pleased, he began to hum.

Laine forced herself to keep her eyes open as Dillon began his descent. There was a brief impression of greens and browns melding with blue, and again the swift rise of mountains be-

fore they were bouncing on asphalt and gliding to a stop.
Dazed, she surveyed the hangars and lines of aircraft, Piper
Cubs and cabin planes, twin engines and passenger jets. *There's
some mistake,* she thought. *This cannot belong to my father.*

"Don't get any ideas, Duchess," Dillon remarked, noting
her astonished stare. His mouth tightened. "You've forfeited
your share. And even if the captain was inclined to be generous, his partner would make things very difficult. You're
going to have to look someplace else for an easy ride."

He jumped to the ground as Laine stared at him with disbelief. Disengaging her belt, she prepared to lower herself to
the ground. His hands gripped her waist before her feet made
contact. For a moment, he held her suspended. With their
faces only inches apart, Laine found his eyes her jailer. She
had never known eyes so green or so compelling.

"Watch your step," he commanded, then dropped her to
the ground.

Laine stepped back, retreating from the hostility in his
voice. Gathering her courage, she lifted her chin and held
her ground. "Mr. O'Brian, would you please tell me where
I might find my father?"

He stared for a moment, and she thought he would simply
refuse and leave her. Abruptly, he gestured toward a small
white building. "His office is in there," he barked before he
turned to stride away.

chapter two

The building which Laine approached was a midsize hut. Fanning palms and flaming anthurium skirted its entrance. Hands trembling, Laine entered. She felt as though her knees might dissolve under her, as though the pounding of her heart would burst through her head. What would she say to the man who had left her floundering in loneliness for fifteen years? What words were there to bridge the gap and express the need which had never died? Would she need to ask questions, or could she forget the whys and just accept?

Laine's image of James Simmons was as clear and vivid as yesterday. It was not dimmed by the shadows of time. *He would be older,* she reminded herself. *She was older as well.* She was not a child trailing after an idol, but a woman meeting her father. They were neither one the same as they had been. Perhaps that in itself would be an advantage.

The outer room of the hut was deserted. Laine had a vague impression of wicker furnishings and woven mats. She stared around her, feeling alone and unsure. Like a ghost of the past, his voice reached out, booming through an open doorway.

Approaching the sound, Laine watched as her father talked on the phone at his desk.

She could see the alterations which age had made on his face, but her memory had been accurate. The sun had darkened his skin and laid its lines upon it, but his features were no stranger to her. His thick brows were gray now, but still prominent over his brown eyes. The nose was still strong and straight over the long, thin mouth. His hair remained full, though as gray as his brows, and she watched as he reached up in a well-remembered gesture and tugged his fingers through it.

She pressed her lips together as he replaced the receiver, then swallowing, Laine spoke in soft memory. "Hello, Cap."

He twisted his head, and she watched surprise flood his face. His eyes ran a quick gamut of emotions, and somewhere between the beginning and the end she saw the pain. He stood, and she noted with a small sense of shock that he was shorter than her child's perspective had made him.

"Laine?" The question was hesitant, colored by a reserve which crushed her impulse to rush toward him. She sensed immediately that his arms would not be open to receive her, and this rejection threatened to destroy her tentative smile.

"It's good to see you." Hating the inanity, she stepped into the room and held out her hand.

After a moment, he accepted it. He held her hand briefly, then released it. "You've grown up." His survey was slow, his smile touching only his mouth. "You've the look of your mother. No more pigtails?"

The smile illuminated her face with such swift impact, her father's expression warmed. "Not for some time. There was no one to pull them." Reserve settled over him again. Feeling the chill, Laine fumbled for some new line of conversation. "You've got your airport; you must be very happy. I'd like to see more of it."

"We'll arrange it." His tone was polite and impersonal, whipping across her face like the sting of a lash.

Laine wandered to a window and stared out through a mist of tears. "It's very impressive."

"Thank you, we're pretty proud of it." He cleared his throat and studied her back. "How long will you be in Hawaii?"

She gripped the windowsill and tried to match his tone. Even at their worst, her fears had not prepared her for this degree of pain. "A few weeks perhaps, I have no definite plans. I came…I came straight here." Turning, Laine began to fill the void with chatter. "I'm sure there are things I should see since I'm here. The pilot who flew me over said Kauai was beautiful, gardens and…" She tried and failed to remember the specifics of Dillon's speech. "And parks." She settled on a generality, keeping her smile fixed. "Perhaps you could recommend a hotel?"

He was searching her face, and Laine struggled to keep her smile from dissolving. "You're welcome to stay with me while you're here."

Burying her pride, she agreed. She knew she could not afford to stay anywhere else. "That's kind of you. I should like that."

He nodded and shuffled some papers on his desk. "How's your mother?"

"She died," Laine murmured. "Three months ago."

Cap glanced up sharply. Laine watched the pain flicker over his face. He sat down. "I'm sorry, Laine. Was she ill?"

"There was…" She swallowed. "There was a car accident."

"I see." He cleared his throat, and his tone was again impersonal. "If you had written, I would have flown over and helped you."

"Would you?" She shook her head and turned back to the window. She remembered the panic, the numbness, the mountain of debts, the auction of every valuable. "I managed well enough."

"Laine, why did you come?" Though his voice had softened, he remained behind the barrier of his desk.

"To see my father." Her words were devoid of emotion.

"Cap." At the voice Laine turned, watching as Dillon's form filled the doorway. His glance scanned her before returning to Cap. "Chambers is leaving for the mainland. He wants to see you before he takes off."

"All right. Laine," Cap turned and gestured awkwardly, "this is Dillon O'Brian, my partner. Dillon, this is my daughter."

"We've met." Dillon smiled briefly.

Laine managed a nod. "Yes, Mr. O'Brian was kind enough to fly me from Oahu. It was a most…fascinating journey."

"That's fine then." Cap moved to Dillon and clasped a

hand to his shoulder. "Run Laine to the house, will you, and see she settles in? I'm sure she must be tired."

Laine watched, excluded from the mystery of masculine understanding as looks were exchanged. Dillon nodded. "My pleasure."

"I'll be home in a couple of hours." Cap turned and regarded Laine in awkward silence.

"All right." Her smile was beginning to hurt her cheeks, so Laine let it die. "Thank you." Cap hesitated, then walked through the door leaving her staring at emptiness. *I will not cry,* she ordered herself. *Not in front of this man.* If she had nothing else left, she had her pride.

"Whenever you're ready, Miss Simmons."

Brushing past Dillon, Laine glanced back over her shoulder. "I hope you drive a car with more discretion than you fly a plane, Mr. O'Brian."

He gave an enigmatic shrug. "Why don't we find out?"

Her bags were sitting outside. She glanced down at them, then up at Dillon. "You seem to have anticipated me."

"I had hoped," he began as he tossed the bags into the rear of a sleek compact, "to pack both them and you back to where you came from, but that is obviously impossible now." He opened his door, slid into the driver's seat and started the engine. Laine slipped in beside him, unaided. Releasing the brake, he shot forward with a speed which jerked her against the cushions.

"What did you say to him?" Dillon demanded, not bothering with preliminaries as he maneuvered skillfully through the airport traffic.

"Being my father's business partner does not entitle you to an account of his personal conversations with me," Laine answered. Her voice was clipped and resentful.

"Listen, Duchess, I'm not about to stand by while you drop into Cap's life and stir up trouble. I didn't like the way he looked when I walked in on you. I gave you ten minutes, and you managed to hurt him. Don't make me stop the car and persuade you to tell me." He paused and lowered his voice. "You'd find my methods unrefined." The threat vibrated in his softly spoken words.

Suddenly Laine found herself too tired to argue. Nights with only patches of sleep, days crowded with pressures and anxiety, and the long, tedious journey had taken their toll. With a weary gesture, she pulled off her hat. Resting her head against the seat, she closed her eyes. "Mr. O'Brian, it was not my intention to hurt my father. In the ten minutes you allowed, we said remarkably little. Perhaps it was the news that my mother had died which upset him, but that is something he would have learned eventually at any rate." Her tone was hollow, and he glanced at her, surprised by the sudden frailty of her unframed face. Her hair was soft and pale against her ivory skin. For the first time, he saw the smudges of mauve haunting her eyes.

"How long ago?"

Laine opened her eyes in confusion as she detected a whisper of sympathy in his voice. "Three months." She sighed and turned to face Dillon more directly. "She ran her car into a telephone pole. They tell me she died instantly." *And painlessly,* she added to herself, *anesthetized with several quarts of vintage champagne.*

Dillon lapsed into silence, and she was grateful that he ignored the need for any trite words of sympathy. She had had enough of those already and found his silence more comforting. She studied his profile, the bronzed chiseled lines and unyielding mouth, before she turned her attention back to the scenery.

The scent of the Pacific lingered in the air. The water was a sparkling blue against the crystal beaches. Screw pines rose from the sand and accepted the lazy breeze, and monkeypods, wide and domelike, spread their shade in invitation. As they drove inland, Laine caught only brief glimpses of the sea. The landscape was a myriad of colors against a rich velvet green. Sun fell in waves of light, offering its warmth so that flowers did not strain to it, but rather basked lazily in its glory.

Dillon turned up a drive which was flanked by two sturdy palms. As they approached the house, Laine felt the first stir of pleasure. It was simple, its lines basic and clean, its walls cool and white. It stood two stories square, sturdy despite its large expanses of glass. Watching the windows wink in the sun, Laine felt her first welcoming.

"It's lovely."

"Not as fancy as you might have expected," Dillon countered as he halted at the end of the drive, "but Cap likes it." The brief truce was obviously at an end. He eased from the car and gave his attention to her luggage.

Without comment, Laine opened her door and slipped out. Shading her eyes from the sun, she stood for a moment and studied her father's home. A set of stairs led to a circling porch. Dillon climbed them, nudged the front door open and strode into the house. Laine entered unescorted.

"Close my door; flies are not welcome."

Laine glanced up and saw, with stunned admiration, an enormous woman step as lightly down the staircase as a young girl. Her girth was wrapped in a colorful, flowing muumuu. Her glossy black hair was pulled tight and secured at the back of her head. Her skin was unlined, the color of dark honey. Her eyes were jet, set deep and widely spaced. Her age might have been anywhere from thirty to sixty. The image of an island priestess, she took a long, uninhibited survey of Laine when she reached the foot of the stairs.

"Who is this?" she asked Dillon as she folded her thick arms over a tumbling bosom.

"This is Cap's daughter." Setting down the bags, he leaned on the banister and watched the exchange.

"Cap Simmons's daughter." Her mouth pursed and her eyes narrowed. "Pretty thing, but too pale and skinny. Don't you eat?" She circled Laine's arm between her thumb and forefinger.

"Why, yes, I…"

"Not enough," she interrupted and fingered a sunlit curl with interest. "Mmm, very nice, very pretty. Why do you wear it so short?"

"I…"

"You should have come years ago, but you are here now." Nodding, she patted Laine's cheek. "You are tired. I will fix your room."

"Thank you. I..."

"Then you eat," she ordered, and hefted Laine's two cases up the stairs.

"That was Miri," Dillon volunteered and tucked his hands in his pockets. "She runs the house."

"Yes, I see." Unable to prevent herself, Laine lifted her hand to her hair and wondered over the length. "Shouldn't you have taken the bags up for her?"

"Miri could carry me up the stairs without breaking stride. Besides, I know better than to interfere with what she considers her duties. Come on." He grabbed her arm and pulled her down the hall. "I'll fix you a drink."

With casual familiarity, Dillon moved to a double-doored cabinet. Laine flexed her arm and surveyed the cream-walled room. Simplicity reigned here as its outer shell had indicated, and she appreciated Miri's obvious diligence with polish and broom. There was, she noted with a sigh, no room for a woman here. The furnishings shouted with masculinity, a masculinity which was well established and comfortable in its solitary state.

"What'll you have?" Dillon's question brought Laine back from her musings. She shook her head and dropped her hat on a small table. It looked frivolous and totally out of place.

"Nothing, thank you."

"Suit yourself." He poured a measure of liquor into a glass and dropped down on a chair. "We're not given to formalities around here, Duchess. While you're in residence, you'll have to cope with a more basic form of existence."

She inclined her head, laying her purse beside her hat. "Perhaps one may still wash one's hands before dinner?"

"Sure," he returned, ignoring the sarcasm. "We're big on water."

"And where, Mr. O'Brian, do you live?"

"Here." He stretched his legs and gave a satisfied smile at her frown. "For a week or two. I'm having some repairs done to my house."

"How unfortunate," Laine commented and wandered the room. "For both of us."

"You'll survive, Duchess." He toasted her with his glass. "I'm sure you've had plenty of experience in surviving."

"Yes, I have, Mr. O'Brian, but I have a feeling you know nothing about it."

"You've got guts, lady, I'll give you that." He tossed back his drink and scowled as she turned to face him.

"Your opinion is duly noted and filed."

"Did you come for more money? Is it possible you're that greedy?" He rose in one smooth motion and crossed the room, grabbing her shoulders before she could back away from his mercurial temper. "Haven't you squeezed enough out of him? Never giving anything in return. Never even disturbing yourself to answer one of his letters. Letting the years pile up without any acknowledgment. What the devil do you want from him now?"

Dillon stopped abruptly. The color had drained from her face, leaving it like white marble. Her eyes were dazed with shock. She swayed as though her joints had melted, and he held her upright, staring at her in sudden confusion. "What's the matter with you?"

"I…Mr. O'Brian, I think I would like that drink now, if you don't mind."

His frown deepened, and he led her to a chair before moving off to pour her a drink. Laine accepted with a murmured thanks, then shuddered at the unfamiliar burn of brandy. The room steadied, and she felt the mists clearing.

"Mr. O'Brian, I…am I to understand…" She stopped and shut her eyes a moment. "Are you saying my father wrote to me?"

"You know very well he did." The retort was both swift and annoyed. "He came to the islands right after you and your mother left him, and he wrote you regularly until five years ago when he gave up. He still sent money," Dillon added, flicking on his lighter. "Oh yes, the money kept right on coming until you turned twenty-one last year."

"You're lying!"

Dillon looked over in astonishment as she rose from her chair. Her cheeks were flaming, her eyes flashing. "Well, well, it appears the ice maiden has melted." He blew out a stream of smoke and spoke mildly. "I never lie, Duchess. I find the truth more interesting."

"He never wrote to me. Never!" She walked to where Dillon sat. "Not once in all those years. All the letters I sent came back because he had moved away without even telling me where."

Slowly, Dillon crushed out his cigarette and rose to face her. "Do you expect me to buy that? You're selling to the wrong person, Miss Simmons. I saw the letters Cap sent, *and* the checks every month." He ran a finger down the lapel of her suit. "You seem to have put them to good use."

"I tell you I never received any letters." Laine knocked his hand away and tilted her head back to meet his eyes. "I have not had one word from my father since I was seven years old."

"Miss Simmons, I mailed more than one letter myself, though I was tempted to chuck them into the Pacific. Presents, too; dolls in the early years. You must have quite a collection of porcelain dolls. Then there was the jewelry. I remember the eighteenth birthday present very clearly. Opal earrings shaped like flowers."

"Earrings," Laine whispered. Feeling the room tilt again, she dug her teeth into her lip and shook her head.

"That's right." His voice was rough as he moved to pour himself another drink. "And they all went to the same place: 17 rue de la Concorde, Paris."

Her color ebbed again, and she lifted a hand to her temple. "My mother's address," she murmured, and turned away to sit before her legs gave way. "I was in school; my mother lived there."

"Yes." Dillon took a quick sip and settled on the sofa again. "Your education was both lengthy and expensive."

Laine thought for a moment of the boarding school with its plain, wholesome food, cotton sheets and leaking roof. She pressed her fingers to her eyes. "I was not aware that my father was paying for my schooling."

"Just who did you think was paying for your French pinafores and art lessons?"

She sighed, stung by the sharpness of his tone. Her hands fluttered briefly before she dropped them into her lap. "Vanessa…my mother said she had an income. I never questioned her. She must have kept my father's letters from me."

Laine's voice was dull, and Dillon moved with sudden impatience. "Is that the tune you're going to play to Cap? You make it very convincing."

"No, Mr. O'Brian. It hardly matters at this point, does it? In any case, I doubt that he would believe me any more than you do. I will keep my visit brief, then return to France." She lifted her brandy and stared into the amber liquid, wondering if it was responsible for her numbness. "I would like a week or two. I would appreciate it if you would not mention this discussion to my father; it would only complicate matters."

Dillon gave a short laugh and sipped from his drink. "I have no intention of telling him any part of this little fairy tale."

"Your word, Mr. O'Brian." Surprised by the anxiety in her voice, Dillon glanced up. "I want your word." She met his eyes without wavering.

"My word, Miss Simmons," he agreed at length.

Nodding, she rose and lifted her hat and bag from the table. "I would like to go up to my room now. I'm very tired."

He was frowning into his drink. Laine, without a backward glance, walked to her room.

chapter three

Laine faced the woman in the mirror. She saw a pale face, dominated by wide, shadowed eyes. Reaching for her rouge, she placed borrowed color in her cheeks.

She had known her mother's faults: the egotism, the shallowness. As a child, it had been easy to overlook the flaws and prize the sporadic, exciting visits with the vibrant, fairy-tale woman. Ice-cream parfaits and party dresses were such a contrast to home-spun uniforms and porridge. As Laine had grown older, the visits had become further spaced and shorter. It became routine for her to spend her vacations from school with the nuns. She had begun to see, through the objectivity of distance, her mother's desperation for youth, her selfish grip on her own beauty. A grown daughter with firm limbs and unlined skin had been more of an obstacle than an accomplishment. A grown daughter was a reminder of one's own mortality.

She was always afraid of losing, Laine thought. Her looks, her youth, her friends, her men. All the creams and potions. She sighed and shut her eyes. All the dyes and lotions. There had been a collection of porcelain dolls, Laine remembered. Vanessa's dolls, or so she had thought. Twelve porcelain dolls, each from a different country. She thought of how beautiful the Spanish doll had been with its high comb and mantilla. And the earrings…Laine tossed down her brush and whirled around the room. Those lovely opal earrings that looked so fragile in Vanessa's ears. I remember seeing her wear them, just as I remember listing them and the twelve porcelain dolls for auction. *How much more that was mine did she keep from me?* Blindly, Laine stared out her window. The incredible array of island blossoms might not have existed.

What kind of woman was she to keep what was mine for her own pleasure? To let me think, year after year, that my father had forgotten me? She kept me from him, even from his words on paper. I resent her for that, how I resent her for that. Not for the money, but for the lies and the loss. She must have used the checks to keep her apartment in Paris, and for all those clothes and all those parties. Laine shut her eyes tight on waves of outrage. At least I know now why she took me with her to France: as an insurance policy. She lived off me for nearly fifteen years, and even then it wasn't enough. Laine felt tears squeezing through her closed lids. Oh, how Cap must hate me. How he must hate me for the ingratitude and the coldness. He would never believe me. She sighed, remembering her father's reaction to her appearance. *"You've the look of your mother."* Opening her eyes, she walked back and studied her face in the mirror.

It was true, she decided as she ran her fingertips along her cheeks. The resemblance was there in the bone structure, in the coloring. Laine frowned, finding no pleasure in her inheritance. *He's only to look at me to see her. He's only to look at me to remember. He'll think as Dillon O'Brian thinks. How could I expect anything else?* For a few moments, Laine and her reflection merely stared at one another. *But perhaps,* she mused, her bottom lip thrust forward in thought, *with a week or two I might salvage something of what used to be, some portion of the friendship. I would be content with that. But he must not think I've come for money, so I must be careful he not find out how little I have left. More than anything, I shall have to be careful around Mr. O'Brian.*

Detestable man, she thought on a fresh flurry of anger. *He is surely the most ill-bred, mannerless man I have ever met. He's worse, much worse, than any of Vanessa's hangers-on. At least they managed to wear a light coat of respectability. Cap probably picked him up off the beach out of pity and made him his partner. He has insolent eyes,* she added, lifting her brush and tugging it through her hair. *Always looking at you as if he knew how you would feel in his arms. He's nothing but a womanizer.* Tossing down the brush, she glared at the woman in the glass. *He's just an unrefined, arrogant womanizer. Look at the way he behaved on the plane.*

The glare faded as she lifted a finger to rub it over her lips. The memory of their turbulent capture flooded back. *You've been kissed before,* she lectured, shaking her head against the echoing sensations. *Not like that,* a small voice insisted. *Never like that.*

"Oh, the devil with Dillon O'Brian!" she muttered aloud,

and just barely resisted the urge to slam her bedroom door on her way out.

Laine hesitated at the sound of masculine voices. It was a new sound for one generally accustomed to female company, and she found it pleasant. There was a mixture of deep blends, her father's booming drum tones and Dillon's laconic drawl. She heard a laugh, an appealing, uninhibited rumble, and she frowned as she recognized it as Dillon's. Quietly, she came down the rest of the steps and moved to the doorway.

"Then, when I took out the carburetor, he stared at it, muttered a stream of incantations and shook his head. I ended up fixing it myself."

"And a lot quicker than the Maui mechanic or any other would have." Cap's rich chuckle reached Laine as she stepped into the doorway.

They were seated easily. Dillon was sprawled on the sofa, her father in a chair. Pipe smoke rose from the tray beside him. Both were relaxed and so content in each other's company that Laine felt the urge to back away and leave them undisturbed. She felt an intruder into some long established routine. With a swift pang of envy, she took a step in retreat.

Her movement caught Dillon's attention. Before she could leave, his eyes held her motionless just as effectively as if his arms had reached out to capture her. She had changed from the sophisticated suit she had worn for the flight into a simple white dress from her own wardrobe. Unadorned and ingenue, it emphasized her youth and her slender innocence. Following the direction of Dillon's unsmiling survey, Cap saw Laine and rose. As he stood, his ease transformed into awkwardness.

"Hello, Laine. Have you settled in all right?"

Laine forced herself to shift her attention from Dillon to her father. "Yes, thank you." The moistening of her lips was the first outward sign of nerves. "The room is lovely. I'm sorry. Did I interrupt?" Her hands fluttered once, then were joined loosely as if to keep them still.

"No…ah, come in and sit down. Just a little shoptalk."

She hesitated again before stepping into the room.

"Would you like a drink?" Cap moved to the bar and jiggled glasses. Dillon remained silent and seated.

"No, nothing, thank you." Laine tried a smile. "Your home is beautiful. I can see the beach from my window." Taking the remaining seat on the sofa, Laine kept as much distance between herself and Dillon as possible. "It must be marvelous being close enough to swim when the mood strikes you."

"I don't get to the water as much as I used to." Cap settled down again, tapping his pipe against the tray. "Used to scuba some. Now, Dillon's the one for it." Laine heard the affection in his voice, and caught it again in his smiling glance at the man beside her.

"I find the sea and the sky have a lot in common," Dillon commented, reaching forward to lift his drink from the table. "Freedom and challenge." He sent Cap an easy smile. "I taught Cap to explore the fathoms; he taught me to fly."

"I suppose I'm more of a land creature," Laine replied,

forcing herself to meet his gaze levelly. "I haven't much experience in the air or on the sea."

Dillon swirled his drink idly, but his eyes held challenge. "You do swim, don't you?"

"I manage."

"Fine." He took another swallow of his drink. "I'll teach you to snorkel." Setting down the glass, he resumed his relaxed position. "Tomorrow. We'll get an early start."

His arrogance shot up Laine's spine like a rod. Her tone became cool and dismissive. "I wouldn't presume to impose on your time, Mr. O'Brian."

Unaffected by the frost in her voice, Dillon continued. "No trouble. I've got nothing scheduled until the afternoon. You've got some extra gear around, haven't you, Cap?"

"Sure, in the back room." Hurt by the apparent relief in his voice, Laine shut her eyes briefly. "You'll enjoy yourself, Laine. Dillon's a fine teacher, and he knows these waters."

Laine gave Dillon a polite smile, hoping he could read between the lines. "I'm sure you know how much I appreciate your time, Mr. O'Brian."

The lifting of his brows indicated that their silent communication was proceeding with perfect understanding. "No more than I your company, Miss Simmons."

"Dinner." Miri's abrupt announcement startled Laine. "You." She pointed an accusing finger at Laine, then crooked it in a commanding gesture. "Come eat, and don't pick at your food. Too skinny," she muttered and whisked away in a flurry of brilliant colors.

Laine's arm was captured as they followed in the wake

of Miri's waves. Dillon slowed her progress until they were alone in the corridor. "My compliments on your entrance. You were the picture of the pure young virgin."

"I have no doubt you would like to offer me to the nearest volcano god, Mr. O'Brian, but perhaps you would allow me to have my last meal in peace."

"Miss Simmons." He bowed with exaggerated gallantry and increased his hold on her arm. "Even I can stir myself on occasion to escort a lady into dinner."

"Perhaps with a great deal of concentration, you could accomplish this spectacular feat without breaking my arm."

Laine gritted her teeth as they entered the glass-enclosed dining room. Dillon pulled out her chair. She glanced coldly up at him. "Thank you, Mr. O'Brian," she murmured as she slid into her seat. Detestable man!

Inclining his head politely, Dillon rounded the table and dropped into a chair. "Hey, Cap, that little cabin plane we've been using on the Maui run is running a bit rough. I want to have a look at it before it goes up again."

"Hmm. What do you think's the problem?"

There began a technical, and to Laine unintelligible, discussion. Miri entered, placing a steaming tray of fish in front of Laine with a meaningful thump. To assure she had not been misunderstood, Miri pointed a finger at the platter, then at Laine's empty plate before she swirled from the room.

The conversation had turned to the intricacies of fuel systems by the time Laine had eaten all she could of Miri's fish. Her silence during the meal had been almost complete as the men enjoyed their mutual interest. She saw, as she watched him, that her father's lack of courtesy was not deliberate, but rather the result of years of living alone. He was, she decided, a man comfortable with men and out of his depth with feminine company. Though she felt Dillon's rudeness was intentional, it was her father's unconscious slight which stung.

"You will excuse me?" Laine rose during a brief lull in the conversation. She felt a fresh surge of regret as she read the discomfort in her father's eyes. "I'm a bit tired. Please." She managed a smile as she started to rise. "Don't disturb yourself, I know the way." As she turned to go, she could almost hear the room sigh with relief at her exit.

Later that evening, Laine felt stifled in her room. The house was quiet. The tropical moon had risen and she could see the curtains flutter with the gentle whispers of perfumed air. Unable to bear the loneliness of the four walls any longer, she stole quietly downstairs and into the night. As she wandered without regard for destination, she could hear the night birds call to each other, piercing the stillness with a strange, foreign music. She listened to the sea's murmur and slipped off her shoes to walk across the fine layer of sand to meet it.

The water fringed in a wide arch, frothing against the sands and lapping back into the womb of midnight blue. Its surface winked with mirrored stars. Laine breathed deeply of its scent, mingling with the flowered air.

But this paradise was not for her. Dillon and her father had banished her. It was the same story all over again. She re-membered how often she had been excluded on her visits to her mother's home in Paris. *Again an intruder,* Laine decided, and wondered if she had either the strength or the will to pursue the smiling masquerade for even a week of her father's company. Her place was not with him any more than it had been with Vanessa. Dropping to the sand, Laine brought her knees to her chest and wept for the years of loss.

"I don't have a handkerchief, so you'll have to cope without one."

At the sound of Dillon's voice, Laine shuddered and hugged her knees tighter. "Please, go away."

"What's the problem, Duchess?" His voice was rough and impatient. If she had had more experience, Laine might have recognized a masculine discomfort with feminine tears. "If things aren't going as planned, sitting on the beach and crying isn't going to help. Especially if there's no one around to sympathize."

"Go away," she repeated, keeping her face buried. "I want you to leave me alone. I want to be alone."

"You might as well get used to it," he returned carelessly. "I intend to keep a close eye on you until you're back in Europe. Cap's too soft to hold out against the sweet, innocent routine for long."

Laine sprang up and launched herself at him. He staggered a moment as the small missile caught him off guard. "He's my father, do you understand? My *father*. I have a right to be with him. I have a right to know him." With useless fury, she beat her fists against his chest. He weathered the attack with some surprise before he caught her arms and dragged her, still swinging, against him.

"There's quite a temper under the ice! You can always try

the routine about not getting his letters—that should further your campaign."

"I don't want his pity, do you hear?" She pushed and shoved and struck out while Dillon held her with minimum effort. "I would rather have his hate than his disinterest, but I would rather have his disinterest than his pity."

"Hold still, blast it," he ordered, losing patience with the battle. "You're not going to get hurt."

"I will not hold still," Laine flung back. "I am not a puppy who washed up on his doorstep and needs to be dried off and given a corner and a pat on the head. I *will* have my two weeks, and I won't let you spoil it for me." She tossed back her head. Tears fell freely, but her eyes now held fury rather than sorrow. "Let me go! I don't want you to touch me." She began to battle with new enthusiasm, kicking and nearly throwing them both onto the sand.

"All right, that's enough." Swiftly, he used his arms to band, his mouth to silence.

He was drawing her into a whirlpool, spinning and spinning, until all sense of time and existence was lost in the current. She would taste the salt of her own tears mixed with some tangy, vital flavor which belonged to him. She felt a swift heat rise to her skin and fought against it as desperately as she fought against his imprisoning arms. His mouth took hers once more, enticing her to give what she did not yet understand. All at once she lost all resistance, all sense of self. She went limp in his arms, her lips softening in surrender. Dillon drew her away and without even being aware of what she was doing, Laine dropped her head to his chest. She trembled as she felt his hand brush lightly through her hair, and nestled closer to him. Suddenly warm and no longer alone, she shut her eyes and let the gamut of emotions run its course.

"Just who are you, Laine Simmons?" Dillon drew her away again. He closed a firm hand under her chin as she stubbornly fought to keep her head lowered. "Look at me," he commanded. The order was absolute. With his eyes narrowed, he examined her without mercy.

Her eyes were wide and brimming, the tears trembling down her cheeks and clinging to her lashes. All layers of her borrowed sophistication had been stripped away, leaving only the vulnerability. His search ended on an impatient oath. "Ice, then fire, now tears. No, don't," he commanded as she struggled to lower her head again. "I'm not in the mood to test my resistance." He let out a deep breath and shook his head. "You're going to be nothing but trouble, I should have seen that from the first look. But you're here, and we're going to have to come to terms."

"Mr. O'Brian…"

"Dillon, for pity's sake. Let's not be any more ridiculous than necessary."

"Dillon," Laine repeated, sniffling and despising herself. "I don't think I can discuss terms with any coherence tonight. If you would just let me go, we could draw up a contract tomorrow."

"No, the terms are simple because they're all mine."

"That sounds exceedingly reasonable." She was pleased that irony replaced tears.

"While you're here," Dillon continued mildly, "we're

going to be together like shadow and shade. I'm your guard-
ian angel until you go back to the Left Bank. If you make a
wrong move with Cap, I'm coming down on you so fast you
won't be able to blink those little-girl eyes."

"Is my father so helpless he needs protection from his own
daughter?" She brushed furiously at her lingering tears.

"There isn't a man alive who doesn't need protection from
you, Duchess." Tilting his head, he studied her damp, glowing face. "If you're an operator, you're a good one. If you're
not, I'll apologize when the time comes."

"You may keep your apology and have it for breakfast.
With any luck, you'll strangle on it."

Dillon threw back his head and laughed, the same appealing rumble Laine had heard earlier. Outraged both with the
laughter and its effect on her, she swung back her hand to
slap his face.

"Oh, no." Dillon grabbed her wrist. "Don't spoil it. I'd
just have to hit you back, and you look fabulous when you're
spitting fire. It's much more to my taste than the cool mademoiselle from Paris. Listen, Laine." He took an exaggerated
breath to control his laughter, and she found herself struggling
to deal with the stir caused by the way her name sounded on
his lips. "Let's try a truce, at least in public. Privately, we can
have a round a night, with or without gloves."

"That should suit you well enough." Laine wriggled out
of his loosened hold and tossed her head. "You have a con-
siderable advantage—given your weight and strength."

"Yeah." Dillon grinned and moved his shoulders. "Learn
to live with it. Come on." He took her hand in a friendly

gesture which nonplussed her. "Into bed; you've got to get up early tomorrow. I don't like to lose the morning."

"I'm not going with you tomorrow." She tugged her hand away and planted her bare heels in the sand. "You'll probably attempt to drown me, then hide my body in some cove."

Dillon sighed in mock exasperation. "Laine, if I have to drag you out of bed in the morning, you're going to find yourself learning a great deal more than snorkeling. Now, are you going to walk back to the house, or do I carry you?"

"If they could bottle your arrogance, Dillon O'Brian, there would be no shortage of fuel in this country!"

With this, Laine turned and fled. Dillon watched until the darkness shrouded her white figure. Then he bent down to retrieve her shoes.

chapter four

The morning was golden. As usual, Laine woke early. For a moment, she blinked in puzzlement. Cool green walls had replaced her white ones, louvered shades hung where she expected faded striped curtains. Instead of her desk stood a plain mahogany bureau topped with a vase of scarlet blossoms. But it was the silence which most confused her. There were no giggles, no rushing feet outside her door. The quiet was broken only by a bird who sang his morning song outside her window. Memory flooded back. With a sigh, Laine lay back against the pillow and wished she could go to sleep again. The habit of early rising was too ingrained. She rose, showered and dressed.

A friend had persuaded her to accept the loan of a swimsuit, and Laine studied the two tiny pieces. She slipped on what had been described as a modified bikini. The silvery blue was flattering, highlighting her subtle curves, but no amount of adjustment could result in a more substantial coverage. There was definitely too much of her and too little suit.

"Silly," Laine muttered and adjusted the halter strings a last time. "Women wear these things all the time, and I've hardly the shape for drawing attention."

Skinny. With a grimace, she recalled Miri's judgment. Laine gave the top a last, hopeless tug. *I don't think all the fish in the Pacific are going to change this inadequacy.* Pulling on white jeans and a scarlet scoop-necked top, she reminded herself that cleavage was not what she needed for dealing with Dillon O'Brian.

As she wandered downstairs, Laine heard the stirrings which accompany an awakening house. She moved quietly, half afraid she would disturb the routine. In the dining room, the sun poured like liquid gold through the windows. Standing in its pool, Laine stared out at soft ferns and brilliant poppies. Charmed by the scene, she decided she would let nothing spoil the perfection of the day. There would be time enough later, on some drizzling French morning, to think of rejections and humiliations, but today the sun was bright and filled with promise.

"So, you are ready for breakfast." Miri glided in from the adjoining kitchen. She managed to look graceful despite her size, and regal despite the glaring flowered muumuu.

"Good morning, Miri." Laine gave her the first smile of the day and gestured toward the sky. "It's beautiful."

"It will bring some color to your skin." Miri sniffed and ran a finger down Laine's arm. "Red if you aren't careful. Now, sit and I will put flesh on your skinny bones." Imperiously, she tapped the back of a chair, and Laine obeyed.

"Miri, have you worked for my father long?"

"Ten years." Miri shook her head and poured steaming

coffee into a cup. "Too long a time for a man not to have a wife. Your mother," she continued, narrowing her dark eyes, "she was skinny too?"

"Well, no, I wouldn't say... That is..." Laine hesitated in an attempt to gauge Miri's estimation of a suitable shape.

Rich laughter shot out. Miri's bosom trembled under pink and orange flowers. "You don't want to say she was not as much woman as Miri." She ran her hands over her well-padded hips. "You're a pretty girl," she said unexpectedly and patted Laine's flaxen curls. "Your eyes are too young to be sad." As Laine stared up at her, speechless under the unfamiliar affection, Miri sighed. "I will bring your breakfast, and you will eat what I give you."

"Make it two, Miri." Dillon strolled in, bronzed and confident in cutoff denims and a plain white T-shirt. "Morning, Duchess. Sleep well?" He dropped into the chair opposite Laine and poured himself a cup of coffee. His movements were easy, without any early-morning lethargy, and his eyes were completely alert. Laine concluded that Dillon O'Brian was one of those rare creatures who moved from sleep to wakefulness instantly. It also occurred to her, in one insistent flash, that he was not only the most attractive man she had ever known, but the most compelling. Struggling against an unexplained longing, Laine tried to mirror his casualness.

"Good morning, Dillon. It appears it's going to be another lovely day."

"We've a large supply of them on this side of the island."

"On this side?" Laine watched as he ran a hand through his hair, sending it into a state of appealing confusion.

"Mmm. On the windward slopes it rains almost every day." He downed half his coffee in one movement, and Laine found herself staring at his long, brown fingers. They looked strong and competent against the cream-colored earthenware. Suddenly, she remembered the feel of them on her chin. "Something wrong?"

"What?" Blinking, she brought her attention back to his face. "No, I was just thinking…I'll have to tour the island while I'm here," she improvised, rushing through the words. "Is your…is your home near here?"

"Not far." Dillon lifted his cup again, studying her over its rim. Laine began to stir her own coffee as if the task required enormous concentration. She had no intention of drinking it, having had her first—and, she vowed, last—encounter with American coffee aboard the plane.

"Breakfast," Miri announced, gliding into the room with a heaping tray. "You will eat." With brows drawn, she began piling portions onto Laine's plate. "And then you go out so I can clean my house. You!" She shook a large spoon at Dillon who was filling his own plate with obvious appreciation. "Don't bring any sand back with you to dirty my floors."

He responded with a quick Hawaiian phrase and a cocky grin. Miri's laughter echoed after her as she moved from the room and into the kitchen.

"Dillon," Laine began, staring at the amount of food on her plate, "I could never eat all of this."

He forked a mouthful of eggs and shrugged. "Better make a stab at it. Miri's decided to fatten you up, and even if you couldn't use it—and you can," he added as he buttered a piece of toast, "Miri is not a lady to cross. Pretend it's bouillabaisse or escargots."

The last was stated with a tangible edge, and Laine stiffened. Instinctively, she put up her defenses. "I have no complaints on the quality of the food, but on the quantity."

Dillon shrugged. Annoyed, Laine attacked her breakfast. The meal progressed without conversation. Fifteen minutes later, she searched for the power to lift yet another forkful of eggs. With a sound of impatience, Dillon rose and pulled her from her chair.

"You look like you'll keel over if you shovel in one more bite. I'll give you a break and get you out before Miri comes back."

Laine gritted her teeth, hoping it would help her to be humble. "Thank you."

As Dillon pulled Laine down the hall toward the front door, Cap descended the stairs. All three stopped as he glanced down from man to woman. "Good morning. It should be a fine day for your snorkeling lesson, Laine."

"Yes, I'm looking forward to it." She smiled, straining for a naturalness she was unable to feel in his presence.

"That's good. Dillon's right at home in the water." Cap's smile gained warmth as he turned to the man by her side. "When you come in this afternoon, take a look at the new twin-engine. I think the modifications you specified worked out well."

"Sure. I'm going to do a bit of work on that cabin plane. Keep Tinker away from it, will you?"

Cap chuckled as they enjoyed some personal joke. When

he turned to Laine, he had a remnant of his smile and a polite nod. "I'll see you tonight. Have a good time."

"Yes, thank you." She watched him move away and, for a moment, her heart lifted to her eyes. Looking back, she found Dillon studying her. His expression was indrawn and brooding.

"Come on," he said with sudden briskness as he captured her hand. "Let's get started." He lifted a faded, long-stringed bag and tossed it over his shoulder as they passed through the front door. "Where's your suit?"

"I have it on." Preferring to trot alongside rather than be dragged, Laine scrambled to keep pace.

The path he took was a well-worn dirt track. Along its borders, flowers and ferns crept to encroach on the walkway. Laine wondered if there was another place on earth where colors had such clarity or where green had so many shades. The vanilla-scented blossoms of heliotrope added a tang to the moist sea air. With a high call, a skylark streaked across the sky and disappeared. Laine and Dillon walked in silence as the sun poured unfiltered over their heads.

After a ten-minute jog, Laine said breathlessly, "I do hope it isn't much farther. I haven't run the decathlon for years."

Dillon turned, and she braced herself for his irritated retort. Instead, he began to walk at a more moderate pace. Pleased, Laine allowed herself a small smile. She felt even a minor victory in dealing with Dillon O'Brian was an accomplishment. Moments later, she forgot her triumph.

The bay was secluded, sheltered by palms and laced with satin-petaled hibiscus. In the exotic beauty of Kauai, it was a stunning diamond. The water might have dripped from the sky that morning. It shone and glimmered like a multitude of fresh raindrops.

With a cry of pleasure, Laine began to pull Dillon through the circling palms and into the white heat of sun and sand. "Oh, it's beautiful!" She turned two quick circles as if to insure encompassing all the new wonders. "It's perfect, absolutely perfect."

She watched his smile flash like a brisk wind. It chased away the clouds and, for one precious moment, there was understanding rather than tension between them. It flowed from man to woman with an ease which was as unexpected as it was soothing. His frown returned abruptly, and Dillon crouched to rummage through the bag. He pulled out snorkels and masks.

"Snorkeling's easy once you learn to relax and breathe properly. It's important to be both relaxed and alert." He began to instruct in simple terms, explaining breathing techniques and adjusting Laine's mask.

"There is no need to be quite so didactic," she said at length, irked by his patronizing tone and frowning face. "I assure you, I have a working brain. Most things don't have to be repeated more than four or five times before I grasp the meaning."

"Fine." He handed her both snorkel and mask. "Let's try it in the water." Pulling off his shirt, he dropped it on the canvas bag. He stood above her adjusting the strap on his own mask.

A fine mat of black hair lay against his bronzed chest. His

skin was stretched tight over his rib cage, then tapered down to a narrow waist. The faded denim hung low over his lean hips. With some astonishment, Laine felt an ache start in her stomach and move warmly through her veins. She dropped her eyes to an intense study of the sand.

"Take off your clothes." Laine's eyes widened. She took a quick step in retreat. "Unless you intend to swim in them," Dillon added. His lips twitched before he turned and moved toward the water.

Embarrassed, Laine did her best to emulate his casualness. Shyly, she stripped off her top. Pulling off her jeans, she folded both and followed Dillon toward the bay. He waited for her, water lapping over his thighs. His eyes traveled over every inch of her exposed skin before they rested on her face.

"Stay close," he commanded when she stood beside him. "We'll skim the surface for a bit until you get the hang of it." He pulled the mask down over her eyes and adjusted it.

Easily, they moved along the shallows where sunlight struck the soft bottom and sea lettuce danced and swayed. Forgetting her instructions, Laine breathed water instead of air and surfaced choking.

"What happened?" Dillon demanded, as Laine coughed and sputtered. "You're going to have to pay more attention to what you're doing," he warned. Giving her a sturdy thump on the back, he pulled her mask back over her eyes. "Ready?" he asked.

After three deep breaths, Laine managed to speak. "Yes." She submerged.

Little by little, she explored deeper water, swimming by

Dillon's side. He moved through the water as a bird moves through the air, with inherent ease and confidence. Before long, Laine learned to translate his aquatic hand signals and began to improvise her own. They were joined in the liquid world by curious fish. As Laine stared into round, lidless eyes, she wondered who had come to gape at whom.

The sun flickered through with ethereal light. It nurtured the sea grass and caused shells and smooth rocks to glisten. It was a silent world, and although the sea bottom teemed with life, it was somehow private and free. Pale pink fingers of coral grouped together to form a hiding place for vivid blue fish. Laine watched in fascination as a hermit crab slid out of its borrowed shell and scurried away. There was a pair of orange starfish clinging contentedly to a rock, and a sea urchin nestled in spiny solitude.

Laine enjoyed isolation with this strange, moody man. She did not pause to appraise the pleasure she took in sharing her new experiences with him. The change in their relationship had been so smooth and so swift, she had not even been aware of it. They were, for a moment, only man and woman cloaked in a world of water and sunlight. On impulse, she lifted a large cone-shaped shell from its bed, its resident long since evicted. First holding it out for Dillon to view, she swam toward the dancing light on the surface.

Shaking her head as she broke water, Laine splattered Dillon's mask with sundrops. Laughing, she pushed her own mask to the top of her head and stood in the waist-high water. "Oh, that was wonderful! I've never seen anything like it." She pushed damp tendrils behind her ears. "All those colors, and so many shades of blue and green molded together. It feels…it feels as if there were nothing else in the world but yourself and where you are."

Excitement had kissed her cheeks with color, her eyes stealing the blue from the sea. Her hair was dark gold, clinging in a sleek cap to her head. Now, without the softening of curls, her face seemed more delicately sculptured, the planes and hollows more fragile. Dillon watched her in smiling silence, pushing his own mask atop his head.

"I've never done anything like that before. I could have stayed down there forever. There's so much to see, so much to touch. Look what I found. It's beautiful." She held the shell in both hands, tracing a finger over its amber lines. "What is it?"

Dillon took it for a moment, turning it over in his hands before giving it back to her. "A music volute. You'll find scores of shells around the island."

"May I keep it? Does this place belong to anyone?"

Dillon laughed, enjoying her enthusiasm. "This is a private bay, but I know the owner. I don't think he'd mind."

"Will I hear the sea? They say you can." Laine lifted the shell to her ear. At the low, drifting echo, her eyes widened in wonder. *"Oh, c'est incroyable."* In her excitement, she reverted to French, not only in speech, but in mannerisms. Her eyes locked on his as one hand held the shell to her ear and the other gestured with her words. *"On entend le bruit de la mer. C'est merveilleux! Dillon, écoute."*

She offered the shell, wanting to share her discovery. He

laughed as she had heard him laugh with her father. "Sorry, Duchess, you lost me a few sentences back."

"Oh, how silly. I wasn't thinking. I haven't spoken English in so long." She brushed at her damp hair and offered him a smile. "It's marvelous, I can really hear the sea." Her words faltered as his eyes lost their amusement. They were darkened by an emotion which caused her heart to jump and pound furiously against her ribs. Her mind shouted quickly to retreat, but her body and will melted as his arms slid around her. Her mouth lifted of its own accord to surrender to his.

For the first time, she felt a man's hands roam over her naked skin. There was nothing between them but the satin rivulets of water which clung to their bodies. Under the streaming gold sun, her heart opened, and she gave. She accepted the demands of his mouth, moved with the caresses of his hands until she thought they would never become separate. She wanted only for them to remain one until the sun died, and the world was still.

Dillon released her slowly, his arms lingering, as if reluctant to relinquish possession. Her sigh was mixed with pleasure and the despair of losing a newly discovered treasure. "I would swear," he muttered, staring down into her face, "you're either a first-rate actress or one step out of a nunnery."

Immediately, the helpless color rose, and Laine turned to escape to the sand of the beach. "Hold on." Taking her arm, Dillon turned her to face him. His brows drew close as he studied her blush. "That's a feat I haven't seen in years. Duchess, you amaze me. Either way," he continued, and his smile held mockery but lacked its former malice, "calculated or innocent, you amaze me. Again," he said simply and drew her into his arms.

This time the kiss was gentle and teasing. But she had less defense against tenderness than passion, and her body was pliant to his instruction. Her hands tightened on his shoulders, feeling the ripple of muscles under her palms as he drew every drop of response from her mouth. With no knowledge of seduction, she became a temptress by her very innocence. Dillon drew her away and gave her clouded eyes and swollen mouth a long examination.

"You're a powerful lady," he said at length, then let out a quick breath. "Let's sit in the sun awhile." Without waiting for her answer, he took her hand and moved toward the beach.

On the sand, he spread a large beach towel and dropped onto it. When Laine hesitated, he pulled her down to join him. "I don't bite, Laine, I only nibble." Drawing a cigarette from the bag beside them, he lit it, then leaned back on his elbows. His skin gleamed with water and sun.

Feeling awkward, Laine sat very still with the shell in her hands. She tried not only to understand what she had felt in Dillon's arms, but why she had felt it. It had been important, and somehow, she felt certain it would remain important for the rest of her life. It was a gift that did not yet have a name. Suddenly, she felt as happy as when the shell had spoken in her ear. Glancing at it, Laine smiled with unrestrained joy.

"You treat that shell as though it were your firstborn." Twisting her head, she saw Dillon grinning. She decided she had never been happier.

"It is my first souvenir, and I've never dived for sunken treasure before."

"Just think of all the sharks you had to push out of the way to get your hands on it." He blew smoke at the sky as she wrinkled her nose at him.

"Perhaps you're only jealous because you didn't get one of your own. I suppose it was selfish of me not to have gotten one for you."

"I'll survive."

"You don't find shells in Paris," she commented, feeling at ease and strangely fresh. "The children will treasure it as much as they would gold doubloons."

"Children?"

Laine was examining her prize, exploring its smooth surface with her fingers. "My students at school. Most of them have never seen anything like this except in pictures."

"You teach?"

Much too engrossed in discovering every angle of the shell, Laine missed the incredulity in his voice. She answered absently, "Yes, English to the French students and French to the English girls who board there. After I graduated, I stayed on as staff. There was really nowhere else to go, and it had always been home in any case. Dillon, do you suppose I could come back sometime and find one or two others, a different type perhaps? The girls would be fascinated; they get so little entertainment."

"Where was your mother?"

"What?" In the transfer of her attention, she saw he was sitting up and staring at her with hard, probing eyes. "What did you say?" she asked again, confused by his change of tone.

"I said, where was your mother?"

"When…when I was in school? She was in Paris." The sudden anger in his tone threw her into turmoil. She searched for a way to change the topic. "I would like to see the airport again; do you think I…"

"Stop it."

Laine jerked at the harsh command, then quickly tried to slip into her armor. "There's no need to shout. I'm quite capable of hearing you from this distance."

"Don't pull that royal routine on me, Duchess. I want some answers." He flicked away his cigarette. Laine saw both the determination and fury in his face.

"I'm sorry, Dillon." Rising and stepping out of reach, Laine remained outwardly calm. "I'm really not in the mood for a cross-examination."

With a muttered oath, Dillon swung to his feet and captured her arms with a swiftness which left her stunned. "You can be a frosty little number. You switch on and off so fast, I can't make up my mind which is the charade. Just who the devil are you?"

"I'm tired of telling you who I am," she answered quietly. "I don't know what you want me to say; I don't know what you want me to be."

Her answer and her mild tone seemed only to make him more angry. He tightened his hold and gave her a quick shake. "What was this last routine of yours?"

She was yanked against him in a sudden blaze of fury, but

before punishment could be meted out, someone called his name. With a soft oath Dillon released her, and turned as a figure emerged from a narrow tunnel of palms.

Laine's first thought was that a spirit from the island was drifting through the shelter and across the sand. Her skin was tawny gold and smooth against a sarong of scarlet and midnight blue. A full ebony carpet of hair fell to her waist, flowing gently with her graceful movements. Almond-shaped amber eyes were fringed with dark velvet. A sultry smile flitted across an exotic and perfect face. She lifted a hand in greeting, and Dillon answered.

"Hello, Orchid."

Her mortality was established in Laine's mind as the beautiful apparition lifted her lips and brushed Dillon's. "Miri said you'd gone snorkeling, so I knew you'd be here." Her voice flowed like soft music.

"Laine Simmons, Orchid King." Dillon's introductions were casual. Laine murmured a response, feeling suddenly as inadequate as a shadow faced with the sun. "Laine's Cap's daughter."

"Oh, I see." Laine was subjected to a more lengthy survey. She saw speculation beneath the practiced smile. "How nice you're visiting at last. Are you staying long?"

"A week or two." Laine regained her poise and met Orchid's eyes. "Do you live on the island?"

"Yes, though I'm off it as often as not. I'm a flight attendant. I'm just back from the mainland, and I've got a few days. I wanted to trade the sky for the sea. I hope you're going back in." She smiled up at Dillon and tucked a hand through his arm. "I would love some company."

Laine watched his charm flow. It seemed he need do nothing but smile to work his own particular magic. "Sure, I've got a couple of hours."

"I think I'll just go back to the house," Laine said quickly, feeling like an intruder. "I don't think I should get too much sun at one time." Lifting her shirt, Laine tugged it on. "Thank you, Dillon, for your time." She bent down and retrieved the rest of her things before speaking again. "It's nice to have met you, Miss King."

"I'm sure we'll see each other again." Undraping her sarong, Orchid revealed an inadequate bikini and a stunning body. "We're all very friendly on this island, aren't we, cousin?" Though it was the standard island form of address, Orchid's use of the word *cousin* implied a much closer relationship.

"Very friendly." Dillon agreed with such ease that Laine felt he must be quite accustomed to Orchid's charms.

Murmuring a goodbye, Laine moved toward the canopy of palms. Hearing Orchid laugh, then speak in the musical tongue of the island, Laine glanced back before the leaves blocked out the view. She watched the golden arms twine around Dillon's neck, pulling his mouth toward hers in invitation.

chapter five

The walk back from the bay gave Laine time to reflect on the varying emotions Dillon O'Brian had managed to arouse in the small amount of time she had known him. Annoyance, resentment and anger had come first. Now, there was a wariness she realized stemmed from her inexperience with men. But somehow, that morning, there had been a few moments of harmony. She had been at ease in his company. And, she admitted ruefully, she had never before been totally at ease in masculine company on a one-to-one basis.

Perhaps it had simply been the novelty of her underwater adventure which had been responsible for her response to him. There had been something natural in their coming together, as if body had been created for body and mouth for mouth. She had felt a freedom in his arms, an awakening. It had been as if walls of glass had shattered and left her open to sensations for the first time.

Stopping, Laine plucked a blush-pink hibiscus, then twirled its stem idly as she wandered up the dirt track. Her tenuous feelings had been dissipated first by Dillon's unexplained anger, then by the appearance of the dark island beauty.

Orchid King, Laine mused. A frown marred her brow as the name of the flirtatious information clerk ran through her brain. *Rose.* Smoothing the frown away, Laine shook off a vague depression. Perhaps Dillon had a predilection for women with flowery names. It was certainly none of her concern. Obviously, she continued, unconsciously tearing off the hibiscus petals, he gave and received kisses as freely as a mouse nibbles cheese. *He simply kissed me because I was there.* Obviously, she went on doggedly, shredding the wounded blossom without thought, *Orchid King has a great deal more to offer than I. She makes me feel like a pale, shapeless wren next to a lush, vibrant flamingo. I would hardly appeal to him as a woman even if he didn't already dislike me. I don't want to appeal to him. Certainly not. The very last thing I want to do is to appeal to that insufferable man.* Scowling, she stared down at the mutilated hibiscus. With something between a sigh and a moan, she tossed it aside and increased her pace.

After depositing the shell in her room and changing out of her bathing suit, Laine wandered back downstairs. She felt listless and at loose ends. In the organized system of classes and meals and designated activities, her time had always been carefully budgeted. She found the lack of demand unsettling. She thought of how often during the course of a busy day she had yearned for a free hour to read or simply to sit alone. Now her time was free, and she wished only for occupation. The difference was, she knew, the fear of idle hours and the tendency to think. She found herself avoiding any attempt to sort out her situation or the future.

No one had shown her through the house since her arrival. After a brief hesitation, she allowed curiosity to lead her and gave herself a tour. She discovered that her father lived simply, with no frills or frippery, but with basic masculine comforts. There were books, but it appeared they were little read. She could see by the quantity and ragged appearance of aeronautical magazines where her father's taste in literature lay. Bamboo shades replaced conventional curtains; woven mats took the place of rugs. While far from primitive, the rooms were simply furnished.

Her mind began to draw a picture of a man content with such a basic existence, who lived quietly and routinely; a man whose main outlet was his love of the sky. Now Laine began to understand why her parents' marriage had failed. Her father's life-style was as unassuming as her mother's had been pretentious. Her mother would never have been satisfied with her father's modest existence, and he would have been lost in hers. Laine wondered, with a small frown, why she herself did not seem to fit with either one of them.

Laine lifted a black-framed snapshot from a desk. A younger version of Cap Simmons beamed out at her, his arm casually tossed around a Dillon who had not yet reached full manhood. Dillon's smile was the same, however—somewhat cocky and sure. If they had stood in the flesh before her, their affection for each other would have seemed no less real. A shared understanding was revealed in their eyes and their easy stance together. It struck Laine suddenly, with a stab of resentment, that they looked like father and son. The years they had shared could never belong to her.

"It's not fair," she murmured, gripping the picture in both hands. With a faint shudder, she shut her eyes. Who am I blaming? she asked herself. Cap for needing someone? Dillon for being here? Blame won't help, and looking for the past is useless. It's time I looked for something new. Letting out a deep breath, Laine replaced the photograph. She turned away and moved farther down the hall. In a moment, she found herself in the kitchen surrounded by gleaming white appliances and hanging copper kettles. Miri turned from the stove and gave Laine a satisfied smile.

"So you have come for lunch." Miri tilted her head and narrowed her eyes. "You have some color from the sun."

Laine glanced down at her bare arms and was pleased with the light tan. "Why, yes, I do. I didn't actually come for lunch, though." She smiled and made an encompassing gesture. "I was exploring the house."

"Good. Now you eat. Sit here." Miri waved a long knife toward the scrubbed wooden table. "And do not make your bed anymore. That is my job." Miri plopped a glass of milk under Laine's nose, then gave a royal sniff.

"Oh, I'm sorry." Laine glanced from the glass of milk up to Miri's pursed lips. "It's just a habit."

"Don't do it again," Miri commanded as she turned to the refrigerator. She spoke again as she began to remove a variety of contents. "Did you make beds in that fancy school?"

"It isn't actually a fancy school," Laine corrected, watching with growing anxiety as Miri prepared a hefty sandwich. "It's really just a small convent school outside Paris."

"You lived in a convent?" Miri stopped her sandwich-building and looked skeptical.

"Well, no. That is, one might say I lived on the fringes of one. Except, of course, when I visited my mother. Miri..." Daunted by the plate set in front of her, Laine looked up helplessly. "I don't think I can manage all this."

"Just eat, Skinny Bones. Your morning with Dillon, it was nice?"

"Yes, very nice." Laine applied herself to the sandwich as Miri eased herself into the opposite chair. "I never knew there was so much to see underwater. Dillon is an expert guide."

"Ah, that one." Miri shook her head and somehow categorized Dillon as a naughty twelve-year-old boy. "He is always in the water or in the sky. He should keep his feet planted on the ground more often." Leaning back, Miri kept a commanding eye on Laine's progress. "He watches you."

"Yes, I know," Laine murmured. "Like a parole officer. I met Miss King," she continued, lifting her voice. "She came to the bay."

"Orchid King." Miri muttered something in unintelligible Hawaiian.

"She's very lovely...very vibrant and striking. I suppose Dillon has known her for a long time." Laine made the comment casually, surprising herself with the intentional probe.

"Long enough. But her bait has not yet lured the fish into the net." Miri gave a sly smile lost on the woman who stared into her milk. "You think Dillon looks good?"

"Looks good?" Laine repeated and frowned, not understanding the nuance. "Yes, Dillon's a very attractive man. At least, I suppose he is; I haven't known many men."

"You should give him more smiles," Miri advised with a wise nod. "A smart woman uses smiles to show a man her mind."

"He hasn't given me many reasons to smile at him," Laine said between bites. "And," she continued, finding she resented the thought, "I would think he gets an abundance of smiles from other sources."

"Dillon gives his attention to many women. He is a very generous man." Miri chuckled, and Laine blushed as she grasped the innuendo. "He has not yet found a woman who could make him selfish. Now you…" Miri tapped a finger aside her nose as if considering. "You would do well with him. He could teach you, and you could teach him."

"I teach Dillon?" Laine shook her head and gave a small laugh. "One cannot teach what one doesn't know. In the first place, Miri, I only met Dillon yesterday. All he's done so far is confuse me. From one moment to the next, I don't know how he's going to make me feel." She sighed, not realizing the sound was wistful. "I think men are very strange, Miri. I don't understand them at all."

"Understand?" Her bright laugh rattled through the kitchen. "What need is there to understand? You need only enjoy. I had three husbands, and I never understood one of them. But—" her smile was suddenly young "—I enjoyed. You are very young," she added. "That alone is attractive to a man used to women of knowledge."

"I don't think…I mean, of course, I wouldn't want him to, but…" Laine fumbled and stuttered, finding her thoughts a mass of confusion. "I'm sure Dillon wouldn't be interested in me. He seems to have a very compatible relationship with Miss King. Besides—" Laine shrugged her shoulders as she felt depression growing, "—he distrusts me."

"It is a stupid woman who lets what is gone interfere with what is now." Miri placed her fingertips together and leaned back in her chair. "You want your father's love, Skinny Bones? Time and patience will give it to you. You want Dillon?" She held up an imperious hand at Laine's automatic protest. "You will learn to fight as a woman fights." She stood, and the flowers on her muumuu trembled with the movement. "Now, out of my kitchen. I have much work to do."

Obediently, Laine rose and moved to the door. "Miri…" Nibbling her lips, she turned back. "You've been very close to my father for many years. Don't you…" Laine hesitated, then finished in a rush. "Don't you resent me just appearing like this after all these years?"

"Resent?" Miri repeated the word, then ran her tongue along the inside of her mouth. "I do not resent because resent is a waste of time. And the last thing I resent is a child." She picked up a large spoon and tapped it idly against her palm. "When you went away from Cap Simmons, you were a child and you went with your mother. Now you are not a child, and you are here. What do I have to resent?" Miri shrugged and moved back to the stove.

Feeling unexpected tears, Laine shut her eyes on them and

drew a small breath. "Thank you, Miri." With a murmur, she retreated to her room.

Thoughts swirled inside Laine's mind as she sat alone in her bedroom. As Dillon's embrace had opened a door to dormant emotions, so Miri's words had opened a door to dormant thoughts. *Time and patience,* Laine repeated silently. Time and patience were Miri's prescription for a daughter's troubled heart. But I have so little time, and little more patience. How can I win my father's love in a matter of days? She shook her head, unable to resolve an answer. *And Dillon,* her heart murmured as she threw herself onto the bed and stared at the ceiling. Why must he complicate an already impossibly complicated situation? Why must he embrace me, making me think and feel as a woman one moment, then push me away and stand as my accuser the next? He can be so gentle when I'm in his arms, so warm. And then... Frustrated, she rolled over, laying her cheek against the pillow. Then he's so cold, and even his eyes are brutal. If only I could stop thinking of him, stop remembering how it feels to be kissed by him. It's only that I have no experience, and he has so much. It's nothing more than a physical awakening. There can be nothing more...nothing more.

The knock on Laine's door brought her up with a start. Pushing at her tousled hair, she rose to answer. Dillon had exchanged cutoffs for jeans, and he appeared as refreshed and alert as she did bemused and heavy-lidded. Laine stared at him dumbly, unable to bring her thoughts and words together. With a frown, he surveyed her sleep-flushed cheeks and soft eyes.

"Did I wake you?"

"No, I…" She glanced back at the clock, and her confusion grew as she noted that an hour had passed since she had first stretched out on the bed. "Yes," she amended. "I suppose the flight finally caught up with me." She reached up and ran a hand through her hair, struggling to orient herself. "I didn't even realize I'd been asleep."

"They're real, aren't they?"

"What?" Laine blinked and tried to sort out his meaning.

"The lashes." He was staring so intently into her eyes, Laine had to fight the need to look away.

Nonchalantly, he leaned against the door and completed his survey. "I'm on my way to the airport. I thought you might want to go. You said you wanted to see it again."

"Yes, I would." She was surprised by his courtesy.

"Well," he said dryly, and gestured for her to come along.

"Oh, I'll be right there. It should only take me a minute to get ready."

"You look ready."

"I need to comb my hair."

"It's fine." Dillon grabbed her hand and pulled her from the room before she could resist further.

Outside she found, to her astonishment, a helmet being thrust in her hands as she faced a shining, trim motorcycle. Clearing her throat, she looked from the helmet, to the machine, to Dillon. "We're going to ride on this?"

"That's right. I don't often use the car just to run to the airport."

"You might find this a good time to do so," Laine advised. "I've never ridden on a motorcycle."

"Duchess, all you have to do is to sit down and hang on." Dillon took the helmet from her and dropped it on her head. Securing his own helmet, he straddled the bike, then kicked the starter into life. "Climb on."

With amazement, Laine found herself astride the purring machine and clutching Dillon's waist as the motorcycle shot down the drive. Her death grip eased slightly as she realized that the speed was moderate, and the motorcycle had every intention of staying upright. It purred along the paved road.

Beside them, a river wandered like an unfurled blue ribbon, dividing patterned fields of taro. There was an excitement in being open to the wind, in feeling the hardness of Dillon's muscles beneath her hands. A sense of liberation flooded her. Laine realized that, in one day, Dillon had already given her experiences she might never have touched. I never knew how limited my life was, she thought with a smile. *No matter what happens, when I leave here, nothing will ever be quite the same again.*

When they arrived at the airport, Dillon wove through the main lot, circling to the back and halting in front of a hangar. "Off you go, Duchess. Ride's over."

Laine eased from the bike and struggled with her helmet. "Here." Dillon pulled it off for her, then dropped it to join his on the seat of the bike. "Still in one piece?"

"Actually," she returned, "I think I enjoyed it."

"It has its advantages." He ran his hands down her arms, then captured her waist. Laine stood very still, unwilling to retreat from his touch. He bent down and moved his mouth with teasing lightness over hers. Currents of pleasure ran over her skin. "Later," he said, pulling back. "I intend to finish that in a more satisfactory manner. But at the moment, I've work to do." His thumbs ran in lazy circles over her hips. "Cap's going to take you around; he's expecting you. Can you find your way?"

"Yes." Confused by the urgency of her heartbeat, Laine stepped back. The break in contact did nothing to slow it. "Am I to go to his office?"

"Yeah, the same place you went before. He'll show you whatever you want to see. Watch your step, Laine." His green eyes cooled abruptly, and his voice lost its lightness. "Until I'm sure about you, you can't afford to make any mistakes."

For a moment, she only stared up at him, feeling her skin grow cold, and her pulse slow. "I'm very much afraid," she admitted sadly, "I've already made one."

Turning, she walked away.

chapter six

Laine walked toward the small, palm-flanked building. Through her mind ran all which had passed in twenty-four hours. She had met her father, learned of her mother's deception and was now readjusting her wishes.

She had also, in the brief span of time it takes the sun to rise and fall, discovered the pleasures and demands of womanhood. Dillon had released new and magic sensations. Again, her mind argued with her heart that her feelings were only the result of a first physical attraction. It could hardly be anything else, she assured herself. One does not fall in love in a day, and certainly not with a man like Dillon O'Brian. We're total opposites. He's outgoing and confident, and so completely at ease with people. I envy him his honest confidence. There's nothing emotional about that. I've simply never met anyone like him before. That's why I'm confused. It has nothing to do with emotions. Laine felt comforted as she entered her father's office building.

As she stepped into the outer lobby, Cap strode from his

office, glancing over his shoulder at a dark girl with a pad in her hand who was following in his wake.

"Check with Dillon on the fuel order before you send that out. He'll be in a meeting for the next hour. If you miss him at his office, try hangar four." As he caught sight of Laine, Cap smiled and slowed his pace. "Hello, Laine. Dillon said you wanted a tour."

"Yes, I'd love one, if you have the time."

"Of course. Sharon, this is my daughter. Laine, this is Sharon Kumocko, my secretary."

Laine observed the curiosity in Sharon's eyes as they exchanged greetings. Her father's tone during the introductions had been somewhat forced. Laine felt him hesitate before he took her arm to lead her outside. She wondered briefly if she had imagined their closeness during her childhood.

"It's not a very big airport," Cap began as they stepped out into the sun and heat. "For the most part, we cater to island hoppers and charters. We also run a flight school. That's essentially Dillon's project."

"Cap." Impulsively, Laine halted his recital and turned to face him. "I know I've put you in an awkward position. I realize now that I should have written and asked if I could come rather than just dropping on your doorstep this way. It was thoughtless of me."

"Laine…"

"Please." She shook her head at his interruption and rushed on. "I realize, too, that you have your own life, your own home, your own friends. You've had fifteen years to settle into a routine. I don't want to interfere with any of that. Believe me, I don't want to be in the way, and I don't want you to feel…" She made a helpless gesture as the impetus ran out of her words. "I would like it if we could be friends."

Cap had studied her during her speech. The smile he gave her at its finish held more warmth than those he had given her before. "You know," he sighed, tugging his fingers through his hair, "it's sort of terrifying to be faced with a grown-up daughter. I missed all the stages, all the changes. I'm afraid I still pictured you as a bad-tempered pigtailed urchin with scraped knees. The elegant woman who walked into my office yesterday and spoke to me with a faint French accent is a stranger. And one," he added, touching her hair a moment, "who brings back memories I thought I'd buried." He sighed again and stuck his hands in his pockets. "I don't know much about women; I don't think I ever did. Your mother was the most beautiful, confusing woman I've ever known. When you were little, and the three of us were still together, I substituted your friendship for the friendship that your mother and I never had. You were the only female I ever understood. I've always wondered if that was why things didn't work."

Tilting her head, Laine gave her father a long, searching look. "Cap, why did you marry her? There seems to be nothing you had in common."

Cap shook his head with a quick laugh. "You didn't know her twenty years ago. She did a lot of changing, Laine. Some people change more than others." He shook his head again, and his eyes focused on some middle distance. "Besides, I loved her. I've always loved her."

"I'm sorry." Laine felt tears burn the back of her eyes, and she dropped her gaze to the ground. "I don't mean to make things more difficult."

"You're not. We had some good years." He paused until Laine lifted her eyes. "I like to remember them now and again." Taking her arm, he began to walk. "Was your mother happy, Laine?"

"Happy?" She thought a moment, remembering the quick-silver moods, the gay bubbling voice with dissatisfaction always under the surface. "I suppose Vanessa was as happy as she was capable of being. She loved Paris and she lived as she chose."

"Vanessa?" Cap frowned, glancing down at Laine's profile. "Is that how you think of your mother?"

"I always called her by name." Laine lifted her hand to shield her eyes from the sun as she watched the descent of a charter. "She said 'mother' made her feel too old. She hated getting older... I feel better knowing you're happy in the life you've chosen. Do you fly anymore, Cap? I remember how you used to love it."

"I still put in my quota of flight hours. Laine." He took both her arms and turned her to face him. "One question, then we'll leave it alone for a while. Have you been happy?"

The directness of both his questions and his eyes caused her to fumble. She looked away as if fascinated by disembarking passengers. "I've been very busy. The nuns are very serious about education."

"You're not answering my question. Or," he corrected, drawing his thick brows together, "maybe you are."

"I've been content," she said, giving him a smile. "I've

learned a great deal, and I'm comfortable with my life. I think that's enough for anyone."

"For someone," Cap returned, "who's reached my age, but not for a very young, very lovely woman." He watched her smile fade into perplexity. "It's not enough, Laine, and I'm surprised you'd settle for it." His voice was stern, laced with a hint of disapproval which put Laine on the defensive.

"Cap, I haven't had the chance…" She stopped, realizing she must guard her words. "I haven't taken the time," she amended, "to chase windmills." She lifted her hands, palms up, in a broad French gesture. "Perhaps I've reached the point in my life when I should begin to do so."

His expression lightened as she smiled up at him. "All right, we'll let it rest for now."

Without any more mention of the past, Cap led Laine through neat rows of planes. He fondled each as if it were a child, explaining their qualities in proud, but to Laine hopelessly technical, terms. She listened, content with his good humor, pleased with the sound of his voice. Occasionally, she made an ignorant comment that made him laugh. She found the laugh very precious.

The buildings were spread out, neat and without pretension; hangars and storage buildings, research and accounting offices, with the high, glass-enclosed control tower dominating all. Cap pointed out each one, but the planes themselves were his consummate interest.

"You said it wasn't big." Laine gazed around the complex and down light-dotted runways. "It looks enormous."

"It's a small, low-activity field, but we do our best to see that it's as well run as Honolulu International."

"What is it that Dillon does here?" Telling herself it was only idle curiosity, Laine surrendered to the urge to question.

"Oh, Dillon does a bit of everything," Cap answered with frustrating vagueness. "He has a knack for organizing. He can find his way through a problem before it becomes one, and he handles people so well they never realize they've been handled. He can also take a plane apart and put it back together again." Smiling, Cap gave a small shake of his head. "I don't know what I'd have done without Dillon. Without his drive, I might have been content to be a crop duster."

"Drive?" Laine repeated, lingering over the word. "Yes, I suppose he has drive when there is something he wants. But isn't he…" She searched for a label and settled on a generality. "Isn't he a very casual person?"

"Island life breeds a certain casualness, Laine, and Dillon was born here." He steered her toward the communications building. "Just because a man is at ease with himself and avoids pretension doesn't mean he lacks intelligence or ability. Dillon has both; he simply pursues his ambitions in his own way."

Later, as they walked toward the steel-domed hangars, Laine realized she and her father had begun to build a new relationship. He was more relaxed with her, his smiles and speech more spontaneous. She knew her shield was dropped as well, and she was more vulnerable.

"I've an appointment in a few minutes." Cap stopped just inside the building and glanced at his watch. "I'll have to turn

you over to Dillon now, unless you want me to have someone take you back to the house."

"No, I'll be fine," she assured him. "Perhaps I can just
wander about. I don't want to be a nuisance."

"You haven't been a nuisance. I enjoyed taking you
through. You haven't lost the curiosity I remember. You
always wanted to know why and how and you always listened. I think you were five when you demanded I explain
the entire control panel of a 707." His chuckle was the same
quick, appealing sound she remembered from childhood.
"Your face would get so serious, I'd swear you had understood everything I'd said." He patted her hand, then smiled
over her head. "Dillon, I thought we'd find you here. Take
care of Laine, will you? I've got Billet coming in."

"It appears I've got the best of the deal."

Laine turned to see him leaning against a plane, wiping his
hand on the loose coveralls he wore.

"Did everything go all right with the union representa-
tive?"

"Fine. You can look over the report tomorrow."

"I'll see you tonight, then." Cap turned to Laine, and after
a brief hesitation, patted her cheek before he walked away.

Smiling, she turned back to encounter Dillon's brooding
stare. "Oh, please," she began, shaking her head. "Don't spoil
it. It's such a small thing."

With a shrug, Dillon turned back to the plane. "Did you
like your tour?"

"Yes, I did." Laine's footsteps echoed off the high ceiling
as she crossed the room to join him. "I'm afraid I didn't un-

derstand a fraction of what he told me. He carried on about aprons and funnel systems and became very expansive on wind drag and thrust." She creased her brow for a moment as she searched her memory. "I'm told struts can withstand comprehensive as well as tensile forces. I didn't have the courage to confess I didn't know one force from the other."

"He's happiest when he's talking about planes," Dillon commented absently. "It doesn't matter if you understood as long as you listened. Hand me that torque wrench."

Laine looked down at the assortment of tools, then searched for something resembling a torque wrench. "I enjoyed listening. Is this a wrench?"

Dillon twisted his head and glanced at the ratchet she offered. With reluctant amusement, he brought his eyes to hers, then shook his head. "No, Duchess. This," he stated, finding the tool himself, "is a wrench."

"I haven't spent a great deal of time under cars or under planes," she muttered. Her annoyance spread as she thought how unlikely it was that he would ask Orchid King for a torque wrench. "Cap told me you've added a flight school. Do you do the instructing?"

"Some."

Pumping up her courage, Laine asked in a rush, "Would you teach me?"

"What?" Dillon glanced back over his shoulder.

"Could you teach me to fly a plane?" She wondered if the question sounded as ridiculous to Dillon as it did to her.

"Maybe." He studied the fragile planes of her face, noting the determined light in her eyes. "Maybe," he repeated. "Why do you want to learn?"

"Cap used to talk about teaching me. Of course—" she spread her hands in a Gallic gesture "—I was only a child, but…" Releasing an impatient breath, Laine lifted her chin and was suddenly very American. "Because I think it would be fun."

The change, and the stubborn set to her mouth, touched off Dillon's laughter. "I'll take one of you up tomorrow." Laine frowned, trying to puzzle out his meaning. Turning back to the plane, Dillon held out the wrench for her to put away. She stared at the grease-smeared handle. Taking his head from the bowels of the plane, Dillon turned back and saw her reluctance. He muttered something she did not attempt to translate, then moved away and pulled another pair of coveralls from a hook. "Here, put these on. I'm going to be a while, and you might as well be useful."

"I'm sure you'd manage beautifully without me."

"Undoubtedly, but put them on anyway." Under Dillon's watchful eye, Laine stepped into the coveralls and slipped her arms into the sleeves. "Good grief, you look swallowed." Crouching down, he began to roll up the pants legs while she scowled at the top of his head.

"I'm sure you'll find me more hindrance than help."

"I figured that out some time ago," he replied. His tone was undeniably cheerful as he rolled up her sleeves half a dozen times. "You shouldn't have quit growing so soon; you don't look more than twelve." He pulled the zipper up to her throat in one swift motion, then looked into her face. She saw his expresion alter. For an instant, she thought she observed a flash of tenderness before he let out an impatient breath. Cursing softly, he submerged into the belly of the plane. "All right," he began briskly, "hand me a screwdriver. The one with the red handle."

Having made the acquaintance of this particular tool, Laine foraged and found it. She placed it in Dillon's outstretched hand. He worked for some time, his conversation limited almost exclusively to the request and description of tools. As time passed, the hum of planes outside became only a backdrop for his voice.

Laine began to ask him questions about the job he was performing. She felt no need to follow his answers, finding pleasure only in the tone and texture of his voice. He was absorbed and she was able to study him unobserved. She surveyed the odd intensity of his eyes, the firm line of his chin and jaw, the bronzed skin which rippled along his arm as he worked. She saw that his chin was shadowed with a day-old beard, that his hair was curling loosely over his collar, that his right brow was lifted slightly higher than his left as he concentrated.

Dillon turned to her with some request, but she could only stare. She was lost in his eyes, blanketed by a fierce and trembling realization.

"What's wrong?" Dillon drew his brows together.

Like a diver breaking water, Laine shook her head and swallowed. "Nothing, I... What did you want? I wasn't paying attention." She bent over the box of tools as if it contained the focus of her world. Silently, Dillon lifted out the one he required and turned back to the engine. Grateful for his preoccupation, Laine closed her eyes. She felt bemused and defenseless.

Love, she thought, *should not come with such quick intensity. It should flow slowly, with tenderness and gentle feelings. It shouldn't stab like a sword, striking without warning, without mercy. How could one love what one could not understand?* Dillon O'Brian was an enigma, a man whose moods seemed to flow without rhyme or reason. And what did she know of him? He was her father's partner, but his position was unclear. He was a man who knew both the sky and the sea, and found it easy to move with their freedom. She knew too that he was a man who knew women and could give them pleasure.

And how, Laine wondered, does one fight love when one has no knowledge of it? Perhaps it was a matter of balance. She deliberately released the tension in her shoulders. *I have to find the way to walk the wire without leaning over either side and tumbling off.*

"It seems you've taken a side trip," Dillon commented, pulling a rag from his pocket. He grinned as Laine gave a start of alarm. "You're a miserable mechanic, Duchess, and a sloppy one." He rubbed the rag over her cheek until a black smudge disappeared. "There's a sink over there; you'd better go wash your hands. I'll finish these adjustments later. The fuel system is giving me fits."

Laine moved off as he instructed, taking her time in removing traces of grime. She used the opportunity to regain her composure. Hanging up the borrowed overalls, she wandered about the empty hangar while Dillon packed away tools and completed his own washing up. She was surprised to see that it had grown late during the time she had inexpertly assisted Dillon. A soft dusk masked the day's brilliance. Along the runways, lights twinkled like small red eyes. As she turned back, Laine found Dillon's gaze on her. She moistened her lips, then attempted casualness.

"Are you finished?"

"Not quite. Come here." Something in his tone caused her to retreat a step rather than obey. He lifted his brows, then repeated the order with a soft, underlying threat. "I said come here."

Deciding voluntary agreement was the wisest choice, Laine crossed the floor. Her echoing footsteps seemed to bounce off the walls like thunder. She prayed the sound masked the furious booming of her heart as she stopped in front of him, and that its beating was in her ears only. She stood in silence as he studied her face, wishing desperately she knew what he was looking for, and if she possessed it. Dillon said nothing, but placed his hands on her hips, drawing her a step closer. Their thighs brushed. His grip was firm, and all the while his eyes kept hers a prisoner.

"Kiss me," he said simply. She shook her head in quick protest, unable to look or break away. "Laine, I said kiss me." Dillon pressed her hips closer, molding her shape to his. His eyes were demanding, his mouth tempting. Tentatively, she lifted her arms, letting her hands rest on his shoulders as she rose to her toes. Her eyes remained open and locked on his as their faces drew nearer, as their breaths began to mingle. Softly, she touched her lips to his.

He waited until her mouth lost its shyness and became mobile on his, waited until her arms found their way around his neck to urge him closer. He increased the pressure, drawing out her sigh as he slid his hands under her blouse to the smooth skin of her back. His explorations were slow and achingly gentle. The hands that caressed her taught rather than demanded. Murmuring his name against the taste of his mouth, Laine strained against him, wanting him, needing him. The swift heat of passion was all-consuming. Her lips seemed to learn more quickly than her brain. They began to seek and demand pleasures she could not yet understand. The rest of the world faded like a whisper. At that moment, there was nothing in her life but Dillon and her need for him.

He drew her away. Neither spoke, each staring into the other's eyes as if to read a message not yet written. Dillon brushed a stray curl from her cheek. "I'd better take you home."

"Dillon," Laine began, completely at a loss as to what could be said. Unable to continue, she closed her eyes on her own inadequacy.

"Come on, Duchess, you've had a long day." Dillon circled her neck with his hand and massaged briefly. "We're not dealing on equal footing at the moment, and I like to fight fair under most circumstances."

"Fight?" Laine managed, struggling to keep her eyes open and steady on his. "Is that what this is, Dillon? A fight?"

"The oldest kind," he returned with a small lift to his mouth. His smile faded before it was truly formed, and suddenly his hand was firm on her chin. "It's not over, Laine, and when we have the next round, I might say the devil with the rules."

chapter seven

When Laine came down for breakfast the next morning, she found only her father. "Hello, Skinny Bones," Miri called out before Cap could greet her. "Sit and eat. I will fix you tea since you do not like my coffee."

Unsure whether to be embarrassed or amused, Laine obeyed. "Thank you, Miri," she said to the retreating back.

"She's quite taken with you." Looking over, Laine saw the light of mirth in Cap's eyes. "Since you've come, she's been so wrapped up with putting pounds on you, she hasn't made one comment about me needing a wife."

With a wry smile, Laine watched her father pour his coffee. "Glad to help. I showed myself around a bit yesterday. I hope you don't mind."

"No, of course not." His smile was rueful. "I guess I should've taken you around the house myself. My manners are a little rusty."

"I didn't mind. Actually," she tilted her head and returned his smile, "wandering around alone gave me a sort of fresh perspective. You said you'd missed all the stages and still thought of me as a child. I think…" Her fingers spread as she tried to clarify her thoughts. "I think I missed them too—that is, I still had my childhood image of you. Yesterday, I began to see James Simmons in flesh and blood."

"Disappointed?" There was more ease in his tone and a lurking humor in his eyes.

"Impressed," Laine corrected. "I saw a man content with himself and his life, who has the love and respect of those close to him. I think my father must be a very nice man."

He gave her an odd smile which spoke both of surprise and pleasure. "That's quite a compliment coming from a grown daughter." He added more coffee to his cup, and Laine let the silence drift. Her gaze lingered on Dillon's empty seat a moment. "Ah…is Dillon not here?"

"Hmm? Oh, Dillon had a breakfast meeting. As a matter of fact, he has quite a few things to see to this morning." Cap drank his coffee black, and with an enjoyment Laine could not understand.

"I see," she responded, trying not to sound disappointed. "I suppose the airport keeps both of you very busy."

"That it does." Cap glanced at his watch and tilted his head in regret. "Actually, I have an appointment myself very shortly. I'm sorry to leave you alone this way, but…"

"Please," Laine interrupted. "I don't need to be entertained, and I meant what I said yesterday about not wanting to interfere. I'm sure I'll find plenty of things to keep me occupied."

"All right then. I'll see you this evening." Cap rose, then paused at the doorway with sudden inspiration. "Miri can arrange a ride for you if you'd like to do some shopping in town."

"Thank you." Laine smiled, thinking of her limited funds. "Perhaps I will." She watched him stroll away, then sighed, as her gaze fell again on Dillon's empty chair.

Laine's morning was spent lazily. She soon found out that Miri would not accept or tolerate any help around the house. Following the native woman's strong suggestion that she go out, Laine gathered her stationery and set out for the bay. She found it every bit as perfect as she had the day before—the water clear as crystal, the sand white and pure. Spreading out a blanket, Laine sat down and tried to describe her surroundings with words on paper. The letters she wrote to France were long and detailed, though she omitted any mention of her troubled situation.

As she wrote, the sun rose high overhead. The air was moist and ripe. Lulled by the peace and the rays of the sun, she curled up on the blanket and slept.

Her limbs were languid, and behind closed lids was a dull red mist. She wondered hazily how the reverend mother had urged so much heat out of the ancient furnace. Reluctantly, she struggled to toss off sleep as a hand shook her shoulder. *"Un moment, ma soeur,"* she murmured, and sighed with the effort. *"J'arrive."* Forcing open her leaden lids, she found Dillon's face inches above hers.

"I seem to have a habit of waking you up." He leaned back on his heels and studied her cloudy eyes. "Don't you know better than to sleep in the sun with that complexion? You're lucky you didn't burn."

"Oh." At last realizing where she was, Laine pushed herself into a sitting position. She felt the odd sense of guilt of the napper caught napping. "I don't know why I fell asleep like that. It must have been the quiet."

"Another reason might be exhaustion," Dillon countered, then frowned. "You're losing the shadows under your eyes."

"Cap said you were very busy this morning." Laine found his continued survey disconcerting and shuffled her writing gear.

"Hmm, yes, I was. Writing letters?"

She glanced up at him, then tapped the tip of her pen against her mouth. "Hmm, yes, I was."

"Very cute." His mouth twitched slightly as he hauled her to her feet. "I thought you wanted to learn how to fly a plane."

"Oh!" Her face lit up with pleasure. "I thought you'd forgotten. Are you sure you're not too busy? Cap said…"

"No, I hadn't forgotten, and no, I'm not too busy." He cut her off as he leaned down to gather her blanket. "Stop babbling as if you were twelve and I were taking you to the circus for cotton candy."

"Of course," she replied, amused by his reaction.

Dillon let out an exasperated breath before grabbing her hand and pulling her across the sand. She heard him mutter something uncomplimentary about women in general.

Less than an hour later, Laine found herself seated in Dillon's plane. "Now, this is a single-prop monoplane with a reciprocating engine. Another time, I'll take you up in the jet, but…"

"You have another plane?" Laine interrupted.

"Some people collect hats," Dillon countered dryly, then pointed to the variety of gauges. "Basically, flying a plane is no more difficult than driving a car. The first thing you have to do is understand your instruments and learn how to read them."

"There are quite a few, aren't there?" Dubiously, Laine scanned numbers and needles.

"Not really. This isn't exactly an X-15." He let out a long breath at her blank expression, then started the engine. "O.K., as we climb, I want you to watch this gauge. It's the altimeter. It…"

"It indicates the height of the plane above sea level or above ground," Laine finished for him.

"Very good." Dillon cleared his takeoff with the tower, and the plane began its roll down the runway. "What did you do, grab one of Cap's magazines last night?"

"No. I remember some of my early lessons. I suppose I stored away all the things Cap used to ramble about when I was a child. This is a compass, and this…" Her brow furrowed in her memory search. "This is a turn and bank indicator, but I'm not sure I remember quite what that means."

"I'm impressed, but you're supposed to be watching the altimeter."

"Oh, yes." Wrinkling her nose at the chastisement, she obeyed.

"All right." Dillon gave her profile a quick grin, then turned his attention to the sky. "The larger needle's going to make one turn of the dial for every thousand feet we climb. The smaller one makes a turn for every ten thousand. Once you learn your gauges, and how to use each one of them, your job's less difficult than driving, and there's generally a lot less traffic."

"Perhaps you'll teach me to drive a car next," Laine suggested as she watched the large needle round the dial for the second time.

"You don't know how to drive?" Dillon demanded. His voice was incredulous.

"No. Is that a crime in this country? I assure you, there are some people who believe me to be marginally intelligent. I'm certain I can learn to fly this machine in the same amount of time it takes any of your other students."

"It's possible," Dillon muttered. "How come you never learned to drive a car?"

"Because I never had one. How did you break your nose?" At his puzzled expression, Laine merely gave him a bland smile. "My question is just as irrelevant as yours."

Laine felt quite pleased when he laughed, almost as though she had won a small victory.

"Which time?" he asked, and it was her turn to look puzzled. "I broke it twice. The first time I was about ten and tried to fly a cardboard plane I had designed off the roof of the garage. I didn't have the propulsion system perfected. I only broke my nose and my arm, though I was told it should've been my neck."

"Very likely," Laine agreed. "And the second time?"

"The second time, I was a bit older. There was a disagreement over a certain girl. My nose suffered another insult, and the other guy lost two teeth."

"Older perhaps, but little wiser," Laine commented. "And who got the girl?"

Dillon flashed his quick grin. "Neither of us. We decided she wasn't worth it after all and went off to nurse our wounds with a beer."

"How gallant."

"Yeah, I'm sure you've noticed that trait in me. I can't seem to shake it. Now, watch your famous turn and bank indicator, and I'll explain its function."

For the next thirty minutes, he became the quintessential teacher, surprising Laine with his knowledge and patience. He answered the dozens of questions she tossed out as flashes of her early lessons skipped through her memory. He seemed to accept her sudden thirst to know as if it were not only natural, but expected. They cruised through a sky touched with puffy clouds and mountain peaks and skimmed the gaping mouth of the multihued Waimea Canyon. They circled above the endless, whitecapped ocean. Laine began to see the similarity between the freedom of the sky and the freedom of the sea. She began to feel the fascination Dillon had spoken of, the need to meet the challenge, the need to explore. She listened with every ounce of her concentration, determined to understand and remember.

"There's a little storm behind us," Dillon announced casually. "We're not going to beat it back." He turned to Laine with a faint smile on his lips. "We're going to get tossed around a bit, Duchess."

"Oh?" Trying to mirror his mood, Laine shifted in her seat and studied the dark clouds in their wake. "Can you fly through that?" she asked, keeping her voice light while her stomach tightened.

"Oh, maybe," he returned. She jerked her head around swiftly. When she saw the laughter in his eyes, she let out a long breath.

"You have an odd sense of humor, Dillon. Very unique," she added, then sucked in her breath as the clouds overtook them. All at once, they were shrouded in darkness, rain pelting furiously on all sides. As the plane rocked, Laine felt a surge of panic.

"You know, it always fascinates me to be in a cloud. Nothing much to them, just vapor and moisture, but they're fabulous." His voice was calm and composed. Laine felt her heartbeat steadying. "Storm clouds are the most interesting, but you really need lightning."

"I think I could live without it," Laine murmured.

"That's because you haven't seen it from up here. When you fly above lightning, you can watch it kicking up inside the clouds. The colors are incredible."

"Have you flown through many storms?" Laine looked out her windows, but saw nothing but swirling black clouds.

"I've done my share. The front of this one'll be waiting for us when we land. Won't last long, though." The plane bucked again, and Laine looked on in bewilderment as Dillon grinned.

"You enjoy this sort of thing, don't you? The excitement, the sense of danger?"

"It keeps the reflexes in tune, Laine." Turning, he smiled at her without a trace of cynicism. "And it keeps life from being boring." The look held for a moment, and Laine's heart did a series of jumping jacks. "There's plenty of stability in life," he continued, making adjustments to compensate for the wind. "Jobs, bills, insurance policies, that's what gives you balance. But sometimes, you've got to ride a roller coaster, run a race, ride a wave. That's what makes life fun. The trick is to keep one end of the scope from overbalancing the other."

Yes, Laine thought. Vanessa never learned the trick. She was always looking for a new game and never enjoyed the one she was playing. And perhaps I've overcompensated by thinking too much of the stability. Too many books, and not enough doing. Laine felt her muscles relax and she turned to Dillon with a hint of a smile. "I haven't ridden a roller coaster for a great many years. One could say that I'm due. Look!" She pressed her face against the side window and peered downward. "It's like something out of *Macbeth,* all misty and sinister. I'd like to see the lightning, Dillon. I really would."

He laughed at the eager anticipation on her face as he began his descent. "I'll see if I can arrange it."

The clouds seemed to swirl and dissolve as the plane lost altitude. Their thickness became pale gray cobwebs to be dusted out of the way. Below, the landscape came into view as they dropped below the mist. The earth was rain-drenched and vivid with color. As they landed, Laine felt her pleasure fade into a vague sense of loss. She felt like a child who had just blown out her last birthday candle.

"I'll take you back up in a couple days if you want," said Dillon, taxiing to a halt.

"Yes, please, I'd like that very much. I don't know how to thank you for…"

"Do your homework," he said as he shut off the engine. "I'll give you some books and you can read up on instrumentation."

"Yes, sir," Laine said with suspicious humility. Dillon glared at her briefly before swinging from the plane. Laine's lack of experience caused her to take more time with her exit. She found herself swooped down before she could complete the journey on her own.

In the pounding rain they stood close, Dillon's hands light on her waist. She could feel the heat of his body through the dampness of her blouse. Dark tendrils of hair fell over his forehead, and without thought, Laine lifted her hand to smooth them back. There was something sweetly ordinary about being in his arms, as if it were a place she had been countless times before and would come back to countless times again. She felt her love bursting to be free.

"You're getting wet," she murmured, dropping her hand to his cheek.

"So are you." Though his fingers tightened on her waist, he drew her no closer.

"I don't mind."

With a sigh, Dillon rested his chin on the top of her head. "Miri'll punch me out if I let you catch a chill."

"I'm not cold," she murmured, finding indescribable pleasure in their closeness.

"You're shivering." Abruptly, Dillon brought her to his side and began to walk. "We'll go into my office, and you can dry out before I take you home."

As they walked, the rain slowed to a mist. Fingers of sunlight began to strain through, brushing away the last stubborn drops. Laine surveyed the complex. She remembered the building which housed Dillon's office from the tour she had taken with her father. With a grin, she pushed damp hair from her eyes and pulled away from Dillon. "Race you," she challenged, and scrambled over wet pavement.

He caught her, laughing and breathless, at the door. With a new ease, Laine circled his neck as they laughed together. She felt young and foolish and desperately in love.

"You're quick, aren't you?" Dillon observed, and she tilted her head back to meet his smile.

"You learn to be quick when you live in a dormitory. Competition for the bath is brutal." Laine thought she saw his smile begin to fade before they were interrupted.

"Dillon, I'm sorry to disturb you."

Glancing over, Laine saw a young woman with classic bone structure, her raven hair pulled taut at the nape of a slender neck. The woman returned Laine's survey with undisguised curiosity. Blushing, Laine struggled out of Dillon's arms.

"It's all right, Fran. This is Laine Simmons, Cap's daughter. Fran's my calculator."

"He means secretary," Fran returned with an exasperated

sigh. "But this afternoon I feel more like an answering service. You have a dozen phone messages on your desk."

"Anything urgent?" As he asked, he moved into an adjoining room.

"No." Fran gave Laine a friendly smile. "Just several people who didn't want to make a decision until they heard from Mount Olympus. I told them all you were out for the day and would get back to them tomorrow."

"Good." Walking back into the room, Dillon carried a handful of papers and a towel. He tossed the towel at Laine before he studied the papers.

"I thought you were supposed to be taking a few days off," Fran stated while Dillon muttered over his messages.

"Um-hum. There doesn't seem to be anything here that can't wait."

"I've already told you that." Fran snatched the papers out of his hand.

"So you did." Unabashed, Dillon grinned and patted her cheek. "Did you ask Orchid what she wanted?"

Across the room, Laine stopped rubbing the towel against her hair, then began again with increased speed.

"No, though after the *third* call, I'm afraid I became a bit abrupt with her."

"She can handle it," Dillon returned easily, then switched his attention to Laine. "Ready?"

"Yes." Feeling curiously deflated, Laine crossed the room and handed Dillon the towel. "Thank you."

"Sure." Casually, he tossed the damp towel to Fran. "See you tomorrow, cousin."

"Yes, master." Fran shot Laine a friendly wave before Dillon hustled her from the building.

With a great deal of effort, Laine managed to thrust Orchid King from her mind during the drive home and throughout the evening meal. The sun was just setting when she settled on the porch with Dillon and her father.

The sky's light was enchanting. The intense, tropical blue was breaking into hues of gold and crimson, the low, misted clouds streaked with pinks and mauves. There was something dreamlike and soothing in the dusk. Laine sat quietly in a wicker chair, thinking over her day as the men's conversation washed over her. Even had she understood their exchange, she was too lazily content to join in. She knew that for the first time in her adult life, she was both physically and mentally relaxed. Perhaps, she mused, it was the adventures of the past few days, the testing of so many untried feelings and emotions.

Mumbling about coffee, Cap rose and slipped inside the house. Laine gave him an absent smile as he passed her, then curled her legs under her and watched the first stars blink into life.

"You're quiet tonight." As Dillon leaned back in his chair, Laine heard the soft click of his lighter.

"I was just thinking how lovely it is here." Her sigh drifted with contentment. "I think it must be the loveliest place on earth."

"Lovelier than Paris?"

Hearing the edge in his voice, Laine turned to look at him questioningly. The first light of the moon fell gently over her face. "It's very different from Paris," she answered. "Parts of Paris are beautiful, mellowed and gentled with age. Other parts are elegant or dignified. She is like a woman who has been often told she is enchanting. But the beauty here is more primitive. The island is ageless and innocent at the same time."

"Many people tire of innocence." Dillon shrugged and drew deeply on his cigarette.

"I suppose that's true," she agreed, unsure why he seemed so distant and so cynical.

"In this light, you look a great deal like your mother," he said suddenly, and Laine felt her skin ice over.

"How do you know? You never met my mother."

"Cap has a picture." Dillon turned toward her, but his face was in shadows. "You resemble her a great deal."

"She certainly does." Cap sauntered out with a tray of coffee in his hands. Setting it on a round glass table, he straightened and studied Laine. "It's amazing. The light will catch you a certain way, or you'll get a certain expression on your face. Suddenly, it's your mother twenty years ago."

"I'm not Vanessa." Laine sprang up from her seat, and her voice trembled with rage. "I'm nothing like Vanessa." To her distress, tears began to gather in her eyes. Her father looked on in astonishment. "I'm nothing like her. I won't be compared to her." Furious with both the men and herself, Laine turned and slammed through the screen door. On her dash for the stairs, she collided with Miri's substantial form. Stuttering an apology, she streaked up the stairs and into her room.

★ ★ ★

Laine was pacing around her room for the third time when Miri strolled in.

"What is all this running and slamming in my house?" Miri asked, folding her arms across her ample chest.

Shaking her head, Laine lowered herself to the bed, then, despising herself, burst into tears. Clucking her tongue and muttering in Hawaiian, Miri crossed the room. Soon Laine found her head cradled against a soft, pillowing bosom. "That Dillon," Miri muttered as she rocked Laine to and fro.

"It wasn't Dillon," Laine managed, finding the maternal comfort new and overwhelming. "Yes, it was…it was both of them." Laine had a sudden desperate need for reassurance. "I'm nothing like her, Miri. I'm nothing like her at all."

"Of course you are not." Miri patted Laine's blond curls. "Who is it you are not like?"

"Vanessa." Laine brushed away tears with the back of her hand. "My mother. Both of them were looking at me, saying how much I look like her."

"What is this? What is this? All these tears because you look like someone?" Miri pulled Laine away by the shoulders and shook her. "Why do you waste your tears on this? I think you're a smart girl, then you act stupid."

"You don't understand." Laine drew up her knees and rested her chin on them. "I won't be compared to her, not to her. Vanessa was selfish and self-centered and dishonest."

"She was your mother," Miri stated with such authority that Laine's mouth dropped open. "You will speak with respect of your mother. She is dead, and whatever she did is over now. You must bury it," Miri commanded, giving Laine another shake, "or you will never be happy. Did they say you were selfish and self-centered and dishonest?"

"No, but…"

"What did Cap Simmons say to you?" Miri demanded.

Laine let out a long breath. "He said I looked like my mother."

"And do you, or does he lie?"

"Yes, I suppose I do, but…"

"So, your mother was a pretty woman, you are a pretty woman." Miri lifted Laine's chin with her thick fingers. "Do you know who you are, Laine Simmons?"

"Yes, I think I do."

"Then you have no problem." Miri patted her cheek and rose.

"Oh, Miri." Laine laughed and wiped her eyes again. "You make me feel very foolish."

"You make yourself feel foolish," Miri corrected. "I did not slam doors."

Laine sighed over Miri's logic. "I suppose I'll have to go down and apologize."

As Laine stood, Miri folded her arms and blocked her way. "You will do no such thing."

Staring at her, Laine let out a frustrated breath. "But you just said…"

"I said you were stupid, and you were. Cap Simmons and Dillon were also stupid. No woman should be compared to another woman. You are special, you are unique. Sometimes men see only the face." Miri tapped a finger against each of her cheeks. "It takes them longer to see what is inside. So—" she gave Laine a white-toothed smile "—you will not apologize, you will let them apologize. It is the best way."

"I see," Laine said, not seeing at all. Suddenly, she laughed and sat back on the bed. "Thank you, Miri, I feel much better."

"Good. Now go to bed. I will go lecture Cap Simmons and Dillon." There was an unmistakable note of anticipation in her voice.

chapter eight

The following morning Laine descended the stairs, her Nile-green sundress floating around her, leaving her arms and shoulders bare. Feeling awkward after the previous evening's incident, Laine paused at the doorway of the dining room. Her father and Dillon were already at breakfast and deep in discussion.

"If Bob needs next week off, I can easily take his shift on the charters." Dillon poured coffee as he spoke.

"You've got enough to do at your own place without taking that on, too. Whatever happened to those few days off you were going to take?" Cap accepted the coffee and gave Dillon a stern look.

"I haven't exactly been chained to my desk the past week." Dillon grinned, then shrugged as Cap's expression remained unchanged. "I'll take some time off next month."

"Where have I heard that before?" Cap asked the ceiling. Dillon's grin flashed again.

"I didn't tell you I was retiring next year, did I?" Dillon sipped coffee casually, but Laine recognized the mischief in his voice. "I'm going to take up hang gliding while you slave away behind a desk. Who are you going to nag if I'm not around every day?"

"When you can stay away for more than a week at a time," Cap countered, "that's when *I'm* going to retire. The trouble with you—" he wagged a spoon at Dillon in admonishment "—is that your mind's too good and you've let too many people find it out. Now you're stuck because nobody wants to make a move without checking with you first. You should've kept that aeronautical-engineering degree a secret. Hang gliding." Cap chuckled and lifted his cup. "Oh, hello, Laine."

Laine jolted at the sound of her name. "Good morning," she replied, hoping that her outburst the evening before had not cost her the slight progress she had made with her father.

"Is it safe to ask you in?" His smile was sheepish, but he beckoned her forward. "As I recall, your explosions were frequent, fierce, but short-lived."

Relieved he had not offered her a stilted apology, Laine took her place at the table. "Your memory is accurate, though I assure you, I explode at very infrequent intervals these days." She offered Dillon a tentative smile, determined to treat the matter lightly. "Good morning, Dillon."

"Morning, Duchess. Coffee?" Before she could refuse, he was filling her cup.

"Thank you," she murmured. "It's hard to believe, but I think today is more beautiful than yesterday. I don't believe I'd ever grow used to living in paradise."

"You've barely seen any of it yet," Cap commented. "You should go up to the mountains, or to the center. You know, the center of Kauai is one of the wettest spots in the world. The rain forest is something to see."

"The island seems to have a lot of variety." Laine toyed with her coffee. "I can't imagine any of it is more beautiful than right here."

"I'll take you around a bit today," Dillon announced. Laine glanced sharply at him.

"I don't want to interfere with your routine. I've already taken up a great deal of your time." Laine had not yet regained her balance with Dillon. Her eyes were both wary and unsure.

"I've a bit more to spare." He rose abruptly. "I'll have things cleared up and be back around eleven. See you later, Cap." He strode out without waiting for her assent.

Miri entered with a full plate and placed it in front of Laine. She scowled at the coffee. "Why do you pour coffee when you aren't going to drink it?" With a regal sniff, she picked up the cup and swooped from the room. With a sigh, Laine attacked her breakfast and wondered how the day would pass. She was to find the morning passed quickly.

As if granting a royal boon, Miri agreed to allow Laine to refresh the vases of flowers which were scattered throughout the house. Laine spent her morning hours in the garden. It was not a garden as Laine remembered from her early American years or from her later French ones. It was a spreading, sprawling, wild tangle of greens and tempestuous hues. The plants would not be organized or dictated to by plot or plan.

Inside again, Laine took special care in the arranging of the vases. Her mind drifted to the daffodils which would be blooming outside her window at school. She found it odd that she felt no trace of homesickness, no longing for the soft French voices of the sisters or the high, eager ones of her students. She knew that she was dangerously close to thinking of Kauai as home. The thought of returning to France and the life she led there filled her with a cold, dull ache.

In her father's den, Laine placed the vase of frangipani on his desk and glanced at the photograph of Cap and Dillon. *How strange,* she thought, *that I should need both of them so badly.* With a sigh, she buried her face in the blossoms.

"Do flowers make you unhappy?"

She whirled, nearly upsetting the vase. For a moment, she and Dillon stared at each other without speaking. Laine felt the tension between them, though its cause and meaning were unclear to her. "Hello. Is it eleven already?'"

"It's nearly noon. I'm late." Dillon thrust his hands in his pockets and watched her. Behind her, the sun poured through the window to halo her hair. "Do you want some lunch?"

"No, thank you," she said with conviction. She saw his eyes smile briefly.

"Are you ready?"

"Yes, I'll just tell Miri I'm going."

"She knows." Crossing the room, Dillon slid open the glass door and waited for Laine to precede him outside.

Laine found Dillon in a silent mood as they drove from the house. She gave his thoughts their privacy and concentrated on the view. Ridges of green mountains loomed on either side. Dillon drove along a sheer precipice where the earth surrendered abruptly to the sky to fall into an azure sea.

"They used to toss Kukui oil torches over the cliffs to entertain royalty," Dillon said suddenly, after miles of silence. "Legend has it that the menehune lived here. The pixie people," he elaborated at her blank expression. "You see there?" After halting the car, he pointed to a black precipice lined with grooves. "That's their staircase. They built fishponds by moonlight."

"Where are they now?" Laine smiled at him.

Dillon reached across to open her door. "Oh, they're still here. They're hiding."

Laine joined him to walk to the edge of the cliff. Her heart flew to her throat as she stared from the dizzying height down to the frothing power of waves on rock. For an instant, she could feel herself tumbling helplessly through miles of space.

Unaffected by vertigo, Dillon looked out to sea. The breeze teased his hair, tossing it into confusion. "You have the remarkable capacity of knowing when to be quiet and making the silence comfortable," he remarked.

"You seemed preoccupied." The wind tossed curls in her eyes, and Laine brushed them away. "I thought perhaps you were working out a problem."

"Did you?" he returned, and his expression seemed both amused and annoyed. "I want to talk to you about your mother."

The statement was so unexpected that it took Laine a moment to react. "No." She turned away, but he took her arm and held her still.

"You were furious last night. I want to know why."

"I overreacted." She tossed her head as her curls continued to dance around her face. "It was foolish of me, but sometimes my temper gets the better of me." She saw by his expression that her explanation would not placate him. She wanted badly to tell him how she had been hurt, but the memory of their first discussion in her father's house, and his cold judgment of her, prevented her. "Dillon, all my life I've been accepted for who I am." Speaking slowly, she chose her words carefully. "It annoys me to find that changing now. I do not want to be compared with Vanessa because we share certain physical traits."

"Is that what you think Cap was doing?"

"Perhaps, perhaps not." She tilted her chin yet farther. "But that's what you were doing."

"Was I?" It was a question which asked for no answer, and Laine gave none. "Why are you so bitter about your mother, Laine?"

She moved her shoulders and turned back toward the sea. "I'm not bitter, Dillon, not any longer. Vanessa's dead, and that part of my life is over. I don't want to talk about her until I understand my feelings better."

"All right." They stood silent for a moment, wrapped in the wind.

"I'm having a lot more trouble with you than I antici-pated," Dillon muttered.

"I don't know what you mean."

"No," he agreed, looking at her so intently she felt he read her soul. "I'm sure you don't." He walked away, then stopped. After a hesitation too brief to measure, he turned toward her again and held out his hand. Laine stared at it, unsure what he was offering. Finding it did not matter, she accepted.

During the ensuing drive, Dillon spoke easily. His mood had altered, and Laine moved with it. The world was lush with ripe blossoms. Moss clung, green and vibrant, to cliffs— a carpet on stone. They passed elephant ears whose leaves were large enough to use as a canopy against rain or sun. The frangipani became more varied and more brilliant. When Dillon stopped the car again, Laine did not hesitate to take his hand.

He led her along a path that was sheltered by palms, moving down it as though he knew the way well. Laine heard the rush of water before they entered the clearing. Her breath caught at the sight of the secluded pool circled by thick trees and fed by a shimmering waterfall.

"Oh, Dillon, what a glorious place! There can't be another like it in the world!" Laine ran to the edge of the pool, then dropped down to feel the texture of the water. It was warm silk. "If I could, I would come here to swim in the moonlight." With a laugh, she rose and tossed water to the sky. "With flowers in my hair and nothing else."

"That's the only permissible way to swim in a moonlit pool. Island law."

Laughing again, she turned to a bush and plucked a scarlet

hibiscus. "I suppose I'd need long black hair and honey skin to look the part."

Taking the bloom from her, Dillon tucked it behind her ear. After studying the effect, he smiled and ran a finger down her cheek. "Ivory and gold work very nicely. There was a time you'd have been worshiped with all pomp and ceremony, then tossed off a cliff as an offering to jealous gods."

"I don't believe that would suit me." Utterly enchanted, Laine twirled away. "Is this a secret place? It feels like a secret place." Stepping out of her shoes, she sat on the edge of the pool and dangled her feet in the water.

"If you want it to be." Dropping down beside her, Dillon sat Indian-fashion. "It's not on the tourist route, at any rate."

"It feels magic, the same way that little bay feels magic. Do you feel it, Dillon? Do you realize how lovely this all is, how fresh, or are you immune to it by now?"

"I'm not immune to beauty." He lifted her hand, brushing his lips over her fingertips. Her eyes grew wide as currents of pleasure jolted up her arm. Smiling, Dillon turned her hand over and kissed her palm. "You can't have lived in Paris for fifteen years and not have had your hand kissed. I've seen movies."

The lightness of his tone helped her regain her balance. "Actually, everyone's always kissing my left hand. You threw me off when you kissed my right." She kicked water in the air and watched the drops catch the sun before they were swallowed by the pool. "Sometimes, when the rain drizzles in the fall, and the dampness creeps through the windows,

I'll remember this." Her voice had changed, and there was something wistful, something yearning in her tone. "Then when spring comes, and the buds flower, and the air smells of them, I'll remember the fragrance here. And when the sun shines on a Sunday, I'll walk near the Seine and think of a waterfall."

Rain came without warning, a shower drenched in sun. Dillon scrambled up, pulling Laine under a sheltering cluster of palms.

"Oh, it's warm." She leaned out from the green ceiling to catch rain in her palm. "It's as if it's dropping from the sun."

"Islanders call it liquid sunshine." Dillon gave an easy tug on her hand to pull her back as she inched forward. "You're getting soaked. I think you must enjoy getting drenched in your clothes." He ruffled her hair and splattered the air with shimmering drops.

"Yes, I suppose I do." She stared out, absorbed with the deepening colors. Blossoms trembled under their shower. "There's so much on the island that remains unspoiled, as if no one had ever touched it. When we stood on the cliff and looked down at the sea, I was frightened. I've always been a coward. But still, it was beautiful, so terrifyingly beautiful I couldn't look away."

"A coward?" Dillon sat on the soft ground and pulled her down to join him. Her head naturally found the curve of his shoulder. "I would have said you were remarkably intrepid. You didn't panic during the storm yesterday."

"No, I just skirted around the edges of panic."

His laugh was full of pleasure. "You also survived the little show in the plane on the way from Oahu without a scream or a faint."

"That's because I was angry." She pushed at her damp hair and watched the thin curtain of rain. "It was unkind of you."

"Yes, I suppose it was. I'm often unkind."

"I think you're kind more often than not. Though I also think you don't like being labeled a kind man."

"That's a very odd opinion for a short acquaintance." Her answering shrug was eloquent and intensely Gallic. A frown moved across his brow. "This school of yours," he began, "what kind is it?"

"Just a school, the same as any other, with giggling girls and rules which must be broken."

"A boarding school?" he probed, and she moved her shoulders again.

"Yes, a boarding school. Dillon, this is not the place to think of schedules and classes. I shall have to deal with them again soon enough. This is a magic place, and for now I want to pretend I belong here. *Ah, regarde!*" Laine shifted, gesturing in wonder. *"Un arc-en-ciel."*

"I guess that means rainbow." He glanced at the sky, then back at her glowing face.

"There are two! How can there be two?"

They stretched, high and perfect, in curving arches from one mountain ridge to another. The second's shimmering colors were the reverse of the first's. As the sun glistened on raindrops, the colors grew in intensity, streaking across the cerulean sky like a trail from an artist's many-tinted brush.

"Double bows are common here," Dillon explained, relaxing against the base of the palm. "The trade winds blow against the mountains and form a rain boundary. It rains on one side while the sun shines on the other. Then, the sun strikes the raindrops, and…"

"No, don't tell me," Laine interrupted with a shake of her head. "It would spoil it if I knew." She smiled with the sudden knowledge that all things precious should be left unexplained. "I don't want to understand," she murmured, accepting both her love and the rainbows without question, without logic. "I just want to enjoy." Tilting back her head, Laine offered her mouth. "Will you kiss me, Dillon?"

His eyes never left hers. He brought his hands to her face, and gently, his fingers stroked the fragile line of her cheek. In silence, he explored the planes and hollows of her face with his fingertips, learning the texture of fine bones and satin skin. His mouth followed the trail of his fingers, and Laine closed her eyes, knowing nothing had ever been sweeter than his lips on her skin. Still moving slowly, still moving gently, Dillon brushed his mouth over hers in a whisperlike kiss which drugged her senses. He seemed content to taste, seemed happy to sample rather than devour. His mouth moved on, lingering on the curve of her neck, nibbling at the lobe of her ear before coming back to join hers. His tongue teased her lips apart as her heartbeat began to roar in her ears. He took her to the edge of reason with a tender, sensitive touch. As her need grew, Laine drew him closer, her body moving against his in innocent temptation.

Dillon swore suddenly before pulling her back. She kept her arms around his neck, her fingers tangled in his hair as he stared down at her. Her eyes were deep and cloudy with growing passion. Unaware of her own seductive powers, Laine sighed his name and placed a soft kiss on both of his cheeks.

"I want you," Dillon stated in a savage murmur before his mouth crushed hers. She yielded to him as a young willow yields to the wind.

His hands moved over her as if desperate to learn every aspect, every secret, and she who had never known a man's intimate touch delighted in the seeking. Her body was limber under his touch, responsive and eager. She was the student, and he the teacher. Her skin grew hot as her veins swelled with pounding blood. As the low, smoldering fire burst into quick flame, her demands rose with his. She trembled and murmured his name, as frightened of the new sensation as she had been at the edge of the cliff.

Dillon lifted his mouth from hers, resting it on her hair before she could search for the joining again. He held her close, cradling her head against his chest. His heart drummed against her ear, and Laine closed her eyes with the pleasure. Drawing her away, he stood. He moved his hands to his pockets as he turned his back on her.

"It's stopped raining." She thought his voice sounded strange and heard him take a long breath before he turned back to her. "We'd better go."

His expression was unfathomable. Though she searched, Laine could find no words to fill the sudden gap and close the distance which had sprung between them. Her eyes met his, asking questions her lips could not. Dillon opened his mouth as if to speak, then closed it again before he reached down to pull her to her feet. Her eyes faltered. Dillon lifted her chin with his fingertips, then traced the lips still soft from his. Briskly, he shook his head. Without a word, he lay his mouth gently on hers before he led her away from the palms.

chapter nine

A generous golden ball, the sun dominated the sky as the car moved along the highway. Dillon made easy conversation, as if passion belonged only to a rain-curtained pool. While her brain fidgeted, Laine tried to match his mood.

Men, she decided, must be better able to deal with the demands of the body than women are with those of the heart. He had wanted her; even if he had not said it, she would have known. The urgency, the power of his claim had been unmistakable. Laine felt her color rise as she remembered her unprotesting response. Averting her head as if absorbed in the view, she tried to decide what course lay open to her.

She would leave Kauai in a week's time. Now, she would not only have to abandon the father whom she had longed for all of her life, but the man who held all claim to her heart. Perhaps, she reflected with a small sigh, I'm always destined to love what can never be mine. Miri said I should fight as a woman fights, but I don't know where to begin. Perhaps with honesty. I should find the place and time to tell Dillon of my feelings. If he knew I wanted nothing from him but his affection, we might make a beginning. I could find a way to stay here at least a while longer. I could take a job. In time, he might learn to really care for me. Laine's mood lightened at the thought. She focused again on her surroundings.

"Dillon, what is growing there? Is it bamboo?" Acres upon acres of towering stalks bordered the road. Clumps of cylindrical gold stretched out on either side.

"Sugarcane," he answered, without glancing at the fields.

"It's like a jungle." Fascinated, Laine leaned out the window, and the wind buffeted her face. "I had no idea it grew so tall."

"Gets to be a bit over twenty feet, but it doesn't grow as fast as a jungle in this part of the world. It takes a year and a half to two years to reach full growth."

"There's so much." Laine turned to face him, absently brushing curls from her cheeks. "It's a plantation, I suppose, though it's hard to conceive of one person owning so much. It must take tremendous manpower to harvest."

"A bit." Dillon swerved off the highway and onto a hard-packed road. "The undergrowth is burned off, then machines cut the plants. Hand cutting is time consuming so machinery lowers production costs even when labor costs are low. Besides, it's one miserable job."

"Have you ever done it?" She watched a quick grin light his face.

"A time or two, which is why I prefer flying a plane."

Laine glanced around at the infinity of fields, wondering when the harvest began, trying to picture the machines slicing through the towering stalks. Her musings halted as the brilliant white of a house shone in the distance. Tall, with graceful colonial lines and pillars, it stood on lush lawns. Vines dripped from scrolled balconies; the high and narrow windows were shuttered in soft gray. The house looked comfortably old and lived in. Had it not been for South Sea foliage, Laine might have been seeing a plantation house in old Louisiana.

"What a beautiful home. One could see for miles from the balcony." Laine glanced at Dillon in surprise as he halted the car and again leaned over to open her door. "This is a private home, is it not? Are we allowed to walk around?"

"Sure." Opening his own door, Dillon slid out. "It's mine." He leaned against the car and looked down at her. "Are you going to sit there with your mouth open or are you going to come inside?" Quickly, Laine slid out and stood beside him. "I gather you expected a grass hut and hammock?"

"Why, no, I don't precisely know what I expected, but..." With a helpless gesture of her hands, she gazed about. A tremor of alarm trickled through her. "The cane fields," she began, praying she was mistaken. "Are they yours?"

"They go with the house."

Finding her throat closed, Laine said nothing as Dillon led her up stone steps and through a wide mahogany door. Inside, the staircase dominated the hall. Wide and arching in a deep half circle, its wood gleamed. Laine had a quick, confused impression of watercolors and wood carvings as Dillon strode straight down the hall and led her into a parlor.

The walls were like rich cream; the furnishings were dark and old. The carpet was a delicately faded needlepoint over a glistening wood floor. Nutmeg sheers were drawn back from the windows to allow the view of a manicured lawn.

"Sit down." Dillon gestured to a chair. "I'll see about something cold to drink." Laine nodded, grateful for the time alone to organize her scattered thoughts. She listened until Dillon's footsteps echoed into silence.

Her survey of the room was slow. She seated herself in a high-backed chair and let her eyes roam. The room had an undeniable air of muted wealth. Laine had not associated wealth with Dillon O'Brian. Now she found it an insurmountable obstacle. Her protestations of love would never be accepted as pure. He would think his money had been her enticement. She closed her eyes on a small moan of desperation. Rising, she moved to a window and tried to deal with dashed hopes.

What was it he called me once? *An operator.* With a short laugh, she rested her brow against the cool glass. I'm afraid I make a very poor one. I wish I'd never come here, never seen what he has. At least then I could have hung on to hope a bit longer. Hearing Dillon's approach, Laine struggled for composure. As he entered, she gave him a careful smile.

"Dillon, your home is very lovely." After accepting the tall glass he offered, Laine moved back to her chair.

"It serves." He sat opposite her. His brow lifted fractionally at the formality of her tone.

"Did you build it yourself?"

"No, my grandfather." With his customary ease, Dillon leaned back and watched her. "He was a sailor and decided Kauai was the next best thing to the sea."

"So. I thought it looked as if it had known generations." Laine sipped at her drink without tasting it. "But you found planes more enticing than the sea or the fields."

"The fields serve their purpose." Dillon frowned momentarily at her polite, impersonal interest. "They yield a marketable product, assist in local employment and make use of the land. It's a profitable crop and its management takes only a portion of my time." As Dillon set down his glass, Laine thought he appeared to come to some decision. "My father died a couple of months before I met Cap. We were both floundering, but I was angry, and he was…" Dillon hesitated, then shrugged. "He was as he always is. We suited each other. He had a cabin plane and used to pick up island hoppers. I couldn't learn about flying fast enough, and Cap needed to teach. I needed balance, and he needed to give it. A couple of years later, we began planning the airport."

Laine dropped her eyes to her glass. "And it was the money from your fields which built the airport?"

"As I said, the cane has its uses."

"And the bay where we swam?" On a sudden flash of intuition, she lifted her eyes to his. "That's yours, too, isn't it?"

"That's right." She could see no change of expression in his eyes.

"And my father's house?" Laine swallowed the dryness building in her throat. "Is that also on your property?"

She saw annoyance cross his face before he smoothed it away. His answer was mild. "Cap had a fondness for that strip of land, so he bought it."

"From you?"

"Yes, from me. Is that a problem?"

"No," she replied. "It's simply that I begin to see things more clearly. Much more clearly." Laine set down her drink and folded her empty hands. "It appears that you are more my father's son than I shall ever be his daughter."

"Laine…" Dillon let out a short breath, then rose and paced the room with a sudden restlessness. "Cap and I understand each other. We've known each other for nearly fifteen years. He's been part of my life for almost half of it."

"I'm not asking you for justifications, Dillon. I'm sorry if it seemed as if I were." Laine stood, trying to keep her voice steady. "When I return to France next week, it will be good to know that my father has you to rely on."

"Next week?" Dillon stopped pacing. "You're planning to leave next week?"

"Yes." Laine tried not to think of how quickly seven days could pass. "We agreed I would stay for two weeks. It's time I got back to my own life."

"You're hurt because Cap hasn't responded to you the way you'd hoped."

Surprised both by his words and the gentleness of his tone, Laine felt the thin thread of her control straining. She struggled to keep her eyes calm and level with his. "I have changed my mind…on a great many matters. Please don't, Dillon." She shook her head as he started to speak. "I would rather not talk of this; it's only more difficult."

"Laine." He placed his hands on her shoulders to prevent her from turning away. "There are a lot of things that you and I have to talk about, whether they're difficult or not. You can't keep shutting away little parts of yourself. I want…" The ringing of the doorbell interrupted his words. With a quick, impatient oath, he dropped his hands and strode away to answer.

A light, musical voice drifted into the room. When Orchid King entered the parlor on Dillon's arm, Laine met her with a polite smile.

It struck Laine that Orchid and Dillon were a perfectly matched couple. Orchid's tawny, exotic beauty suited his ruggedness, and her fully rounded curves were all the more stunning against his leanness. Her hair fell in an ebony waterfall, cascading down a smooth bare back to the waist of close-fitting pumpkin-colored shorts. Seeing her, Laine felt dowdy and provincial.

"Hello, Miss Simmons." Orchid tightened her hand on Dillon's arm. "How nice to see you again so soon."

"Hello, Miss King." Annoyed by her own insecurities, Laine met Orchid's amusement with eyes of a cool spring morning. "You did say the island was small."

"Yes, I did." She smiled, and Laine was reminded of a tawny cat. "I hope you've been able to see something of it."

"I took Laine around a bit this morning." Watching Laine, Dillon missed the flash of fire in Orchid's amber eyes.

"I'm sure she couldn't find a better guide." Orchid's expression melted into soft appeal. "I'm so glad you were home, Dillon. I wanted to make certain you'd be at the luau tomorrow night." Turning more directly to face him, she subtly but effectively excluded Laine from the conversation. "It wouldn't be any fun without you."

"I'll be there." Laine watched a smile lift one corner of his mouth. "Are you going to dance?"

"Of course." The soft purr of her voice added to Laine's image of a lithesome feline. "Tommy expects it."

Dillon's smile flashed into a grin. He lifted his eyes over Orchid's head to meet Laine's. "Tommy is Miri's nephew. He's having his annual luau tomorrow. You should find both the food and the entertainment interesting."

"Oh, yes," Orchid agreed. "No tourist should leave the islands without attending a luau. Do you plan to see the other islands during your vacation?"

"I'm afraid that will have to wait for another time. I'm sorry to say I haven't lived up to my obligations as a tourist. The purpose of my visit has been to see my father and his home."

Somewhat impatiently, Dillon disengaged his arm from Orchid's grasp. "I have to see my foreman. Why don't you keep Laine company for a few minutes?"

"Certainly." Orchid tossed a lock of rain-straight hair behind her back. "How are the repairs coming?"

"Fine. I should be able to move back in a couple of days without being in the way." With an inclination of his head for Laine, he turned and strode from the room.

"Miss Simmons, do make yourself at home." Assuming the role of hostess with a graceful wave of her hand, Orchid glided farther into the room. "Would you care for anything? A cold drink perhaps?"

Infuriated at being placed in the position of being Orchid's guest, Laine forced down her temper. "Thank you, no. Dillon has already seen to it."

"It seems you spend a great deal of time in Dillon's company," Orchid commented as she dropped into a chair. She crossed long, slender legs, looking like an advertisement for Hawaii's lush attractions. "Especially for one who comes to visit her father."

"Dillon has been very generous with his time." Laine copied Orchid's action and hoped she was equipped for a feminine battle of words.

"Oh, yes, Dillon's a generous man." Her smile was indulgent and possessive. "It's quite easy to misinterpret his generosity unless one knows him as well as I do. He can be so charming."

"Charming?" Laine repeated, and looked faintly skeptical. "How odd. Charming is not the adjective which comes to my mind. But then," she paused and smiled, "you know him better than I do."

Orchid placed the tips of her fingers together, then regarded Laine over the tips. "Miss Simmons, maybe we can dispense with the polite small talk while we have this time alone."

Wondering if she was sinking over her head, Laine nodded. "Your option, Miss King."

"I intend to marry Dillon."

"A formidable intention," Laine managed as her heart constricted. "I assume Dillon is aware of your goal."

"Dillon knows I want him." Irritation flickered over the

exotic face at Laine's easy answer. "I don't appreciate all the time you've been spending with him."

"That's a pity, Miss King." Laine picked up her long-abandoned glass and sipped. "But don't you think you're discussing this with the wrong person? I'm sure speaking to Dillon would be more productive."

"I don't believe that's necessary." Orchid gave Laine a companionable smile, showing just a hint of white teeth. "I'm sure we can settle this between us. Don't you think telling Dillon you wanted to learn to fly a plane was a little trite?"

Laine felt a flush of fury that Dillon had discussed her with Orchid. "Trite?"

Orchid made an impatient gesture. "Dillon's diverted by you at the moment, perhaps because you're such a contrast to the type of woman he's always preferred. But the milk-and-honey looks won't keep Dillon interested for long." The musical voice hardened. "Cool sophistication doesn't keep a man warm, and Dillon is very much a man."

"Yes, he's made that very clear," Laine could not resist interjecting.

"I'm warning you…once," Orchid hissed. "Keep your distance. I can make things very uncomfortable for you."

"I'm sure you can," Laine acknowledged. She shrugged. "I've been uncomfortable before."

"Dillon can be very vindictive when he thinks he's being deceived. You're going to end up losing more than you bargained for."

"Nom de Dieu!" Laine rose. "Is this how the game is played?" She made a contemptuous gesture with the back of

her hand. "I want none of it. Snarling and hissing like two cats over a mouse. This isn't worthy of Dillon."

"We haven't started to play yet." Orchid sat back, pleased by Laine's agitation. "If you don't like the rules, you'd better leave. I don't intend to put up with you any longer."

"Put up with me?" Laine stopped, her voice trembling with rage. "No one, Miss King, no one *puts up* with me. You hardly need concern yourself with a woman who will be gone in a week's time. Your lack of confidence is as pitiful as your threats." Orchid rose at that, her fists clenched by her sides.

"What do you want from me?" Laine demanded. "Do you want my assurance that I won't interfere with your plans? Very well, I give it freely and with pleasure. Dillon is yours."

"That's generous of you." Spinning, Laine saw Dillon leaning against the doorway. His arms were crossed, his eyes dangerously dark.

"Oh, Dillon, how quick you were." Orchid's voice was faint.

"Apparently not quick enough." His eyes were locked on Laine's. "What's the problem?"

"Just a little feminine talk, Dillon." Recovered, Orchid glided to his side. "Laine and I were just getting to know each other."

"Laine, what's going on?"

"Nothing important. If it's convenient, I should like to go back now." Without waiting for a reply, Laine picked up her bag and moved to the doorway.

Dillon halted her by a hand on her arm. "I asked you a question."

"And I have given you the only answer I intend to give."
She wrenched free and faced him. "I will not be questioned
any longer. You have no right to question me; I am nothing
to you. You have no right to criticize me as you have done
from the first moment. You have no right to judge." The
anger in her tone was now laced with despair. "You have no
right to make love to me just because it amuses you."

She ran in a flurry of flying skirts, and he watched the door
slam behind her.

chapter ten

Laine spent the rest of the day in her room. She attempted not to dwell on the scene in Dillon's home, or on the silent drive which followed it. She was not sure which had been more draining. It occurred to her that she and Dillon never seemed to enjoy a cordial relationship for more than a few hours at a time. It was definitely time to leave. She began to plan for her return to France. Upon a review of her finances, she discovered that she had barely enough for a return ticket.

It would, she realized with a sigh, leave her virtually penniless. Her own savings had been sorely dented in dealing with her mother's debts, and plane fare had eaten at what remained. She could not, she determined, return to France without a franc in her pocket. If there was a complication of any kind, she would be helpless to deal with it. *Why didn't I stop to think before I came here?* she demanded of herself. *Now I've placed myself in an impossible situation.*

Sitting on the bed, Laine rubbed an aching temple and tried to think. She didn't want to ask her father for money.

Pride prevented her from wiring to any friends to ask for a loan. She stared down at the small pile of bills in frustration. They won't proliferate of their own accord, she reflected, so I must plan how to increase their number.

She moved to her dresser and opened a small box. For some minutes, she studied the gold locket it contained. It had been a gift from her father to her mother, and Vanessa had given it to her on her sixteenth birthday. She remembered the pleasure she had felt upon receiving something, however indirectly, from her father. She had worn it habitually until she had dressed for her flight to Hawaii. Feeling it might cause her father pain, Laine had placed it in its box, hoping that unhappy memories would be buried. It was the only thing of value she owned, and now she had to sell it.

Her door swung open. Laine held the box behind her back. Miri glided in, a swirling mountain of color. She regarded Laine's flushed face with raised brows.

"Did you mess something up?"

"No."

"Then don't look guilty. Here." She laid a sheath of brilliant blue and sparkling white on the bedspread. "It's for you. You wear this to the luau tomorrow."

"Oh." Laine stared at the exquisite length of silk, already feeling its magic against her skin. "It's beautiful. I couldn't." She raised her eyes to Miri's with a mixture of desire and regret. "I couldn't take it."

"You don't like my present?" Miri demanded imperiously. "You are very rude."

"Oh, no." Struck with alarm at the unintentional offense,

Laine fumbled with an explanation. "It's beautiful…really. It's only that…"

"You should learn to say thank-you and not argue. This will suit your skinny bones." Miri gave a nod of satisfaction encompassing both the woman and the silk. "Tomorrow, I will show you how to wrap it."

Unable to prevent herself, Laine moved over to feel the cool material under her fingers. The combination of longing and Miri's dark, arched brows proved too formidable for pride. She surrendered with a sigh. "Thank you, Miri. It's very good of you."

"That's much better," Miri approved and patted Laine's halo of curls. "You are a pretty child. You should smile more. When you smile, the sadness goes away."

Feeling the small box weighing like a stone in her hand, Laine held it up and opened it. "Miri, I wonder if you might tell me where I could sell this."

One large brown finger traced the gold before Miri's jet eyes lifted. Laine saw the now familiar pucker between her brows. "Why do you want to sell a pretty thing like this? You don't like it?"

"No, no, I like it very much." Helpless under the direct stare, Laine moved her shoulders. "I need the money."

"Money? Why do you need money?"

"For my passage and expenses…to return to France."

"You don't like Kauai?" Her indignant tone caused Laine to smile and shake her head.

"Kauai is wonderful; I'd like nothing better than to stay here forever. But I must get back to my job."

"What do you do in that place?" Miri dismissed France with a regal gesture and settled her large frame into a chair. She folded her hands across the mound of her belly.

"I teach." Laine sat on the bed and closed the lid on the face of the locket.

"Don't they pay you to teach?" Miri pursed her lips in disapproval. "What did you do with your money?"

Laine flushed, feeling like a child who had been discovered spending her allowance on candy. "There…there were debts, and I…"

"You have debts?"

"Well, no, I…not precisely." Laine's shoulders drooped with frustration. Seeing Miri was prepared to remain a permanent fixture of her room until she received an explanation, Laine surrendered. Slowly, she began to explain the financial mountain which she had faced at her mother's death, the necessity to liquidate assets, the continuing drain on her own resources. In the telling, Laine felt the final layers of her resentment fading. Miri did not interrupt the recital, and Laine found that confession had purged her of bitterness.

"Then, when I found my father's address among her personal papers, I took what I had left and came here. I'm afraid I didn't plan things well, and in order to go back…" She shrugged again and trailed off. Miri nodded.

"Why have you not told Cap Simmons? He would not have his daughter selling her baubles. He's a good man, he would not have you in a strange country counting your pennies."

"He doesn't owe me anything."

"He is your father," Miri stated, lifting her chin and peering down her nose at Laine.

"But he's not responsible for a situation brought on by Vanessa's carelessness and my own impulsiveness. He would think… No." She shook her head. "I don't want him to know. It's very important to me that he *not* know. You must promise not to speak of this to him."

"You are a very stubborn girl." Miri crossed her arms and glared at Laine. Laine kept her eyes level. "Very well." Miri's bosom lifted and fell with her sigh. "You must do what you must do. Tomorrow, you will meet my nephew, Tommy. Ask him to come look at your bauble. He is a jeweler and will give you a fair price."

"Thank you, Miri." Laine smiled, feeling a portion of her burden ease.

Miri rose, her muumuu trembling at the movement. "You had a nice day with Dillon?"

"We went by his home," Laine returned evasively. "It's very impressive."

"Very nice place," Miri agreed and brushed an infinitesimal speck of dust from the chair's back. "My cousin cooks there, but not so well as Miri."

"Miss King dropped by." Laine strove for a casual tone, but Miri's brows rose.

"Hmph." Miri stroked the tentlike lines of her flowered silk.

"We had a rather unpleasant discussion when Dillon left us alone. When he came back…" Laine paused and drew her brows together. "I shouted at him."

Miri laughed, holding her middle as if it would split from the effort. For several moments, her mirth rolled comfortably around the room. "So you can shout, Skinny Bones? I would like to have seen that."

"I don't think Dillon found it that amusing." In spite of herself, Laine smiled.

"Oh, that one." She wiped her eyes and shook her head. "He is too used to having his own way with women. He is too good-looking and has too much money." She placed a comforting hand over the barrel of her belly. "He's a fair boss, and he works in the fields when he's needed. He has big degrees and many brains." She tapped her finger on her temple, but looked unimpressed. "He was a very bad boy, with many pranks." Laine saw her lips tremble as she tried not to show amusement at the memories. "He is still a bad boy," she said firmly, regaining her dignity. "He is very smart and *very* important." She made a circling movement with both hands to indicate Dillon's importance, but her voice was full of maternal criticism. "But no matter what he thinks, he does not know women. He only knows planes." She patted Laine's head and pointed to the length of silk. "Tomorrow, you wear that and put a flower in your hair. The moon will be full."

It was a night of silver and velvet. From her window, Laine could see the dancing diamonds of moonlight on the sea. Allowing the breeze to caress her bare shoulders, Laine reflected that the night was perfect for a luau under the stars.

She had not seen Dillon since the previous day. He had returned to the house long after she had retired, and had left again before she had awakened. She was determined, however, not to permit their last meeting to spoil the beauty of the evening. If she had only a few days left in his company, she would make every effort to see that they were pleasant.

Turning from her window, Laine gave one final look at the woman in the mirror. Her bare shoulders rose like marble from the brilliant blue of the sarong. She stared at the woman in the glass, recognizing some change, but unable to discern its cause. She was not aware that over the past few days she had moved from girlhood to womanhood. After a final touch of the brush to her hair, Laine left the room. Dillon's voice rose up the staircase, and she moved to meet it. All at once, it seemed years since she had last heard him speak.

"We'll be harvesting next month, but if I know the schedule of meetings far enough in advance, I can…"

His voice trailed away as Laine moved into the doorway. Pausing in the act of pouring a drink, he made a slow survey. Laine felt her pulse triple its rate as his eyes lingered along their route before meeting hers.

Glancing up from filling his pipe, Cap noted Dillon's absorption. He followed his gaze. "Well, Laine." He rose, surprising her by crossing the room and taking both her hands in his. "What a beautiful sight."

"Do you like it?" Smiling first at him, she glanced down at the sarong. "I'm not quite used to the way it feels."

"I like it very much, but I was talking about you. My

daughter is a very beautiful woman, isn't she, Dillon?" His eyes were soft and smiled into Laine's.

"Yes." Dillon's voice came from behind him. "Very beautiful."

"I'm glad she's here." He pressed her fingers between the warmth of his hands. "I've missed her." He bent and kissed her cheek, then turned to Dillon. "You two run along. I'll see if Miri's ready, which she won't be. We'll be along later."

Laine watched him stride away. She lifted one hand to her cheek, unable to believe she could be so deeply affected by one small gesture.

"Are you ready?" She nodded, unable to speak, then felt Dillon's hands descend to her shoulders. "It isn't easy to bridge a fifteen-year gap, but you've made a start."

Surprised by the support in his voice, Laine blinked back tears and turned to face him. "Thank you. It means a great deal to me for you to say that. Dillon, yesterday, I…"

"Let's not worry about yesterday right now." His smile was both an apology and an acceptance of hers. It was easy to smile back. He studied her a moment before lifting her hand to his lips. "You are incredibly beautiful, like a blossom hanging on a branch just out of reach." Laine wanted to blurt out that she was not out of reach, but a thick blanket of shyness covered her tongue. She could do no more than stare at him.

"Come on." Keeping her hand in his, Dillon moved to the door. "You should try everything once." His tone was light again as they slid into his car. "You know, you're a very small lady."

"Only because you look from an intimidating height," she

returned, feeling pleased with the ease of their relationship. "What does one do at a luau, Dillon? I'm very much afraid I'll insult a local tradition if I refuse to eat raw fish. But—" resting her head against the seat, she smiled at the stars "—I shall refuse to do so."

"We don't hurl mainlanders into the sea anymore for minor offenses. You haven't much hip," he commented, dropping his eyes for a moment. "But you could have a stab at a hula."

"I'm sure my hips are adequate and will no doubt be more so if Miri has her way." Laine sent him a teasing glance. "Do you dance, Dillon?"

He grinned and met her look. "I prefer to watch. Dancing the hula properly takes years of practice. These dancers are very good."

"I see." She shifted in her seat to smile at him. "Will there be many people at the luau?"

"Mmm." Dillon tapped his finger absently against the wheel. "About a hundred, give or take a few."

"A hundred," Laine echoed. She fought off unhappy memories of her mother's overcrowded, overelegant parties. So many people, so many demands, so many measuring eyes.

"Tommy has a lot of relatives."

"How nice for him," she murmured and considered the advantages of small families.

chapter eleven

The hollow, primitive sound of drums vibrated through air pungent with roasting meat. Torches were set on high stakes, their orange flames shooting flickering light against a black sky. To Laine it was like stepping back in time. The lawn was crowded with guests—some in traditional attire and others, like Dillon, in the casual comfort of jeans. Laughter rose from a myriad of tones and mixed languages. Laine gazed around, enthralled by the scene and the scents.

Set on a huge, woven mat were an infinite variety of mysterious dishes in wooden bowls and trays. Ebony-haired girls in native dress knelt to spoon food onto the plates and serving dishes. Diverse aromas lifted on the night air and lingered to entice. Men, swathed at the waist and bare-chested, beat out pulsating rhythms on high, conical drums.

Introduced to an impossible blur of faces, Laine merely floated with the mood of the crowd. There seemed to be a universal friendliness, an uncomplicated joy in simply being.

Soon sandwiched between her father and Dillon, Laine

sat on the grass and watched her plate being heaped with unknown wonders. A roar of approval rose over the music as the pig was unearthed from the *imu* and carved. Dutifully, she dipped her fingers in poi and sampled. She shrugged her shoulders as Dillon laughed at her wrinkled nose.

"Perhaps it's an acquired taste," she suggested as she wiped her fingers on a napkin.

"Here." Dillon lifted a fork and urged its contents into Laine's reluctant mouth.

With some surprise, she found the taste delightful. "That's very good. What is it?"

"*Laulau.*"

"This is not illuminating."

"If it's good, what else do you have to know?" His logic caused her to arch her brows. "It's pork and butterfish steamed in *ti* leaves," he explained, shaking his head. "Try this." Dillon offered the fork again, and Laine accepted without hesitation.

"Oh, what is it? I've never tasted anything like it."

"Squid," he answered, then roared with laughter at her gasp of alarm.

"I believe," Laine stated with dignity, "I shall limit myself to pork and pineapple."

"You'll never grow hips that way."

"I shall learn to live without them. What is this drink…? No," she decided, smiling as she heard her father's chuckle. "I believe I'm better off not knowing."

Avoiding the squid, Laine found herself enjoying the informal meal. Occasionally, someone stopped and crouched beside them, exchanging quick greetings or a long story. Laine was treated with a natural friendliness which soon put her at her ease. Her father seemed comfortable with her, and though he and Dillon enjoyed an entente which eluded her, she no longer felt like an intruder. Music and laughter and the heady perfume of night swam around her. Laine thought she had never felt so intensely aware of her surroundings.

Suddenly, the drummers beat a rapid tempo, reaching a peak, then halting. Their echo fell into silence as Orchid stepped into view. She stood in a circle of torchlight, her skin glowing under its touch. Her eyes were gold and arrogant. Tantalizing and perfect, her body was adorned only in a brief top and a slight swatch of scarlet silk draped low over her hips. She stood completely still, allowing the silence to build before she began slowly circling her hips. A single drum began to follow the rhythm she set.

Her hair, crowned with a circlet of buds, fell down her bare back. Her hands and lithesome curves moved with a hypnotic power as the bare draping of silk flowed against her thighs. Sensuous and tempting, her gestures moved with the beat, and Laine saw that her golden eyes were locked on Dillon's. The faint smile she gave him was knowledgeable. Almost imperceptibly, her dance grew in speed. As the drum became more insistent, her movements became more abandoned. Her face remained calm and smiling above her undulating body. Then, abruptly, sound and movement halted into stunning silence.

Applause broke out. Orchid threw Laine a look of triumph before she lifted the flower crown from her head and tossed it into Dillon's lap. With a soft, sultry laugh, she retreated to the shadows.

"Looks like you've got yourself an invitation," Cap commented, then pursed his lips in thought. "Amazing. I wonder how many RPMs we could clock her at."

Shrugging, Dillon lifted his glass.

"You like to move like that, Skinny Bones?" Laine turned to where Miri sat in the background. She looked more regal than ever in a high-backed rattan chair. "You eat so you don't rattle, and Miri will teach you."

Flushed with a mixture of embarrassment and the longing to move with such free abandonment, Laine avoided Dillon's eyes. "I don't rattle now, but I think Miss King's ability is natural."

"You might pick it up, Duchess." Dillon grinned at Laine's lowered lashes. "I'd like to sit in on the lessons, Miri. As you well know, I've got a very discerning eye." He dropped his gaze to her bare legs, moving it up the length of blue and white silk, before meeting her eyes.

Miri muttered something in Hawaiian, and Dillon chuckled and tossed back a retort in the same tongue. "Come with me," Miri commanded. Rising, she pulled Laine to her feet.

"What did you say to him?" Laine moved in the wake of Miri's flowing gown.

"I said he is a big hungry cat cornering a small mouse."

"I am not a mouse," Laine returned indignantly.

Miri laughed without breaking stride. "Dillon says no, too. He says you are a bird whose beak is sometimes sharp under soft feathers."

"Oh." Unsure whether to be pleased or annoyed with the description, Laine lapsed into silence.

"I have told Tommy you have a bauble to sell," Miri announced. "You will talk to him now."

"Yes, of course," Laine murmured, having forgotten the locket in the enchantment of the night.

Miri paused in front of the luau's host. He was a spare, dark-haired man with an easy smile and friendly eyes. Laine judged him to be in the later part of his thirties, and she had seen him handle his guests with a practiced charm. "You will talk to Cap Simmons's daughter," Miri commanded as she placed a protective hand on Laine's shoulder. "You do right by her, or I will box your ears."

"Yes, Miri," he agreed, but his subservient nod was not reflected in his laughing eyes. He watched the graceful mountain move off before he tossed an arm around Laine's shoulders. He moved her gently toward the privacy of trees. "Miri is the matriarch of our family," he said with a laugh. "She rules with an iron hand."

"Yes, I've noticed. It's impossible to say no to her, isn't it?" The celebrating sounds of the luau drifted into a murmur as they walked.

"I've never tried. I'm a coward."

"I appreciate your time, Mr. Kinimoko," Laine began.

"Tommy, please, then I can call you Laine." She smiled, and as they walked on, she heard the whisper of the sea. "Miri said you had a bauble to sell. I'm afraid she wasn't any more specific."

"A gold locket," Laine explained, finding his friendly manner had put her at ease. "It's heart-shaped and has a braided chain. I have no idea of its value." She paused, wishing there was another way. "I need the money."

Tommy glanced at the delicate profile, then patted her shoulder. "I take it you don't want Cap to know? Okay," he continued as she shook her head. "I have some free time in the morning. Why don't I come by and have a look around ten? You'll find it more comfortable than coming into the shop."

Laine heard leaves rustle and saw Tommy glance idly toward the sound. "It's very good of you." He turned back to her and she smiled, relieved that the first hurdle was over. "I hope I'm not putting you to any trouble."

"I enjoy troubling for beautiful wahines." He kept his arm over her shoulders as he led her back toward the sound of drums and guitars. "You heard Miri. You don't want me to get my ears boxed, do you?"

"I would never forgive myself if I were responsible for that. I'll tell Miri you've done right by Cap Simmons's daughter, and your ears will be left in peace." Laughing, Laine tilted her face to his as they broke through the curtain of trees.

"Your sister's looking for you, Tommy." At Dillon's voice, Laine gave a guilty start.

"Thanks, Dillon. I'll just turn Laine over to you. Take good care of her," he advised gravely. "She's under Miri's protection."

"I'll keep that in mind." Dillon watched in silence as Tommy merged back into the crowd, then he turned back to study Laine. "There's an old Hawaiian custom," he began slowly, and she heard annoyance color his tone, "which I have just invented. When a woman comes to a luau with a man, she doesn't walk in monkeypod trees with anyone else."

"Will I be tossed to the sharks if I break the rules?" Her teasing smile faded as Dillon took a step closer.

"Don't, Laine." He circled her neck with his hand. "I haven't had much practice in restraint."

She swayed toward him, giving in to the sudden surging need. "Dillon," she murmured, offering her mouth in simple invitation. She felt the strength of his fingers as they tightened on her neck. She rested her hands against his chest and felt his heartbeat under her palms. The knowledge of his power over her, and her own longing, caused her to tremble. Dillon made a soft sound, a lingering expulsion of breath. Laine watched him struggle with some emotion, watched something flicker in his eyes and fade before his fingers relaxed again.

"A wahine who stands in the shadows under a full moon must be kissed."

"Is this another old Hawaiian tradition?" Laine felt his arms slip around her waist and melted against him.

"Yes, about ten seconds old."

With unexpected gentleness, his mouth met hers. At the first touch, her body went fluid, mists of pleasure shrouding her. As from a distant shore, Laine heard the call of the drums, their rhythm building to a crescendo as did her heartbeat. Feeling the tenseness of Dillon's shoulders under her hands, she stroked, then circled his neck to bring his face closer to hers. Too soon, he lifted his mouth, and his arms relinquished his hold of her.

"More," Laine murmured, unsatisfied, and pulled his face back to hers.

She was swept against him. The power of his kiss drove all but the need from her mind. She could taste the hunger on his lips, feel the heat growing on his flesh. The air seemed to tremble around them. In that moment, her body belonged more to him than to her. If there was a world apart from seeking lips and caressing hands it held no meaning for her. Again, Dillon drew her away, but his voice was low and uneven.

"We'll go back before another tradition occurs to me."

In the morning, Laine lingered under the sun's streaming light, unwilling to leave her bed and the warm pleasure which still clung from the evening before. The taste of Dillon's mouth still lingered on hers, and his scent remained fresh and vital on her senses. She relived the memory of being in his arms. Finally, with a sigh, she abandoned the luxury of her bed and rose to face the day. Just as she was securing the belt of her robe, Miri glided into the room.

"So, you have decided to get up. The morning is half gone while you lay in your bed." Miri's voice was stern, but her eyes twinkled with indulgence.

"It made the night last longer," Laine replied, smiling at the affectionate scold.

"You liked the roast pig and poi?" Miri asked with a wise nod and a whisper of a smile.

"It was wonderful."

With her lilting laugh floating through the room, Miri

turned to leave. "I am going to the market. My nephew is here to see your bauble. Do you want him to wait?"

"Oh." Forcing herself back down to earth, Laine ran her fingers through her hair. "I didn't realize it was that late. I don't want to inconvenience him. I...is anyone else at home?"

"No, they are gone."

Glancing down at her robe, Laine decided it was adequate coverage. "Perhaps he could come up and look at it. I don't want to keep him waiting."

"He will give you a fair price," Miri stated as she drifted through the doorway. "Or, you will tell me."

Laine took the small box from her drawer and opened the lid. The locket glinted under a ray of sunshine. There were no pictures to remove but, nonetheless, she opened it and stared at its emptiness.

"Laine."

Turning, she managed to smile at Tommy as he stood in the doorway. "Hello. It was good of you to come. Forgive me, I slept rather late this morning."

"A compliment to the host of the luau." He made a small, rather dapper bow as she approached him.

"It was my first, and I have no doubt it will remain my favorite." Laine handed him the box, then gripped her hands together as he made his examination.

"It's a nice piece," he said at length. Lifting his eyes, Tommy studied her. "Laine, you don't want to sell this—it's written all over your face."

"No." She saw from his manner she need not hedge. "It's necessary that I do."

Detecting the firmness in her voice, Tommy shrugged and placed the locket back in its box. "I can give you a hundred for it, though I think it's worth a great deal more to you."

Laine nodded and closed the lid as he handed the box back to her. "That will be fine. Perhaps you'd take it now. I would rather you kept it."

"If that's what you want." Tommy drew out his wallet and counted out bills. "I brought some cash. I thought you'd find it easier than a check."

"Thank you." After accepting the money, Laine stared down at it until he rested a hand on her shoulder.

"Laine, I've known Cap a long time. Would you take this as a loan?"

"No." She shook her head, then smiled to ease the sharpness of the word. "No. It's very kind of you, but I must do it this way."

"Okay." He took the offered box and pocketed it. "I will, however, hold this for a while in case you have second thoughts."

"Thank you. Thank you for not asking questions."

"I'll see myself out." He took her hand and gave it a small squeeze. "Just tell Miri to get in touch with me if you change your mind."

"Yes, I will."

After he had gone, Laine sat heavily on the bed and stared at the money she held clutched in her hand. There was nothing else I could do, she told herself. It was only a piece of metal. Now, it's done, I can't dwell on it.

"Well, Duchess, it seems you've had a profitable morning."

Laine's head snapped up. Dillon's eyes were frosted like an ice-crusted lake, and she stared at him, unable to clear her thoughts. His gaze raked her scantily clad body, and she reached a hand to the throat of her robe in an automatic gesture. Moving toward her, he pulled the bills from her hand and dropped the money on the nightstand.

"You've got class, Duchess." Dillon pinned her with his eyes. "I'd say that's pretty good for a morning's work."

"What are you talking about?" Her thoughts were scattered as she searched for a way to avoid telling him about the locket.

"Oh, I think that's clear enough. I guess I owe Orchid an apology." He thrust his hands in his pockets and rocked back on his heels. The easy gesture belied the burning temper in his eyes. "When she told me about this little arrangement, I came down on her pretty hard. You're a fast worker, Laine. You couldn't have been with Tommy for more than ten minutes last night; you must have made quite a sales pitch."

"I don't know why you're so angry," she began, confused as to why the sale of her locket would bring on such fury. "I suppose Miss King listened to our conversation last night." Suddenly, Laine remembered the quick rustle of leaves. "But why she should feel it necessary to report to you on my business…"

"How'd you manage to get rid of Miri while you conducted your little business transaction?" Dillon demanded. "She has a rather strict moral code, you know. If she finds out how you're earning your pin money, she's liable to toss you out on your ear."

"What do you…" Realization dawned slowly. *Not my locket,* Laine thought dumbly, *but myself.* All trace of color fled from her face. "You don't really believe that I…" Her voice broke as she read the condemnation in his eyes. "This is despicable of you, Dillon. Nothing you've accused me of, nothing you've said to me since we first met compares with this." The words trembled with emotion as she felt a vicelike pressure around her heart. "I won't be insulted this way by you."

"Oh, won't you?" Taking her arm, Dillon dragged Laine to her feet. "Have you a more plausible explanation up your sleeve for Tommy's visit and the wad you're fondling? Go ahead, run it by me. I'm listening."

"Oh, yes, I can see you are. Forgive me for refusing, but Tommy's visit and my money are my business. I owe you no explanation, Dillon. Your conclusions aren't worthy of my words. The fact that you gave enough credence to whatever lie Orchid told you to come check on me, means we have nothing more to say to each other."

"I didn't come here to check on you." He was towering menacingly over her, but Laine met his eyes without flinching. "I came by because I thought you'd want to go up again. You said you wanted to learn to fly, and I said I'd teach you. If you want an apology, all you have to do is give me a reasonable explanation."

"I've spent enough time explaining myself to you. More than you deserve. Questions, always questions. Never *trust*." Her eyes smoldered with blue fire. "I want you to leave my room. I want you to leave me alone for the rest of the time I have in my father's house."

"You had me going." His fingers tightened on her arms, and she caught her breath at the pressure. "I bought it all. The big, innocent eyes, the virginal frailty, the pictures you painted of a woman looking for her father's affection and nothing else. *Trust?*" he flung back at her. "You'd taken me to the point where I trusted you more than myself. You knew I wanted you, and you worked on me. All those trembles and melting bones and artless looks. You played it perfectly, right down to the blushes." He pulled her against him, nearly lifting her off her feet.

"Dillon, you're hurting me." She faltered.

"I wanted you," he went on, as if she had not spoken. "Last night I was aching for you, but I treated you with a restraint and respect I've never shown another woman. You slip on that innocent aura that drives a man crazy. You shouldn't have used it on me, Duchess."

Terror shivered along her skin. Her breath was rapid and aching in her lungs.

"Game's over. I'm going to collect." He silenced her protest with a hard, punishing kiss. Though she struggled against his imprisoning arms, she made no more ripple than a leaf battling a whirlpool. The room tilted, and she was crushed beneath him on the mattress. She fought against the intimacy as his mouth and hands bruised her. He was claiming her in fury, disposing of the barrier of her robe and possessing her flesh with angry demand.

Slowly, his movements altered in texture. Punishment became seduction as his hands began to caress rather than bruise. His mouth left hers to trail down her throat. With a sob ending on a moan, Laine surrendered. Her body became pliant under his, her will snapping with the weight of sensations never tasted. Tears gathered, but she made no more effort to halt them than she did the man who urged them from her soul.

All movement stopped abruptly, and Dillon lay still. The room was thrown into a tortured silence, broken only by the sound of quick breathing. Lifting his head, Dillon studied the journey of a tear down Laine's cheek. He swore with sudden eloquence, then rose. He tugged a hand through his hair as he turned his back on her.

"This is the first time I've been driven to nearly forcing myself on a woman." His voice was low and harsh as he swung around and stared at her. Laine lay still, emotionally drained. She made no effort to cover herself, but merely stared up at him with the eyes of a wounded child. "I can't deal with what you do to me, Laine."

Turning on his heel, he strode from the room. Laine thought the slamming of her door the loneliest sound she had ever heard.

chapter twelve

It was raining on the new spring grass. From her dormitory window Laine watched the green brighten with its morning bath. Outside her door, she heard girls trooping down the hall toward breakfast, but she did not smile at their gay chattering in French and English. She found smiles still difficult.

It had not yet been two weeks since Miri had met Laine's packed cases with a frown and drawn brows. She had met Laine's sketchy explanations with crossed arms and further questions. Laine had remained firm, refusing to postpone her departure or to give specific answers. The note she had left for her father had contained no more details, only an apology for her abrupt leave-taking and a promise to write once she had settled back in France. As of yet, Laine had not found the courage to put pen to paper.

Memories of her last moments with Dillon continued to haunt her. She could still smell the perfume of island blossoms, still feel the warm, moist air rise from the sea to move over her skin. Watching the moon wane, she could remember its lush fullness over the heads of palms. She had hoped her memories would fade with time. She reminded herself that Kauai and its promises were behind her.

It's better this way, she told herself, picking up her brush and preparing herself for the day's work. *Better for everyone.* Her father was settled in his life and would be content to exchange occasional letters. One day, perhaps, he would visit her. Laine knew she could never go back. She, too, had her own life, a job, the comfort of familiar surroundings. Here, she knew what was expected of her. Her existence would be tranquil and unmarred by storms of emotions. She closed her eyes on Dillon's image.

It's too soon, she told herself. Too soon to test her ability to think of him without pain. Later, when the memory had dulled, she would open the door. When she allowed herself to think of him again, it would be to remember the beauty.

It was easier to forget if she followed a routine. Laine scheduled each day to allow for a minimum of idle time. Classes claimed her mornings and early afternoons, and she spent the remainder of her days with chores designed to keep her mind and hands busy.

Throughout the day, the rain continued. With a musical plop, the inevitable leak dripped into the basin on Laine's classroom floor. The school building was old and rambling. Repairs were always either just completed, slated to be done or in vague consideration for the future. The windows were shut against the damp, but the gloom crept into the room. The students were languid and inattentive. Her final class of the day was made up of English girls just entering adolescence. They

were thoroughly bored by their hour lesson on French gram-
mar. As it was Saturday, there was only a half day of classes,
but the hours dragged. Hugging her navy blazer closer, Laine
reflected that the afternoon would be better employed with
a good book and a cheerful fire than by conjugating verbs in
a rain-dreary classroom.

"Eloise," Laine said, recalling her duty. "One must postpone naps until after class."

The girl's eyes blinked open. She gave a groggy, self-conscious smile as her classmates giggled. "Yes, Mademoiselle
Simmons."

Laine bit back a sigh. "You will have your freedom in ten
minutes," she reminded them as she perched on the edge of her
desk. "If you have forgotten, it is Saturday. Sunday follows."

This information brought murmurs of approval and a few
straightened shoulders. Seeing she had at least momentarily captured their attention, Laine went on. *"Maintenant,* the verb
chanter. To sing. *Attendez, ensuite répétez. Je chante, tu chantes, il
chante, nous chantons, vous…"* Her voice faded as she saw the man
leaning against the open door in the rear of the classroom.

"Vous chantez."

Laine forced her attention back to young Eloise. *"Oui, vous
chantez, et ils chantent. Répétez."*

Obediently, the music of high girlish voices repeated the
lesson. Laine retreated behind her desk while Dillon stood
calmly and watched. As the voices faded into silence, Laine
wracked her brain for the assignment she had planned.

"Bien. You will write, for Monday, sentences using this

verb in all its forms. Eloise, we will not consider *'Il chante'* an imaginative sentence."

"Yes, Mademoiselle Simmons."

The bell rang signaling the end of class.

"You will not run," she called over the furious clatter of shuffling desks and scurrying feet. Gripping her hands in her lap, Laine prepared herself for the encounter.

She watched the girls giggle and whisper as they passed by Dillon, and saw, as her heart spun circles, his familiar, easy grin. Crossing the room with his long stride, he stood before her.

"Hello, Dillon." She spoke quickly to cover her confusion. "You seem to have quite an effect on my students."

He studied her face in silence as she fought to keep her smile in place. The flood of emotion threatened to drown her.

"You haven't changed," he said at length. "I don't know why I was afraid you would." Reaching in his pocket, he pulled out the locket and placed it on her desk. Unable to speak, Laine stared at it. As her eyes filled, her hand closed convulsively over the gold heart. "Not a very eloquent apology, but I haven't had a lot of practice. For pity's sake, Laine." His tone shifted into anger so quickly, she lifted her head in shock. "If you needed money, why didn't you tell me?"

"And confirm your opinion of my character?" she retorted.

Turning away, Dillon moved to a window and looked into the insistent mist of rain. "I had that one coming," he murmured, then rested his hands on the sill and lapsed into silence.

She was moved by the flicker of pain that had crossed his face. "There's no purpose in recriminations now, Dillon. It's best to leave all that in the past." Rising, she kept the desk between them. "I'm very grateful to you for taking the time and the trouble to return my locket. It's more important to me than I can tell you. I don't know when I'll be able to pay you. I…"

Dillon whirled, and Laine stepped away from the fury on his face. She watched him struggle for control. "No, don't say anything, just give me a minute." His hands retreated to his pockets. For several long moments, he paced the room. Gradually, his movements grew calmer. "The roof leaks," he said idly.

"Only when it rains."

He gave a short laugh and turned back to her. "Maybe it doesn't mean much, but I'm sorry. No." He shook his head to ward her off as she began to answer. "Don't be so blasted generous. It'll only make me feel more guilty." He started to light a cigarette, remembered where he was and let out a long breath. "After my exhibition of stupidity, I went up for a while. I find that I think more clearly a few thousand feet off the ground. You might find this hard to believe, and I suppose it's even more ridiculous to expect you to forgive me, but I did manage to get a grip on reality. I didn't even believe the things I was saying to you when I was saying them." He rubbed his hands over his face, and Laine noticed for the first time that he looked tired and drawn. "I only know that I went a little crazy from the first minute I saw you.

"I went back to the house with the intention of offering a series of inadequate apologies. I tried to rationalize that all the accusations I tossed at you about Cap were made for his sake." He shook his head, and a faint smile touched his mouth. "It didn't help."

"Dillon…"

"Laine, don't interrupt. I haven't the patience as it is." He paced again, and she stood silent. "I'm not very good at this, so just don't say anything until I'm finished." Restless, he continued to roam around the room as he spoke. "When I got back, Miri was waiting for me. I couldn't get anything out of her at first but a detailed lecture on my character. Finally, she told me you'd gone. I didn't take that news very well, but it's no use going into that now. After a lot of glaring and ancient curses, she told me about the locket. I had to swear a blood oath not to tell Cap. It seems you had her word on that. I've been in France for ten days trying to find you." Turning back, he gestured in frustration. "Ten days," he repeated as if it were a lifetime. "It wasn't until this morning that I traced the maid who worked for your mother. She was very expansive once I settled her into broken English. I got an earful about debts and auctions and the little mademoiselle who stayed in school over Christmas vacations while Madame went to Saint Moritz. She gave me the name of your school." Dillon paused. For a moment there was only the sound of water dripping from the ceiling into the basin. "There's nothing you can say to me that I haven't already said to myself, in more graphic terms. But I figured you should have the chance."

Seeing he was finished, Laine drew a deep breath and prepared to speak. "Dillon, I've thought carefully on how my position would have looked to you. You knew only one side, and your heart was with my father. I find it difficult, when I'm calm, to resent that loyalty or your protection of his welfare. As for what happened on the last morning—" Laine swallowed, striving to keep her voice composed. "I think it was as difficult for you as it was for me, perhaps more difficult."

"You'd make it a whole lot easier on my conscience if you'd yell or toss a few things at me."

"I'm sorry." She managed a smile and lifted her shoulders with the apology. "I'd have to be very angry to do that, especially here. The nuns frown on displays of temper."

"Cap wants you to come home."

Laine's smile faded at his quiet words. He watched her eyes go bleak before she shook her head and moved to the window. "This is my home."

"Your home's in Kauai. Cap wants you back. Is it fair to him to lose you twice?"

"Is it fair to ask me to turn my back on my own life and return?" she countered, trying to block out the pain his words were causing. "Don't talk to me about fair, Dillon."

"Look, be as bitter as you want about me. I deserve it. Cap doesn't. How do you think he feels knowing what your childhood was like?"

"You told him?" She whirled around, and for the first time since he had come into the room, Dillon saw her mask of control slip. "You had no right…"

"I had every right," he interrupted. "Just as Cap had every right to know. Laine, listen to me." She had started to turn away, but his words and quiet tone halted her. "He loves you. He never stopped, not all those years. I guess that's why I reacted to you the way I did." With an impatient sound, he ran his hands through his hair again. "For fifteen years, loving you hurt him."

"Don't you think I know that?" she tossed back. "Why must he be hurt more?"

"Laine, the few days you were with him gave him back his daughter. He didn't ask why you never answered his letters, he never accused you of any of the things I did." He shut his eyes briefly, and again she noticed fatigue. "He loved you without needing explanations or apologies. It would have been wrong to prolong the lies. When he found you'd left, he wanted to come to France himself to bring you back. I asked him to let me come alone because I knew it was my fault that you left."

"There's no blame, Dillon." With a sigh, Laine slipped the locket into her blazer pocket. "Perhaps you were right to tell Cap. Perhaps it's cleaner. I'll write him myself tonight; it was wrong of me to leave without seeing him. Knowing that he is really my father again is the greatest gift I've ever had. I don't want either one of you to think that my living in France means I hold any resentment. I very much hope that Cap visits me soon. Perhaps you'd carry a note back for me."

Dillon's eyes darkened. His voice was tight with anger when he spoke. "He isn't going to like knowing you're buried in this school."

Laine turned away from him and faced the window.

"I'm not buried, Dillon. The school is my home and my job."

"And your escape?" he demanded impatiently, then swore as he saw her stiffen. He began to pace again. "I'm sorry, that was a cheap shot."

"No more apologies, Dillon. I don't believe the floors can stand the wear."

He stopped his pacing and studied her. Her back was still to him, but he could just see the line of her chin against the pale cap of curls. In the trim navy blazer and white pleated skirt, she looked more student than teacher. He began to speak in a lighter tone. "Listen, Duchess, I'm going to stay around for a couple of days, play tourist. How about showing me around? I could use someone who speaks the language."

Laine shut her eyes, thinking of what a few days in his company would mean. There was no point in prolonging the pain. "I'm sorry, Dillon, I'd love to take you around, but I haven't the time at the moment. My work here has backed up since I took the time off to visit Kauai."

"You're going to make this difficult, aren't you?"

"I'm not trying to do that, Dillon." Laine turned, with an apologetic smile. "Another time, perhaps."

"I haven't got another time. I'm trying my best to do this right, but I'm not sure of my moves. I've never dealt with a woman like you before. All the rules are different." She saw, with curiosity, that his usual confidence had vanished. He took a step toward her, stopped, then walked to the black-board. For some moments, he studied the conjugation of several French verbs. "Have dinner with me tonight."

"No, Dillon, I…" He whirled around so swiftly, Laine swallowed the rest of her words.

"If you won't even have dinner with me, how the devil am I supposed to talk you into coming home so I can struggle through this courting routine? Any fool could see I'm no good at this sort of thing. I've already made a mess of it. I don't know how much longer I can stand here and be reasonably coherent. I love you, Laine, and it's driving me crazy. Come back to Kauai so we can be married."

Stunned into speechlessness, Laine stared at him. "Dillon," she began, "did you say you love me?"

"Yes, I said I love you. Do you want to hear it again?" His hands descended to her shoulders, his lips to her hair. "I love you so much I'm barely able to do simple things like eat and sleep for thinking of you. I keep remembering how you looked with a shell held to your ear. You stood there with the water running from your hair, and your eyes the color of the sky and the sea, and I fell completely in love with you. I tried not to believe it, but I lost ground every time you got near me. When you left, it was like losing part of myself. I'm not complete anymore without you."

"Dillon." His name was only a whisper.

"I swore I wasn't going to put any pressure on you." She felt his brow lower to the crown of her head. "I wasn't going to say all these things to you at once like this. I'll give you whatever you need, the flowers, the candlelight. You'd be surprised how conventional I can be when it's necessary. Just come back with me, Laine. I'll give you some time before I start pressuring you to marry me."

"No." She shook her head, then took a deep breath. "I won't come back with you unless you marry me first."

"Listen." Dillon tightened his grip, then with a groan of pleasure lowered his mouth to hers. "You drive a hard bargain," he murmured as he tasted her lips. As if starved for the flavor, he lingered over the kiss.

"I'm not going to give you the opportunity to change your

mind." Lifting her arms, Laine circled his neck, then laid her cheek against his. "You can give me the flowers and candle-light after we're married."

"Duchess, you've got a deal. I'll have you married to me before you realize what you're getting into. Some people might tell you I have a few faults—such as, I occasionally lose my temper—"

"Really?" Laine lifted an incredulous face. "I've never known anyone more mild and even-tempered. However—" she trailed her finger down his throat and toyed with the top button of his shirt "—I suppose I should confess that I am by nature very jealous. It's just something I can't control. And if I ever see another woman dance the hula especially for you, I shall probably throw her off the nearest cliff!"

"Would you?" Dillon gave a self-satisfied masculine grin as he framed her face in his hands. "Then I think Miri should start teaching you as soon as we get back. I warn you, I plan to sit in on every lesson."

"I'm sure I'll be a quick learner." Rising to her toes, Laine pulled him closer. "But right now there are things I would rather learn. Kiss me again, Dillon!"

★ ★ ★ ★ ★

Less of a Stranger

For my friend Joanne

chapter one

He watched her coming. Though she wore jeans and a jacket, with a concealing helmet over her head, Katch recognized her femininity. She rode a small Honda motorcycle. He drew on his thin cigar and appreciated the competent way she swung into the market's parking lot.

Settling the bike, she dismounted. She was tall, Katch noted, perhaps five feet eight, and slender. He leaned back on the soda machine and continued to watch her out of idle curiosity. Then she removed the helmet. Instantly, his curiosity was intensified. She was a stunner.

Her hair was loose and straight, swinging nearly to her shoulders, with a fringe of bangs sweeping over her forehead. It was a deep, rich brunette that showed glints of red and gold from the sun. Her face was narrow, the features sharp and distinct. He'd known models who'd starved themselves to get the angles and shadows that were in this woman's face. Her mouth, however, was full and generous.

Katch recognized the subtleties of cosmetics and knew that none had been used to add interest to the woman's features.

…e didn't need them. Her eyes were large, and even with the distance of the parking lot between them, he caught the depth of dark brown. They reminded him of a colt's eyes— deep and wide and aware. Her movements were unaffected. They had an unrefined grace that was as coltish as her eyes. She was young, he decided, barely twenty. He drew on the cigar again. She was definitely a stunner.

"Hey, Megan!"

Megan turned at the call, brushing the bangs from her eyes as she moved. Seeing the Bailey twins pull to the curb in their Jeep, she smiled.

"Hi." Clipping the helmet onto a strap on her bike, Megan walked to the Jeep. She was very fond of the Bailey twins.

Like herself, they were twenty-three and had golden, beach-town complexions, but they were petite, blue-eyed and pertly blond. The long, baby-fine hair they shared had been tossed into confusion by the wind. Both pairs of blue eyes drifted past Megan to focus on the man who leaned against the soda machine. In reflex, both women straightened and tucked strands of hair behind their ears. Tacitly, they agreed their right profile was the most comely.

"We haven't seen you in a while." Teri Bailey kept one eye cocked on Katch as she spoke to Megan.

"I've been trying to get some things finished before the season starts." Megan's voice was low, with the gentle flow of coastal South Carolina. "How've you been?"

"Terrific!" Jeri answered, shifting in the driver's seat. "We've got the afternoon off. Why don't you come shopping with us?" She, too, kept Katch in her peripheral vision.

"I'd like to—" Megan was already shaking her head "—but I've got to pick up a few things here."

"Like the guy over there with terrific gray eyes?" Jeri demanded.

"What?" Megan laughed.

"And shoulders," Teri remarked.

"He hasn't taken those eyes off her, has he, Teri?" Jeri remarked. "And we spent twelve-fifty for this blouse." She fingered the thin strap of the pink camisole top which matched her twin's.

"What," Megan asked, totally bewildered, "are you talking about?"

"Behind you," Teri said with a faint inclination of her fair head. "The hunk by the soda machine. Absolutely gorgeous." But as Megan began to turn her head, Teri continued in a desperate whisper, "Don't turn around, for goodness sake!"

"How can I see if I don't look?" Megan pointed out reasonably as she turned.

His hair was blond, not pale like the twins', but dusky and sun-streaked. It was thick and curled loosely and carelessly around his face. He was lean, and the jeans he wore were well faded from wear. His stance was negligent, completely relaxed as he leaned back against the machine and drank from a can. But his face wasn't lazy, Megan thought as he met her stare without a blink. It was sharply aware. He needed a shave, certainly, but his bone structure was superb. There was the faintest of clefts in his chin, and his mouth was long and thin.

Normally, Megan would have found the face fascinating—strongly sculpted, even handsome in a rough-and-ready fashion.

But the eyes were insolent. They were gray, as the twins had stated, dark and smoky. And, Megan decided with a frown, rude. She'd seen his type before—drifters, loners, looking for the sun and some fleeting female companionship. Under her bangs, her eyebrows drew together. He was openly staring at her. As the can touched his lips, he sent Megan a slow wink.

Hearing one of the twins giggle, Megan whipped her head back around.

"He's adorable," Jeri decided.

"Don't be an idiot." Megan swung her hair back with a toss of her head. "He's typical."

The twins exchanged a look as Jeri started the Jeep's engine. "Too choosy," she stated. They gave Megan mirror smiles as they pulled away from the curb. "Bye!"

Megan wrinkled her nose at them, but waved before she turned away. Purposefully ignoring the man who loitered beside the concessions, Megan walked into the market.

She acknowledged the salute from the clerk behind the counter. Megan had grown up in Myrtle Beach. She knew all the small merchants in the five-mile radius around her grandfather's amusement park.

After choosing a basket, she began to push it down the first aisle. Just a few things, she decided, plucking a quart of milk from a shelf. She had only the saddlebags on the bike for transporting. If the truck hadn't been acting up… She let her thoughts drift away from that particular problem. Nothing could be done about it at the moment.

Megan paused in the cookie section. She'd missed lunch and the bags and boxes looked tempting. Maybe the oatmeal…

"These are better."

Megan started as a hand reached in front of her to choose a bag of cookies promising a double dose of chocolate chips. Twisting her head, she looked up into the insolent gray eyes.

"Want the cookies?" He grinned much as he had outside.

"No," she said, giving a meaningful glance at his hand on her basket. Shrugging, he took his hand away but, to Megan's irritation, he strolled along beside her.

"What's on the list, Meg?" he asked companionably as he tore open the bag of cookies.

"I can handle it alone, thanks." She started down the next aisle, grabbing a can of tuna. He walked, Megan noted, like a gunslinger—long, lanky strides with just a hint of swagger.

"You've got a nice bike." He bit into a cookie as he strolled along beside her. "Live around here?"

Megan chose a box of tea bags. She gave it a critical glance before tossing it into the basket. "It lives with me," she told him as she moved on.

"Cute," he decided and offered her a cookie. Megan ignored him and moved down the next aisle. When she reached for a loaf of bread, however, he laid a hand on top of hers. "Whole wheat's better for you." His palm was hard and firm on the back of her hand. Megan met his eyes indignantly and tried to pull away.

"Listen, I have…"

"No rings," he commented, lacing his fingers through hers and lifting her hand for a closer study. "No entanglements. How about dinner?"

"No way." She shook her hand but found it firmly locked in his.

"Don't be unfriendly, Meg. You have fantastic eyes." He smiled into them, looking at her as though they were the only two people on earth. Someone reached around her, with an annoyed mutter, to get a loaf of rye.

"Will you go away?" she demanded in an undertone. It amazed her that his smile was having an effect on her even though she knew what was behind it. "I'll make a scene if you don't."

"That's all right," he said genially, "I don't mind scenes."

He wouldn't, she thought, eyeing him. He'd thrive on them. "Look," she began angrily, "I don't know who you are, but..."

"David Katcherton," he volunteered with another easy smile. "Katch. What time should I pick you up?"

"You're not going to pick me up," she said distinctly. "Not now, not later." Megan cast a quick look around. The market was all but empty. She couldn't cause a decent scene if she'd wanted to. "Let go of my hand," she ordered firmly.

"The Chamber of Commerce claims Myrtle Beach is a friendly town, Meg." Katch released her hand. "You're going to give them a bad name."

"And stop calling me Meg," she said furiously. "I don't know you."

She stomped off, wheeling the basket in front of her.

"You will." He made the claim quietly, but she heard him.

Their eyes met again, hers dark with temper, his assured. Turning away, she quickened her pace to the check-out counter.

"You wouldn't believe what happened at the market." Megan set the bag on the kitchen table with a thump.

Her grandfather sat at the table, on one of the four matching maple chairs, earnestly tying a fly. He grunted in acknowledgment but didn't glance up. Wires and feathers and weights were neatly piled in front of him.

"This man," she began, pulling the bread from the top bag. "This incredibly rude man tried to pick me up. Right in the cookie section." Megan frowned as she stored tea bags in a canister. "He wanted me to go to dinner with him."

"Hmm." Her grandfather meticulously attached a yellow feather to the fly. "Have a nice time."

"Pop!" Megan shook her head in frustration, but a smile tugged at her mouth.

Timothy Miller was a small, spare man in his mid-sixties. His round, lined face was tanned, surrounded by a shock of white hair and a full beard. The beard was soft as a cloud and carefully tended. His blue eyes, unfaded by the years, were settled deeply into the folds and lines of his face. They missed little. Megan could see he was focused on his lures. That he had heard her at all was a tribute to his affection for his granddaughter.

Moving over, she dropped a kiss on the crown of his head. "Going fishing tomorrow?"

"Yessiree, bright and early." Pop counted out his assortment of lures and mentally reviewed his strategy. Fishing was a serious business. "The truck should be fixed this evening. I'll be back before supper."

Megan nodded, giving him a second kiss. He needed his fishing days. The amusement parks opened for business on weekends in the spring and fall. In the three summer months they worked seven days a week. The summer kept the town alive; it drew tourists, and tourists meant business. For one-fourth of the year, the town swelled from a population of thirteen or fourteen thousand to three hundred thousand. The bulk of those three hundred thousand people had come to the small coastal town to have fun.

To provide it, and make his living, her grandfather worked hard. He always had, Megan mused. It would have been a trial if he hadn't loved the park so much. It had been part of her life for as long as she could remember.

Megan had been barely five when she had lost her parents. Over the years, Pop had been mother, father and friend to her. And Joyland was home to her as much as the beach-side cottage they lived in. Years before, they had turned to each other in grief. Now, their love was bedrock firm. With the exclusion of her grandfather, Megan was careful with her emotions, for once involved, they were intense. When she loved, she loved totally.

"Trout would be nice," she murmured, as she gave him a last, quick hug. "We'll have to settle for tuna casserole tonight."

"Thought you were going out."

"Pop!" Megan leaned back against the stove and pushed

her hair from her face with both hands. "Do you think I'd spend the evening with a man who tried to pick me up with a bag of chocolate chip cookies?" With a jerk of her wrist, she flicked on the burner under the teakettle.

"Depends on the man." She saw the twinkle in his eye as he glanced up at her. Megan knew she finally had his full attention. "What'd he look like?"

"A beach bum," she retorted, although she knew the answer wasn't precisely true. "With a bit of cowboy thrown in." She smiled then in response to Pop's grin. "Actually, he had a great face. Lean and strong, very attractive in an unscrupulous sort of way. He'd do well in bronze."

"Sounds interesting. Where'd you meet him again?"

"In the cookie section."

"And you're going to fix tuna casserole instead of having dinner out?" Pop gave a heavy sigh and shook his head. "I don't know what's the matter with this girl," he addressed a favored lure.

"He was cocky," Megan claimed and folded her arms. "And he *leered* at me. Aren't grandfathers supposed to tote shotguns around for the purpose of discouraging leerers?"

"Want to borrow one and go hunting for him?"

The shrill whistling of the kettle drowned out her response. Pop watched Megan as she rose to fix the tea.

She was a good girl, he mused. A bit too serious about things at times, but a good girl. And a beauty, too. It didn't surprise him that a stranger had tried to make a date with her. He was more surprised that it hadn't happened more often. But Megan could discourage a man without opening her mouth, he recalled. All she had to do was aim one of her "I beg your pardon" looks and most of them backed off. That seemed to be the way she wanted it.

Between the amusement park and her art, she never seemed to have time for much socializing. Or didn't make time, Pop amended thoughtfully. Still, he wasn't certain that he didn't detect more than just annoyance in her attitude toward the man in the market. Unless he missed his guess, she had been amused and perhaps a touch attracted. Because he knew his granddaughter well, he decided to let the subject ride for the time being.

"The weather's supposed to hold all weekend," he commented as he carefully placed his lures in his fishing box. "There should be a good crowd in the park. Are you going to work in the arcade?"

"Of course." Megan set two cups of tea on the table and sat again. "Have those seats been adjusted on the Ferris wheel?"

"Saw to it myself this morning." Pop blew on his tea to cool it, then sipped.

He was relaxed, Megan saw. Pop was a simple man. She'd always admired his unassuming manner, his quiet humor, his lack of pretensions. He loved to watch people enjoy. More, she added with a sigh, than he liked to charge them for doing so. Joyland never made more than a modest profit. He was, Megan concluded, a much better grandfather than businessman.

To a large extent, it was she who handled the profit-and-loss aspect of the park. Though the responsibility took time away from her art, she knew it was the park that supported them. And, more important, it was the park that Pop loved.

At the moment, the books were teetering a bit too steeply into the red for comfort. Neither of them spoke of it at any length with the other. They mentioned improvements during the busy season, talked vaguely about promoting business during the Easter break and over Memorial Day weekend.

Megan sipped at her tea and half listened to Pop's rambling about hiring summer help. She would see to it when the time came. Pop was a whiz in dealing with cranky machines and sunburned tourists, but he tended to overpay and underwork his employees. Megan was more practical. She had to be.

I'll have to work full-time myself this summer, she reflected. She thought fleetingly of the half-completed sculpture in her studio over the garage. It'll just have to wait for December, she told herself and tried not to sigh. There's no other way until things are on a more even keel again. Maybe next year…it was always next year. There were things to do, always things to do. With a small shrug, she turned back to Pop's monologue.

"So, I figure we'll get some of the usual college kids and drifters to run the rides."

"I don't imagine that'll be a problem," Megan murmured. Pop's mention of drifters had led her thoughts back to David Katcherton.

Katch, she mused, letting his face form in her mind again. Ordinarily, she'd have cast his type as a drifter, but there had been something more than that. Megan prided herself on her observations, her characterizations of people. It annoyed her that she wasn't able to make a conclusive profile on this man. It annoyed her further that she was again thinking of a silly encounter with a rude stranger.

"Want some more tea?" Pop was already making his way to the stove when Megan shook herself back.

"Ah…yeah, sure." She scolded herself for dwelling on the insignificant when there were things to do. "I guess I'd better start dinner. You'll want an early night if you're going fishing in the morning."

"That's my girl." Pop turned the flame back on under the kettle as he glanced out the window. He cast a quick look at his unsuspecting granddaughter. "I hope you've got enough for three," he said casually. "It looks like your beach-cowboy found his way to the ranch."

"What?" Megan's brows drew together as she stood up.

"A perfect description, as usual, Megan," Pop complimented her as he watched the man approach, loose-limbed with a touch of a swashbuckler, a strong, good-looking face. Pop liked his looks. He turned with a grin as Megan walked to the window to stare out. Pop suppressed a chuckle at her expression.

"It *is* him," she whispered, hardly believing her eyes as she watched Katch approach her kitchen door.

"I thought it might be," Pop said mildly.

"Of all the nerve," she muttered darkly. "Of all the *incredible* nerve!"

chapter two

Before her grandfather could comment, Megan took the few
strides necessary to bring her to the kitchen door. She swung
it open just as Katch stepped up on the stoop. There was a
flicker, only a flicker, of surprise in the gray eyes.

"You have a nerve," she said coolly.

"So I've been told," he agreed easily. "You're prettier than
you were an hour ago." He ran a finger down her cheek.
"There's a bit of rose under the honey now. Very becoming."
He traced the line of her chin before dropping his hand. "Do
you live here?"

"You know very well I do," she retorted. "You followed
me."

Katch grinned. "Sorry to disappoint you, Meg. Finding
you here's just a bonus. I'm looking for Timothy Miller.
Friend of yours?"

"He's my grandfather." She moved, almost imperceptibly,
positioning herself between Katch and the doorway. "What
do you want with him?"

Katch recognized the protective move, but before he could comment, Pop spoke from behind her.

"Why don't you let the man in, Megan? He can tell me himself."

"I'm basically human, Meg," Katch said quietly. The tone of his voice had her looking at him more closely.

She glanced briefly over her shoulder, then turned back to Katch. The look she gave him was a warning. Don't do anything to upset him.

She noticed something in his eyes she hadn't expected— gentleness. It was more disconcerting than his earlier arrogance. Megan backed into the kitchen, holding open the door in silent invitation.

Katch smiled at her, casually brushing a strand of hair from her cheek as he walked by and into the kitchen. Megan stood for a moment, wondering why she should be so moved by a stranger's touch.

"Mr. Miller?" She heard the unaffected friendliness in Katch's voice and glanced over as he held out a hand to her grandfather. "I'm David Katcherton."

Pop nodded in approval. "You're the fellow who called me a couple of hours ago." He shot a look past Katch's shoulder to Megan. "I see you've already met my granddaughter."

His eyes smiled in response. "Yes. Charming."

Pop chuckled and moved toward the stove. "I was just about to make some more tea. How about a cup?"

Megan noticed the faint lift of his brow. Tea, she thought, was probably not his first choice.

"That'd be nice. Thanks." He walked to the table and sat,

Megan decided, as if his acquaintance were long-standing and personal. Half reluctant, half defiant, she sat next to him. Her eyes asked him questions behind Pop's back.

"Did I tell you before that you have fabulous eyes?" he murmured. Without waiting for her answer, he turned his attention to Pop's tackle box. "You've got some great lures here," he observed to Pop, picking up a bone squid, then a wood plug painted to simulate a small frog. "Do you make any of your own?"

"That's half the sport," Pop stated, bringing a fresh cup to the table. "Have you done much fishing?"

"Here and there. I'd guess you'd know the best spots along the Grand Strand."

"A few of them," Pop said modestly.

Megan scowled into her tea. Once the subject of fishing had been brought up, Pop could go on for hours. And hours.

"I thought I'd do some surf casting while I'm here," Katch mentioned offhandedly. Megan was surprised to catch a shrewdly measuring expression in his eyes.

"Well now—" Pop warmed to the theme "—I might just be able to show you a spot or two. Do you have your own gear?"

"Not with me, no."

Pop brushed this off as inconsequential. "Where are you from, Mr. Katcherton?"

"Katch," he corrected, leaning back in his chair. "California originally."

That, Megan decided, explained the beachboy look. She

drank her cooling tea with a casual air while studying him over the rim.

"You're a long way from home," Pop commented. He shifted comfortably, then brought out a pipe he saved for interesting conversations. "Do you plan to be in Myrtle Beach long?"

"Depends. I'd like to talk with you about your amusement park."

Pop puffed rapidly on his pipe while holding a match to the bowl. The tobacco caught, sending out cherry-scented smoke. "So you said on the phone. Funny, Megan and I were just talking about hiring on help for the summer. Only about six weeks before the season starts." He puffed and let the smoke waft lazily. "Less than three until Easter. Ever worked rides or a booth?"

"No." Katch sampled his tea.

"Well…" Pop shrugged his inexperience away. "It's simple enough to learn. You look smart." Again, Megan caught the flash of Katch's grin. She set down her cup.

"We can't pay more than minimum to a novice," she said dampeningly.

He made her nervous, she was forced to admit. With any luck, she could discourage him from Joyland so that he'd try his luck elsewhere. But something nagged at her. He didn't look the type to take a job running a roller coaster or hawking a pitch-and-toss for a summer. There were hints of authority in his face, touches of casual power in his stance. Yet there was something not altogether respectable in his raffish charm.

He met her stare with a complete lack of self-consciousness. "That seems reasonable. Do you work in the park, Meg?"

She bit back a retort to his familiarity. "Often," she said succinctly.

"Megan's got a good business head," Pop interjected. "She keeps me straight."

"Funny," Katch said speculatively. "Somehow I thought you might be a model. You've the face for it." There was no flirtatiousness in his tone.

"Megan's an artist," Pop said, puffing contentedly at his pipe.

"Oh?"

She watched Katch's eyes narrow and focus on her. Uncomfortable, she shifted in her chair. "We seem to be drifting away from the subject," she said crisply. "If you've come about a job—"

"No."

"But…didn't you say—"

"I don't think so," he cut her off again and added a smile. He turned to Pop now, and Megan recognized a subtle change in his manner. "I don't want a job in your park, Mr. Miller. I want to buy it."

Both men were intent on each other. Pop was surprised, unmistakably so, but there was also a look of consideration in his eyes. Neither of them noticed Megan. She stared at Katch, her face open and young, and just a little frightened. She wanted to laugh and say he was making a foolish joke, but she knew better. Katch said exactly what he meant.

She'd recognized the understated authority and power

beneath the glib exterior. This was business, pure and simple. She could see it on his face. There was a flutter of panic in her stomach as she looked at her grandfather.

"Pop?" Her voice was very small, and he made no sign that he heard her.

"You're a surprise," the old man said eventually. Then he began to puff on his pipe again. "Why my park?"

"I've done some research on the amusements here." Katch shrugged off the details. "I like yours."

Pop sighed and blew smoke at the ceiling. "I can't say I'm interested in selling out, son. A man gets used to a certain way of life."

"With the offer I'm prepared to make, you might find it easy to get used to another."

Pop gave a quiet laugh. "How old are you, Katch?"

"Thirty-one."

"That's just about how long I've been in this business. How much do you know about running a park?"

"Not as much as you do." Katch grinned and leaned back again. "But I could learn fast with the right teacher."

Megan saw that her grandfather was studying Katch carefully. She felt excluded from the conversation and resented it. Her grandfather was capable of doing this very subtly. She recognized that David Katcherton had the same talent. Megan sat silently; natural courtesy forbade her interrupting private conversation.

"Why do you want to own an amusement park?" Pop asked suddenly. Megan could tell he was interested in David Katcherton. A warning bell began to ring in her head. The last thing she wanted was for her grandfather to become too involved with Katch. He was trouble, Megan was sure of it.

"It's good business," Katch answered Pop's question after a moment. "And fun." He smiled. "I like things that put fun into life."

He knows how to say the right thing, Megan acknowledged grudgingly, noting Pop's expression.

"I'd appreciate it if you'd think about it, Mr. Miller," Katch continued. "We could talk about it again in a few days."

And how to advance and retreat, she thought.

"I can't refuse to think about it," Pop agreed, but shook his head. "Still, you might take another look around. Megan and I've run Joyland for a good many years. It's home to us." He looked to his granddaughter teasingly. "Weren't you two going out to dinner?"

"No!" She flashed him a scowl.

"Exactly what I had in mind," Katch said smoothly. "Come on, Meg, I'll buy you a hamburger." As he rose, he took her hand, pulling her to her feet. Feeling her temper rise with her, Megan attempted to control it.

"I can't tell you how I hate to refuse such a charming invitation," she began.

"Then don't," Katch cut her off before turning to Pop. "Would you like to join us?"

Pop chuckled and motioned them away with the back of his hand. "Go on. I've got to get my gear together for the morning."

"Want company?"

Pop studied Katch over the bowl of his pipe. "I'm leaving at five-thirty," he said after a moment. "I have extra gear."

"I'll be here."

Megan was so astonished that she allowed Katch to lead her outside without making another protest. Pop never invited anyone along on his fishing mornings. They were his relaxation, and he enjoyed his solitude too much to share it.

"He never takes anyone with him," she murmured, thinking aloud.

"Then I'm flattered."

Megan noticed that Katch still had her hand, his fingers comfortably laced with hers.

"I'm not going out with you," she said positively and stopped walking. "You might be able to charm Pop into taking you fishing, but—"

"So you think I'm charming?" His smile was audacious as he took her other hand.

"Not in the least," she said firmly, repressing an answering smile.

"Why won't you have dinner with me?"

"Because," she said, meeting his eyes directly, "I don't like you."

His smile broadened. "I'd like the chance to change your mind."

"You couldn't." Megan started to draw her hands away, but he tightened his fingers.

"Wanna bet?" Again, she squashed the desire to smile. "If

I change your mind, you'll go to the park with me Friday night."

"And if I don't change my mind?" she asked. "What then?"

"I won't bother you anymore." He grinned, as persuasive, she noted, as he was confident.

Her brow lifted in speculation. It might, she reflected, it just might be worth it.

"All you have to do is have dinner with me tonight," Katch continued, watching Megan's face. "Just a couple of hours."

"All right," she agreed impulsively. "It's a deal." She wriggled her fingers, but he didn't release them. "We could shake on it," she said, "but you still have my hands."

"So I do," he agreed. "We'll seal it my way then."

With a quick tug, he had her colliding against his chest. She felt a strength there which wasn't apparent in the lean, somewhat lanky frame. Before she could express annoyance, his mouth had taken hers.

He was skillful and thorough. She never knew whether she had parted her lips instinctively or if he had urged her to do so with the gently probing tip of his tongue.

From the instant of contact, Megan's mind had emptied, to be filled only with thoughts she couldn't center on. Her body dominated, taking command in simple surrender. She was melted against him, aware of his chest hard against her breasts…aware of his mouth quietly savaging hers. There was nothing else. She found there was nothing to hold on to. No anchor to keep her from veering off into wild water. Megan gave a small, protesting moan and drew away.

His eyes were darker than she'd thought, and too smoky to read clearly. Why had she thought them so decipherable? Why had she thought him so manageable? Nothing was as she had thought it had been minutes before. Her breath trembled as she fought to collect herself.

"You're very warm," Katch said softly. "It's a pity you struggle so hard to be remote."

"I'm not. I don't…" Megan shook her head, wishing desperately for her heartbeat to slow.

"You are," he corrected, "and you do." Katch gave her hands a companionable squeeze before releasing one of them. The other he kept snugly in his as he turned toward his car.

Panic was welling up inside Megan, and she tried to suppress it. *You've been kissed before,* she reminded herself. This was just unexpected. It just caught you off guard. Even as the excuse ran through her mind, she knew it for a lie. She'd never been kissed like that before. And the situation was no longer under her control.

"I don't think I'll go after all," she told him in calmer tones.

Katch turned, smiling at her as he opened the car door. "A bet's a bet, Meg."

chapter three

Katch drove a black Porsche. Megan wasn't surprised. She wouldn't have expected him to drive anything ordinary. It wasn't difficult to deduce that David Katcherton could afford the best of everything.

He'd probably inherited his money, she decided as she settled back against the silver gray seat cushion. He'd probably never worked a day in his life. She remembered the hard, unpampered feel of his palm. Probably a whiz at sports, she thought. Plays tennis, squash, sails his own yacht. Never does anything worthwhile. Only looks for pleasure. *And finds it,* she thought.

Megan turned to him, pushing her swinging hair back behind her shoulders. His profile was sharply attractive, with the dusky blond hair curling negligently over his ear.

"See something you like?"

Megan flushed in annoyance, aware that she'd been caught staring.

"You need a shave," she said primly.

Katch turned the rearview mirror toward him as if to

check her analysis. "Guess I do." He smiled as they merged into the traffic. "On our next date I'll be sure to remember. Don't say anything," he added, feeling her stiffen at his side. "Didn't your mother ever tell you not to say anything if you couldn't say something pleasant?"

Megan stifled a retort.

Katch smiled as he merged into traffic. "How long have you lived here?"

"Always." With the windows down, Megan could hear the outdoor noises. The music from a variety of car radios competed against each other and merged into a strange sort of harmony. Megan liked the cluttered, indefinable sound. She felt herself relaxing and straightened her shoulders and faced Katch again.

"And what do you do?"

He caught the thread of disdain in the question, but merely lifted a brow. "I own things."

"Really? What sort of things?"

Katch stopped at a red light, then turned, giving her a long, direct look. "Anything I want." The light changed and he deftly slid the car into the parking lot.

"We can't go in there," Megan told him with a glance at the exclusive restaurant.

"Why not?" Katch switched off the ignition. "The food's good here."

"I know, but we're not dressed properly, and—"

"Do you like doing things properly all the time, Meg?"

The question stopped her. She searched his face carefully, wondering if he was laughing at her, and unsure of the answer.

"Tell you what." He eased himself out of the car, then leaned back in the window. "Think about it for a few minutes. I'll be back."

Megan watched him slide through the elegant doors of the restaurant and shook her head. They'll boot him out, she thought. Still, she couldn't help admiring his confidence. There was something rather elusive about it. She crossed her arms over. "Still, I don't really *like* him," she muttered.

Fifteen minutes later, she decided she liked him even less. How impossibly rude! she fumed as she slammed out of his car. Keeping me waiting out here all this time!

She decided to find the nearest phone booth and call her grandfather to ask him to come pick her up. She searched the pockets in her jeans and her jacket. Not a dime, she thought furiously. Not one thin dime to my name. Taking a deep breath, she stared at the doors of the restaurant. She'd have to borrow change, or beg their permission to use the house phone. Anything was better than waiting in the car. Just as she pulled open the door of the restaurant, Katch strolled out.

"Thanks," he said casually and moved past her.

Megan stared after him. He was carrying the biggest picnic basket she'd ever seen. After he'd opened the trunk and settled it inside, he glanced back up at her.

"Well come on." He slammed the lid. "I'm starving."

"What's in there?" she asked suspiciously.

"Dinner." He motioned for her to get in the car. Megan stood beside the closed door on the passenger side.

"How did you get them to do that?"

"I asked. Are you hungry?"

"Well, yes… But how—"

"Then let's go." Katch dropped into the driver's seat and started the engine. The moment she sat beside him, he swung out of the parking lot. "Where's your favorite place?" he demanded.

"My favorite place?" she repeated dumbly.

"You can't tell me you've lived here all your life and don't have a favorite place." Katch turned the car toward the ocean. "Where is it?"

"Toward the north end of the beach," she said. "Not many people go there, except at the height of the season."

"Good. I want to be alone with you."

The simple directness had butterflies dancing in her stomach. Slowly, she turned to look at him again.

"Anything wrong with that?" The smile was back, irreverent and engaging. Megan sighed, feeling like she was just climbing the first hill of a roller coaster.

"Probably," she murmured.

The beach was deserted but for the crying gulls. She stood for a moment facing west, enjoying the rich glow of the dying sun.

"I love this time of day," she said softly. "Everything seems so still. As if the day's holding its breath." She jumped when Katch's hands came to her shoulders.

"Easy," he murmured, kneading the suddenly tense muscles as he stood behind her. He looked over her head to the sunset. "I like it just before dawn, when the birds first start to sing and the light's still soft.

"You should relax more often," he told her. He slid his fingers lazily up her neck and down again. The pleasure became less quiet and more demanding. When she would have slipped away, Katch turned her to face him.

"No," she said immediately, "don't." Megan placed both her hands on his chest. "Don't."

"All right." He relaxed his hold, but didn't release her for a moment. Then he stooped for the picnic basket and pulled out a white tablecloth saying briskly, "Besides, it's time to eat." Megan took it from him, marveling that the restaurant had given him their best linen.

"Here you go." With his head still bent over the basket, he handed her the glasses.

And they're crystal, she thought, dazed as she accepted the elegant wineglasses. There was china next, then silver.

"Why did they give you all this?"

"They were low on paper plates."

"Champagne?" She glanced at the label as he poured. "You must be crazy!"

"What's the matter?" he returned mildly. "Don't you like champagne?"

"Actually I do, though I've only had American."

"Here's to the French." Katch held out a glass to her.

Megan sipped. "It's wonderful," she said before experimenting with another sip. "But you didn't have to…" she gestured expansively.

"I decided I wasn't in the mood for a hamburger." Katch screwed the bottle down into the sand. He placed a small container on the cloth, then dived back into the basket.

"What's this?" Megan demanded as she opened it. She frowned at the shiny black mass inside. He placed toast points on a plate. "Is it…" She paused in disbelief and glanced at him. "Is this caviar?"

"Yeah. Let me have some, will you? I'm starving." Katch took it from her and spread a generous amount on a piece of toast. "Don't you want any?" he asked her as he took a bite.

"I don't know." Megan examined it critically. "I've never tasted it before."

"No?" He offered her his piece. "Taste it." When she hesitated, Katch grinned and held it closer to her mouth. "Go on, Meg, have a bite."

"It's salty," she said with surprise. She plucked the toast from his hand and took another bite. "And it's good," she decided, swallowing.

"You might've left me some," he complained when Megan finished off the toast. She laughed and, heaping caviar onto another piece, handed it to him. "I wondered how it would sound." Katch took the offering, but his attention was on Megan.

"What?" Still smiling, she licked a bit of caviar from her thumb.

"Your laugh. I wondered if it would be as appealing as your face." He took a bite now, still watching her. "It is."

Megan tried to calm her fluttering pulse. "You didn't have to feed me caviar and champagne to hear me laugh." With a casual shrug, she moved out of his reach. "I laugh quite a bit."

"Not often enough."

She looked back at him in surprise. "Why do you say that?"

"Your eyes are so serious. So's your mouth." His glance swept over her face. "Perhaps that's why I feel compelled to make you smile."

"How extraordinary." Megan sat back on her heels and stared at him. "You barely know me."

"Does it matter?"

"I always thought it should," she murmured as he reached into the hamper again. Megan watched, no longer surprised as he drew out lobster tails and fresh strawberries. She laughed again and, pushing back her hair, moved closer to him.

"Here," she said. "Let me help."

The sun sank as they ate. The moon rose. It shot a shimmering white line across the sea. Megan thought it was like a dream—the china and silver gleaming in the moonlight, the exotic tastes on her tongue, the familiar sound of surf and the stranger beside her, who was becoming less of a stranger every minute.

Already Megan knew the exact movement of his face when he smiled, the precise tonal quality of his voice. She knew the exact pattern of the curls over his ear. More than once, bewitched by moonlight and champagne, she had to restrain her fingers from reaching for them, experimenting with them.

"Aren't you going to eat any cheesecake?" Katch gestured with a forkful, then slid it into his mouth.

"I can't." Megan brought her knees up to her chest and rested her chin on them. She watched his obvious enjoyment with dessert. "How do you do it?"

"Dedication." Katch took the last bite. "I try to see every project through to the finish."

"I've never had a picnic like this," she told him with a contented sigh. Leaning back on her elbows, she stretched out her legs and looked up at the stars. "I've never tasted anything so wonderful."

"I'll give Ricardo your compliments." Katch moved to sit beside her. His eyes moved from the crown of her head down the slender arch of her neck. Her face was thrown up to the stars.

"Who's Ricardo?" she asked absently. There was no thought of objection when Katch tucked her hair behind her ear with his fingertip.

"The chef. He loves compliments."

Megan smiled, liking the way the sound of his voice mixed with the sound of the sea. "How do you know?"

"That's how I lured him away from Chicago."

"Lured him away? What do you mean?" It took only an instant for the answer to come to her. "You own that restaurant?"

"Yes." He smiled at the incredulity in her face. "I bought it a couple of years ago."

Megan glanced at the white linen cloth scattered with fine china and heavy silver. She recalled that a little more than two years before, the restaurant had been ready to go under. The food had been overpriced and the service slack. Then it had received a face-lift. The interior had been redesigned, boasting, she was told, a mirrored ceiling. Since its reopening, it had maintained the highest of reputations in a town which prided itself on its quality and variety of restaurants.

She shifted her attention back to him. "*You* bought it?"

"That's right." Katch smiled at her. He sat Indian-style, facing her as she leaned back on her elbows. "Does that surprise you?"

Megan looked at him carefully: the careless toss of curls, the white knees of his jeans, the frayed sneakers. He was not her conception of a successful businessman. Where was the three-piece suit, the careful hairstyling? And yet...she had to admit there was something in his face.

"No," she said at length. "No, I suppose it doesn't." Megan frowned as he shifted his position. In a moment he was close, facing the sea as she did. "You bought it the same way you want to buy Joyland."

"I told you, that's what I do."

"But it's more than owning things, isn't it?" she insisted, not satisfied with his offhand answers. "It's making a success of them."

"That's the idea," he agreed. "There's a certain satisfaction in succeeding, don't you think?"

Megan sat up and turned to him. "But you can't have Joyland, it's Pop's whole life. You don't understand…"

"Maybe not," he said easily. "You can explain it to me later. Not tonight." He covered her hand with his. "This isn't a night for business."

"Katch, you have to—"

"Look at the stars, Meg," he suggested as he did so himself. "Have you ever tried to count them?"

Her eyes were irresistibly drawn upward. "When I was little. But—"

"Star counting isn't just for kids," he instructed in a voice warm and laced with humor. "Do you come here at night?"

The stars were brilliant and low over the sea. "Sometimes," she murmured. "When a project isn't going well and I need to clear my head, or just be alone."

"What sort of artist are you?" His fingers trailed over her knuckles. "Do you paint seascapes? Portraits?"

She smiled and shook her head. "No, I sculpt."

"Ah." He lifted her hand, then examined it—one side, then the other—while she watched him. "Yes, I can see that. Your hands are strong and capable." When he pressed his lips to the center of her palm, she felt the jolt shoot through her entire body.

Carefully, Megan drew her hand away; then, bringing her knees up to her chest, wrapped her arms around them. She could feel Katch smile without seeing it.

"What do you work in? Clay, wood, stone?"

"All three." Turning her head, she smiled again.

"Where did you study?"

"I took courses in college." With a shrug, she passed this off. "There hasn't been much time for it." She looked up at the sky again. "The moon's so white tonight. I like to come here when it's full like this, so that the light's silvery."

When his lips brushed her ear, she would have jerked away, but he slipped an arm around her shoulders. "Relax, Meg." His voice was a whisper at her cheek. "There's a moon and the ocean. That's all there is besides us."

With his lips tingling on her skin, she could almost believe him. Her limbs were heavy, drugged with wine and the magic of his touch. Katch trailed his mouth down to her throat so that she moaned with the leap of her pulse.

"Katch, I'd better go." He was tracing her jaw with light kisses. "Please," she said weakly.

"Later," he murmured, going back to nuzzle her ear. "Much, much later."

"No, I..." Megan turned her head, and the words died. Her lips were no more than a breath from his. She stared at him, eyes wide and aware as he bent closer. Still his mouth didn't touch hers. It hovered, offering, promising. She moaned again, lids lowering as he teased the corners of her lips. His hands never touched her. He had moved his arm so that their only contact was his mouth and tongue on her skin and the mingling of their breath.

Megan felt her resistance peel away, layer by layer until there was only need. She forgot to question the dangers, the consequences. She could only feel. Her mouth sought his. There was no hesitation or shyness now but demand, impatient demand, as she hungered to feel what she had felt before—the delicious confusion, the dark awareness.

When he still didn't touch her, Megan slipped her arms around him. She pulled him close, enjoying his soft sound of pleasure as the kiss deepened. Still, he let her lead, touching her now, but lightly, his fingers in her hair. She could barely hear the hissing of the surf over the pounding of her heart. Finally, she drew away, pulling in a deep breath as their lips separated.

But he wouldn't let her go. "Again?" The question was quiet and seemed to shout through the still night.

Refusal trembled on Megan's tongue. She knew the ground beneath her was far from solid. His hand on the back of her neck brought her a whisper closer.

"Yes," she said, and went into his arms.

This time he was less passive. He showed her there were many ways to kiss. Short and light, long and deep. Tongue and teeth and lips could all bring pleasure. Together, they lowered themselves to the sand.

It was a rough blanket, but she felt only the excitement of his lips on her skin as they wandered to her throat. She ran her fingers through his hair. His mouth returned to hers, harder now, more insistent. She was ready for it, answering it. Craving it.

When his hand took the naked skin of her breast, she murmured in resistance. She hadn't felt him release the zipper of her jacket or the buttons of her shirt. But his hand was gentle, persuasive. He let his fingers trail over her, a whispering touch. Resistance melted into surrender, then heated into passion. It was smoldering just under her skin, threatening to explode into something out of her control. She moved under him and his hands became less gentle.

There was a hunger in the kiss now. She could taste it, a flavor sharper than any she'd known. It was more seductive than soft words or champagne, and more frightening.

"I want you." Katch spoke against her mouth, but the words were not in his easygoing tone. "I want to make love with you."

Megan felt control slipping from her grasp. Her need for him was overpowering, her appetite ravenous. She struggled to climb back to reality, to remember who they were. Names, places, responsibilities. There was more than the moon and the sea. And he was a stranger, a man she barely knew.

"No." Megan managed to free her mouth from his. She struggled to her feet. "No." The repetition was shaky. Quickly, she began to fumble with the buttons of her shirt.

Katch stood and gathered the shirttail in his hands. Surprised, Megan looked up at him. His eyes were no longer calm, but his voice was deadly so. "Why not?"

Megan swallowed. There wasn't lazy arrogance here, but a hint of ruthlessness. She had sensed it, but seeing it was much more potent. "I don't want to."

"Liar," he said simply.

"All right." She nodded, conceding his point. "I don't know you."

Katch inclined his head in agreement but tugged on the tails of her shirt to bring her closer. "You will," he assured her. He kissed her then, searingly. "But we'll wait until you do."

She fought to steady her breathing and stabilize her pulse. "Do you think you should always get what you want?" she demanded. The defiance was back, calming her.

"Yes," he said and grinned. "Of course."

"You're going to be disappointed." She smacked his hands from her shirt and began doing the buttons. Her fingers were unfaltering. "You can't have Joyland and you can't have me. Neither of us is for sale."

The roughness with which he took her arm had her eyes flying back to his face. "I don't buy women." He was angry, his eyes dark with it. The appealing voice had hardened like flint. The artist in her was fascinated by the planes of his face, the woman was uneasy with his harsh tone. "I don't have to. We're both aware that with a bit more persuasion I'd have had you tonight."

Megan pulled out of his hold. "What happened tonight doesn't mean I find you irresistible, you know." She zipped up her jacket with one quick jerk. "I can only repeat, you can't have Joyland and you can't have me."

Katch watched her a moment as she stood in the moonlight, her back to the sea. The smile came again, slowly, arrogantly. "I'll have you both, Meg," he promised quietly. "Before the season begins."

chapter four

The afternoon sun poured into Megan's studio. She was oblivious to it, and to the birdsong outside the windows. Her mind was focused on the clay her hands worked with, or, more precisely, on what she saw in the partially formed mound.

She had put her current project aside, something she rarely did, to begin a new one. The new subject had haunted her throughout the night. She would exorcise David Katcherton by doing a bust of him.

Megan could see it clearly, knew precisely what she wanted to capture: strength and determination behind a surface affability.

Though she had yet to admit it, Katch had frightened her the night before. Not physically—he was too intelligent to use brute force, she acknowledged—but by the force of his personality. Angrily, she stabbed at the clay. Obviously, this was a man who got what he wanted. But she was determined that this time he would not have his way. He would soon find out that she couldn't be pushed around any more than

Pop could. Slowly and meticulously, her fingers worked to mold the planes of his face. It gave her a certain satisfaction to have control over him—if only vicariously with the clay.

Almost without thinking, she shaped a careless curl over the high brow. She stepped back to survey it. Somehow, she had caught a facet of his nature. He was a rogue, she decided. The old-fashioned word suited him. She could picture him with boots and six-guns, dealing cards for stud poker in a Tucson saloon; with a saber, captaining a ship into the Barbary Coast. Her fingers absently caressed the clay curls. He would laugh in the face of the wind, take treasure and women where he found them. *Women*. Megan's thoughts zeroed in on the night before…. On the feel of his lips on hers, the touch of his hand on her skin. She could remember the texture of the sand as they had lain together, the scent and sounds of the sea. And she remembered how the moonlight had fallen on his hair, how her hands had sought it while his lips had wandered over her. How thick and soft it had felt. How…

Megan stopped, appalled. She glanced down to see her fingers in the clay replica of Katch's hair. She swore, and nearly, very nearly, reduced the clay to a formless mass. Controlling herself, she rose, backing away from the forming bust. I should never allow myself to be distracted from my work by petty annoyances, she thought. Her evening with Katch belonged in that category. Just a petty annoyance. Not important.

But it was difficult for Megan to convince herself this was true. Both her intuition and her emotions told her that Katch was important, far more important than a stranger should be to a sensible woman.

And I *am* sensible, she reminded herself. Taking a long breath, she moved to the basin to rinse the clay from her hands. She had to be sensible. Pop needed someone around to remind him that bills had to be paid. A smile crept across her mouth as she dried her hands. Megan thought, as she did from time to time, that she had been almost as much of a savior to her grandfather as he had been to her.

In the beginning, she'd been so young, so dependent upon him. And he hadn't let her down. Then, as she had grown older, Megan had helped by assuming the duties her grand-father had found tiresome: accounts and bank reconciliations. Often, Megan suppressed her own desires in order to fulfill what she thought of as her duty. She dealt with figures, the unromantic process of adding and subtracting. But she also dealt with the illusionary world of art. There were times, when she was deep in her work, that she forgot the rules she had set up for day-to-day living. Often she felt pulled in two directions. She had enough to think about without David Katcherton.

Why a man virtually unknown to her should so success-fully upset the delicate balance of her world, she didn't know. She shook her head. Instead of dwelling on it, she decided, she would work out her frustration by finishing the bust. When it was done, perhaps she would be able to see more clearly exactly how she perceived him. She returned to her work.

The next hour passed quickly. She forgot her irritation

with Katch for going fishing with her grandfather. How annoying to have seen him so eager and well rested when she had peeked through her bedroom curtain at five-thirty that morning! She'd fallen back into her rumpled bed to spend another hour staring, heavy-eyed, at the ceiling. She refused to remember how appealing his laugh had sounded in the hush of dawn.

The planes of his face were just taking shape under her hands when she heard a car drive up. Katch's laugh was followed by the more gravelly tones of her grandfather's.

Because her studio was above the garage, Megan had a bird's-eye view of the house and drive. She watched as Katch lifted their fishing cooler from the back of the pickup. A grin was on his face, but whatever he said was too low for Megan to hear. Pop threw back his head, his dramatic mane of white flying back as he roared his appreciation. He gave Katch a companionable slap on the back. Unaccountably, Megan was miffed. They seemed to be getting along entirely too well.

She continued to watch the man as they unloaded tackle boxes and gear. Katch was dressed much as he had been the day before. The pale blue T-shirt had lettering across the chest, but the words were faded and the distance was too great for Megan to read them. He wore Pop's fishing cap, another source of annoyance for Megan. She was forced to admit the two of them looked good together. There was the contrast between their ages and their builds, but both seemed to her to be extraordinarily masculine men. Their looks were neither smooth nor pampered. She became engrossed with the similarities and differences between them. When Katch looked up, spotting her at the window, Megan continued to stare down, oblivious, absorbed with what she saw in them.

Katch grinned, pushing the fishing cap back so that he had a clearer view. The window was long, the sill coming low at her knees. It had the effect of making Megan seem to be standing in a full-size picture frame. As was her habit when working, she had pulled her hair back in a ribbon. Her face seemed younger and more vulnerable, her eyes wider. The ancient shirt of Pop's she used as a smock dwarfed her.

Her eyes locked on Katch's, and for a moment she thought she saw something flash in them—something she'd seen briefly the night before in the moonlight. A response trembled along her skin. Then his grin was arrogant again, his eyes amused.

"Come on down, Meg." He gestured before he bent to lift the cooler again. "We brought you a present." He turned to carry the cooler around the side of the house.

"I'd rather have emeralds," she called back.

"Next time," Katch promised carelessly, before turning to carry the cooler around the side of the house.

She found Katch alone, setting up for the cleaning of the catch. He smiled when he saw her and set down the knife he held, then pulled her into his arms and kissed her thoroughly, to her utter astonishment. It was a kiss of casual ownership rather than passion, but it elicited a response that surprised her with its force. More than a little shaken, Megan pushed away.

"You can't just…"

"I already did," he pointed out. "You've been working," Katch stated as if the searing kiss had never taken place. "I'd like to see your studio."

It was better, Megan decided, to follow his lead and keep the conversation light. "Where's my grandfather?" she asked as she moved to the cooler and prepared to lift the lid.

"Pop's inside stowing the gear."

Though it was the habit of everyone who knew him to refer to Timothy Miller as Pop, Megan frowned at Katch.

"You work fast, don't you?"

"Yes, I do. I like your grandfather, Meg. You of all people should understand how easy that is to do."

Megan regarded him steadily. She took a step closer, as if testing the air between them. "I don't know if I should trust you."

"You shouldn't." Katch grinned again and ran a finger down the bridge of her nose. "Not for a second." He tossed open the lid of the cooler, then gestured to the fish inside. "Hungry?"

Megan smiled, letting herself be charmed despite the warnings of her sensible self. "I wasn't. But I could be. Especially if I don't have to clean them."

"Pop told me you were squeamish."

"Oh, he *did,* did he?" Megan cast a long, baleful look over her shoulder toward the house. "What else did he tell you?"

"That you like daffodils and used to have a stuffed elephant named Henry."

Megan's mouth dropped open. "He told you that?"

"And that you watch horror movies, then sleep with the blankets over your head."

Megan narrowed her eyes as Katch's grin widened. "Excuse me," she said crossly, pushing Katch aside before racing through the kitchen door. She could hear Katch's laughter behind her.

"Pop!" She found him in the narrow room off the kitchen where he stored his fishing paraphernalia. He gave her an affectionate smile as she stood, hands on hips, in the doorway.

"Hi, Megan. Let me tell you, that boy knows how to fish. Yessiree, he knows how to fish."

His obvious delight with Katch caused Megan to clench her teeth. "That's the best news I've had all day," she said, stepping into the room. "But exactly why did you feel it necessary to tell *that boy* that I had a stuffed elephant and slept with the covers over my head?"

Pop lifted a hand, ostensibly to scratch his head. It wasn't in time, however, to conceal the grin. Megan's brows drew together.

"Pop, really," she said in exasperation. "Must you babble about me as if I were a little girl?"

"You'll always be my little girl," he said maddeningly, and kissed her cheek. "Did you see those trout? We'll have a heck of a fish fry tonight."

"I suppose," Megan began and folded her arms, "*he's* going to eat with us."

"Well, of course." Pop blinked his eyes. "After all, Meg, he caught half the fish."

"That's just peachy."

"We thought you might whip up some of your special blueberry tarts." He smiled ingenuously.

Megan sighed, recognizing defeat.

Within minutes, Pop heard the thumping and banging of pans. He grinned, then slipped out of the room, moving noiselessly through the house and out the front door.

"Whip up some tarts," Megan muttered later as she cut shortening into the flour. *"Men."*

She was bending over to slip the pastry shells into the oven when the screen door slammed shut behind her. Turning, she brushed at the seat of her pants and met the predictable grin.

"I've heard about your tarts," Katch commented, setting the cleaned, filleted fish on the counter. "Pop said he had a few things to see to in the garage and to call him when dinner's ready."

Megan glared through the screen door at the adjoining building. "Oh, he did, did he?" She turned back to Katch. "Well, if you think you can just sit back and be waited on, then you're in for a disappointment."

"You didn't think I'd allow you to cook my fish, did you?" he interrupted.

She stared at his unperturbed face.

"I always cook my own fish. Where's the frying pan?"

Silently, still eyeing him, Megan pointed out the cabinet. She watched as he squatted down to rummage for it.

"It's not that I don't think you're a good cook," he went on as he stood again with the cast-iron skillet in his hand. "It's that I know I am."

"Are you implying I couldn't cook those pathetic little sardines properly?"

"Let's just say I just don't like to take chances with my dinner." He began poking into cupboards. "Why don't you make a salad," he suggested mildly, "and leave the fish to me?" There was a grunt of approval as he located the cracker meal.

Megan watched him casually going through her kitchen cupboards. "Why don't you," she began, "take your trout and…"

Her suggestion was interrupted by the rude buzz of the oven timer.

"Your tarts." Katch walked to the refrigerator for eggs and milk.

With supreme effort, Megan controlled herself enough to deal with the pastry shells. Setting them on the rack to cool, she decided to create the salad of the decade. It would put his pan-fried trout to shame.

For a time there were no words. The hot oil hissed as Katch added his coated trout. Megan tore the lettuce. She sliced raw vegetables. The scent from the pan was enticing. Megan peeled a carrot and sighed. Hearing her, Katch raised a questioning eyebrow.

"You had to be good at it, didn't you?" Megan's smile was reluctant. "You had to do it right."

He shrugged, then snatched the peeled carrot from her

hand. "You'd like it better if I didn't?" Katch took a bite of the carrot before Megan could retrieve it. Shaking her head, she selected another.

"It would have been more gratifying if you'd fumbled around and made a mess of things."

Katch tilted his head as he poked at the sizzling fish with a spatula. "Is that a compliment?"

Megan diced the carrot, frowning at it thoughtfully. "I don't know. It might be easier to deal with you if you didn't seem so capable."

He caught her off guard by taking her shoulders and turning her around to face him. "Is that what you want to do?" His fingers gently massaged her flesh. "Deal with me?" When she felt herself being drawn closer, she placed her hands on his chest. "Do I make you nervous?"

"No." Megan shook her head with the denial. "No, of course not." Katch only lifted a brow and drew her closer. "Yes," she admitted in a rush, and pulled away. "Yes, blast it, you do." Stalking to the refrigerator, she yanked out the blueberry filling she had prepared. "You needn't look so pleased about it," she told him, wishing she could work up the annoyance she thought she should feel.

"Several things make me nervous." Megan moved to the pastry shells and began to spoon in the filling. "Snakes, tooth decay, large unfriendly dogs." When she heard him chuckle, Megan turned her head and found herself grinning at him. "It's difficult to actively dislike you when you make me laugh."

"Do you have to actively dislike me?" Katch flipped the fish expertly and sent oil sizzling.

"That was my plan," Megan admitted. "It seemed like a good idea."

"Why don't we work on a different plan?" Katch suggested, searching through a cupboard again for a platter. "What do you like? Besides daffodils?"

"Soft ice cream," Megan responded spontaneously. "Oscar Wilde, walking barefoot."

"How about baseball?" Katch demanded.

Megan paused in the act of filling the shells. "What about it?"

"Do you like it?"

"Yes," she considered, smiling. "As a matter of fact, I do."

"I knew we had something in common." Katch grinned. He turned the flame off under the pan. "Why don't you call Pop? The fish is done."

There was something altogether too cozy about the three of them sitting around the kitchen table eating a meal each of them had a part in providing, Megan thought. She could sense the growing affection between the two men and it worried her. She was sure that Katch was still as determined as ever to buy Joyland. Yet Pop was so obviously happy in his company. Megan decided that, while she couldn't trust Katch unreservedly, neither could she maintain her original plan. She couldn't dislike him or keep him from touching their lives. She thought it best not to dwell on precisely how he was touching hers.

"Tell you what." Pop sighed over his empty plate and leaned back in his chair. "Since the pair of you cooked dinner, I'll do the dishes." His eyes passed over Megan to Katch. "Why don't you two go for a walk? Megan likes to walk on the beach."

"Pop!"

"I know you young people like to be alone," he continued shamelessly.

Megan opened her mouth to protest, but Katch spoke first. "I'm always willing to take a walk with a beautiful woman, especially if it means getting out of KP," he said.

"You have such a gracious way of putting things," Megan began.

"Actually, I'd really like to see your studio."

"Take Katch up, Megan," Pop insisted. "I've been bragging about your pieces all day. Let him see for himself."

After a moment's hesitation, Megan decided it was simpler to agree. Certainly she didn't mind showing Katch her work. And, there was little doubt that it was safer to let him putter around her studio than to walk with him on the beach.

"All right." She rose. "I'll take you up."

As they passed through the screen door, Katch slipped his arm over her shoulders. "This is a nice place," he commented. He looked around the small trim yard lined with azalea shrubs. "Very quiet and settled."

The weight of his arm was pleasant. Megan allowed it to remain as they walked toward the garage. "I wouldn't think you'd find something quiet and settled terribly appealing."

"There's a time for porch swings and a time for roller

coasters." Katch glanced down at her as she paused at the foot of the steps. "I'd think you'd know that."

"I do," she said, knowing her involvement with him was beginning to slip beyond her control. "I wasn't aware you did." Thoughtful, Megan climbed the stairs. "It's rather a small-scale studio, I suppose, and not very impressive. It's really just a place to work where I won't disturb Pop and he won't disturb me."

Megan opened the door, flicking on the light as the sun was growing dim.

There was much less order here than she permitted herself in other areas of her life. The room was hers, personally, more exclusively than her bedroom in the house next door. There were tools—calipers, chisels, gouges, and an assortment of knives and files. There was the smock she'd carelessly thrown over a chair when Katch had called her downstairs. Future projects sat waiting inside, untouched slabs of limestone and chunks of wood. There was a precious piece of marble she hoarded like a miser. Everywhere, on shelves, tables and even the floor, were samples of her work.

Katch moved past her into the room. Strangely, Megan felt a flutter of nerves. She found herself wondering how to react if he spoke critically, or worse, offered some trite compliment. Her work was important to her and very personal. To her surprise she realized that she cared about his opinion. Quietly, she closed the door behind her, then stood with her back against it.

Katch had gone directly to a small walnut study of a young girl building a sand castle. She was particularly pleased with the piece, as she had achieved exactly the mood she had sought. There was more than youth and innocence in the child's face. The girl saw herself as the princess in the castle tower. The half-smile on her face made the onlooker believe in happy endings.

It was painstakingly detailed, the beginnings of a crenellated roof and the turrets of the castle, the slender fingers of the girl as she sculpted the sand. Her hair was long, falling over her shoulders and wisping into her face as though a breeze teased it. Megan had felt successful when the study had been complete, but now, watching Katch turn it over in his hands, his mouth oddly grave, his eyes intent, she felt a twinge of doubt.

"This is your work?" Because the silence had seemed so permanent, Megan jerked when Katch spoke.

"Well, yes." While she was still searching for something more to say, Katch turned away to prowl the room.

He picked up piece after piece, examining, saying nothing. As the silence dragged on, minute upon minute, Megan became more and more tense. If he'd just say something, she thought. She picked up the discarded smock and folded it, nervously smoothing creases as she listened to the soft sound of his tennis shoes on the wood floor.

"What are you doing here?"

She whirled, eyes wide. Whatever reaction she had expected, it certainly hadn't been anger. And there was anger on his face, a sharp, penetrating anger which caused her to grip the worn material of the smock tighter.

"I don't know what you mean." Megan's voice was calm, but her heart had begun to beat faster.

"Why are you hiding?" he demanded. "What are you afraid of?"

She shook her head in bewilderment. "I'm not hiding, Katch. You're not making any sense."

"I'm not making sense?" He took a step toward her, then stopped, turning away to pace again. She watched in fascination. "Do you think it makes sense to create things like this and lock them up in a room over a garage?" He lifted polished limestone which had been formed into a head-and-shoulders study of a man and a woman in each other's arms. "When you've been given talent like this, you have an obligation. What are you going to do, continue to stack them in here until there isn't any more room?"

His reaction had thrown Megan completely off-balance. She looked around the room. "No, I...I take pieces into an art gallery downtown now and then. They sell fairly well, especially during the season, and—"

Katch's pungent oath cut her off. Megan gave her full attention back to him. Was this furious, disapproving man the same one who had amiably prepared trout in her kitchen a short time ago?

"I don't understand why you're so mad." Annoyed with herself for nervously pleating the material of the smock, Megan tossed it down.

"Waste," he said tersely, placing the limestone back on the shelf. "Waste infuriates me." He came to her, taking her deliberately by the shoulders. "Why haven't you done anything with your work?" His eyes were direct on hers, demanding answers, not evasions.

"It's not as simple as that," she began. "I have responsibilities."

"Your responsibilities are to yourself, to your talent."

"You make it sound as though I've done something wrong." Confused, Megan searched his face. "I've done what I know how to do. I don't understand why you're angry. There are things, like time and money, to be considered," she went on. "A business to run. And reality to face." Megan shook her head. "I can hardly cart my work to a Charleston art gallery and demand a showing."

"That would make more sense than cloistering it up here." He released her abruptly, then paced again.

He was, Megan discovered, much more volatile than her first impression had allowed. She glanced at the clay wrapped in the damp towel. Her fingertips itched to work while fresh impressions were streaming through her brain.

"When's the last time you've been to New York?" Katch demanded, facing her again. "Chicago, L.A.?"

"We can't all be globetrotters," she told him. "Some are born to other things."

He picked up the sand-castle girl again, then strode over to the limestone couple. "I want these two," he stated. "Will you sell them to me?"

They were two of her favorites, though totally opposite in tone. "Yes, I suppose. If you want them."

"I'll give you five hundred." Megan's eyes widened. "Apiece."

"Oh, no, they're not worth—"

"They're worth a lot more, I imagine." Katch lifted the limestone. "Have you got a box I can carry them in?"

"Yes, but, Katch." Megan paused and pushed the bangs from her eyes. "A thousand dollars?"

He set down both pieces and came back to her. He was still angry; she could feel it vibrating from him. "Do you think it's safer to underestimate yourself than to face up to your own worth?"

Megan started to make a furious denial, then stopped. Uncertain, she made a helpless gesture with her hands. Katch turned away again to search for a box himself. She watched him as he wrapped the sculptures in old newspapers. The frown was still on his face, the temper in his eyes.

"I'll bring you a check," he stated, and was gone without another word.

chapter five

There was a long, high-pitched scream. The roller coaster rumbled along the track as it whipped around another curve and tilted its passengers. Lights along the midway were twinkling, and there was noise. Such noise. There was the whirl and whine of machinery, the electronic buzz and beeps from video games, the pop of arcade rifles and the call of concessionaires.

Tinny music floated all over, but for the most part, there was the sound of people. They were laughing, calling, talking, shouting. There were smells: popcorn, peanuts, grilled hot dogs, machine oil.

Megan loaded another clip into the scaled-down rifle and handed it to a would-be Wyatt Earp. "Rabbits are five points, ducks ten, deer twenty-five and the bears fifty."

The sixteen-year-old sharpshooter aimed and managed to bag a duck and a rabbit. He chose a rubber snake as his prize, to the ensuing screams and disgust of his girl.

Shaking her head, Megan watched them walk away. The boy slipped his arm around the girl's shoulders, then pursued the romance by dangling the snake in front of her face. He earned a quick jab in the ribs.

The crowd was thin tonight, but that was to be expected in the off-season. Particularly, Megan knew, when there were so many other parks with more rides, live entertainment and a more sophisticated selection of video games. She didn't mind the slack. Megan was preoccupied, as she had been since the evening Katch had seen her studio. In three days, she hadn't heard a word from him. At first, she had wanted badly to see him, to talk about the things he'd said to her. He had made her think, made her consider a part of herself she had ignored or submerged most of her life.

Her desire to speak with Katch had faded as the days had passed, however. After all, what right did he have to criticize her life-style? What right did he have to make her feel as if she'd committed a crime? He'd accused, tried and condemned her in the space of minutes. Then, he'd disappeared.

Three days, Megan mused, handing another hopeful dead-eye a rifle. Three days without a word. And she'd watched for him—much to her self-disgust. She'd waited for him. As the days had passed, Megan had taken refuge in anger. Not only had he criticized and scolded her, she remembered, but he'd walked out with two of her favorite sculptures. A thousand dollars my foot, she mused, frowning fiercely as she slid a fresh clip into an empty rifle. Just talk, that's all. Talk. He does that very well. It was probably all a line, owning that restaurant. *But why?* Men like that don't need logical reasons, she decided. It's all ego.

"Men," she muttered as she handed a rifle to a new customer.

"I know what you mean, honey." The plump blond woman took the rifle from Megan with a wink.

Megan pushed her bangs back and frowned deeper. "Who needs them?" she demanded.

The woman shouldered the rifle. "We do, honey. That's the problem."

Megan let out a long sigh as the woman earned 125 points. "Nice shooting," she congratulated. "Your choice on the second row."

"Let me have the hippo, sweetie. It looks a little like my second husband."

Laughing, Megan plucked it from the shelf and handed it over. "Here you go." With another wink, the woman tucked the hippo under her arm and waddled off.

Megan settled back while two kids tried their luck. The exchange had been typical of the informality enjoyed by people in amusement parks. She smiled, feeling less grim, if not entirely mollified by the woman's remarks. But she doesn't know Katch, Megan reflected, again exchanging a rifle for a quarter. And neither, she reminded herself, do I.

Automatically, Megan made change when a dollar bill was placed on the counter. "Ten shots for a quarter," she began the spiel. "Rabbits are five, ducks ten…" Megan pushed three quarters back as she reached for a rifle. The moment the fingers pushed the change back to her, she recognized them.

"I'll take a dollar's worth," Katch told her as she looked up in surprise. He grinned, then leaned over to press a quick kiss to her lips. "For luck," he claimed when she jerked away.

Before Megan had pocketed the quarters, Katch had bull's-eyed every one of the bears.

"Wow!" The two boys standing next to Katch were suitably impressed. "Hey, mister, can you do it again?" one asked.

"Maybe." Katch turned to Megan. "Let's have a reload." Without speaking, she handed him the rifle.

"I like the perfume you're wearing," he commented as he sighed. "What is it?"

"Gun oil."

He laughed, then blasted the hapless bears one by one. The two boys gave simultaneous yelps of appreciation. A crowd began to gather.

"Hey, Megan." She glanced up to see the Bailey twins leaning over the counter. Both pairs of eyes drifted meaningfully to Katch. "Isn't he the…"

"Yes," Megan said shortly, not wanting to explain.

"Delicious," Teri decided quietly, giving Katch a flirtatious smile when he straightened.

"Mmm-hmm," Jeri agreed with a twin smile.

Katch gave them a long, appreciative look.

"Here." Megan shoved the rifle at him. "This is your last quarter."

Katch accepted the rifle. "Thanks." He hefted it again. "Going to wish me luck?"

Megan met his eyes levelly. "Why not?"

"Meg, I'm crazy about you."

She dealt with the surge his careless words brought her as he picked off his fourth set of bears. Bystanders broke into raucous applause. Katch set the rifle on the counter, then gave his full attention to Meg.

"What'd I win?"

"Anything you want."

His grin was a flash, and his eyes never left her face. She blushed instantly, hating herself. Deliberately, she stepped to the side and gestured toward the prizes.

"I'll take Henry," he told her. When she gave him a puzzled look, he pointed. "The elephant." Glancing up, Megan spotted the three-foot lavender elephant. She lifted it down from its perch. Even as she set it on the counter for him, Katch took her hands. "And you."

She made her voice prim. "Only the items on display are eligible prizes."

"I love it when you talk that way," he commented.

"Stop it!" she hissed, flushing as she heard the Bailey twins giggle.

"We had a bet, remember?" Katch smiled at her. "It's Friday night."

Megan tried to tug her hands away, but his fingers interlocked with hers. "Who says I lost the bet?" she demanded. The crowd was still milling around the stand so she spoke in an undertone, but Katch didn't bother.

"Come on, Meg, I won fair and square. You're not going to welch, are you?"

"Shh!" She glanced behind him at the curious crowd. "I never welch," she whispered furiously. "And even if I did lose, which I never said I did, I can't leave the stand. I'm sure you can find somebody else to keep you company."

"I want you."

She struggled to keep her eyes steady on his. "Well, I can't leave. Someone has to run the booth."

"Megan." One of the part-timers slipped under the counter. "Pop sent me to relieve you." He smiled innocently when she gave him a disgusted look.

"Perfect timing," she mumbled, then stripped off the change apron and stuffed it in his hands. "Thanks a lot."

"Sure, Megan."

"Hey, keep this back there for me, will you?" Katch dumped the elephant into his arms and captured Megan's hands again as she ducked under the counter. As she straightened, he tugged, tumbling her into his arms.

The kiss was long and demanding. When Katch drew her away, her arms were around his neck. She left them there, staring up into his face with eyes newly aware and darkened.

"I've wanted to do that for three days," he murmured, and rubbed her nose lightly with his.

"Why didn't you?"

He lifted a brow at that, then grinned when her blush betrayed the impetuousness of her words.

"I didn't mean that the way it sounded," Megan began, dropping her arms and trying to wriggle away.

"Yes you did," he countered. Katch released her but dropped a friendly arm over her shoulder. "It was nice, don't spoil it." He took a sweeping glance of the park. "How about a tour?"

"I don't know why you want one. We're not selling."

"We'll see about that," he said, as maddeningly confident as ever. "But in any case, I'm interested. Do you know why people come here? To a place like this?" He gestured with his free arm to encompass the park.

"To be entertained," Megan told him as she followed the movement of his arm.

"You left out two of the most important reasons," he added. "To fantasize and to show off."

They stopped to watch a middle-aged man strip out of his jacket and attempt to ring the bell. The hammer came down with a loud thump, but the ball rose only halfway up the pole. He rubbed his hands together and prepared to try again.

"Yes, you're right." Megan tossed her hair back with a move of her head, then smiled at Katch. "You ought to know."

He tilted his head and shot her a grin. "Want me to ring the bell?"

"Muscles don't impress me," she said firmly.

"No?" He guided her away with his arm still around her. "What does?"

"Poetry," Megan decided all at once.

"Hmm." Katch rubbed his chin and avoided a trio of teenagers. "How about a limerick? I know some great limericks."

"I bet you do." Megan shook her head. "I think I'll pass."

"Coward."

"Oh? Let's ride the roller coaster, then we'll see who's a coward."

"You're on." Taking her hand, he set off in a sprint. He stopped at the ticket booth, and gratefully she caught her breath.

I might as well face it, she reflected as she studied his face. I enjoy him. There isn't any use in pretending I don't.

"What are you thinking?" Katch demanded as he paid for their ride.

"That I could learn to like you—in three or four years. For short periods of time," she added, still smiling.

Katch took both her hands and kissed them, surprising Megan with the shock that raced up her arms. "Flatterer," he murmured, and his eyes laughed at her over their joined hands.

Distressed by the power she felt rushing through her system, Megan tried to tug her hands from his. It was imperative, for reasons only half-formed in her brain, that she keep their relationship casual.

"You have to hold my hand." Katch jerked his head toward the roller coaster. "I'm afraid of heights."

Megan laughed. She let herself forget the tempestuous instant and the hint of danger. She kept her hand in his.

Katch wasn't satisfied with only the roller coaster. He pulled Megan to ride after ride. They were scrambled on the

Mind Maze, spooked in the Haunted Castle and spun lazily on the Ferris wheel.

From the top of the wheel, they watched the colored lights of the park, and the sea stretching out to the right. The wind tossed her hair into her face. Katch took it in his hand as they rose toward the top again. When he kissed her, it felt natural and right…a shared thing, a moment which belonged only to them. The noise and people below were of another world. Theirs was only the gentle movement of the wheel and the dance of the breeze. And the touch of mouth on mouth. There was no demand, only an offering of pleasure.

Megan relaxed against him, finding her head fit naturally in the curve of his shoulder. Held close beside him, she watched the world revolve. Above, the stars were scattered and few. A waning moon shifted in and out of the clouds. The air was cool with a hint of the sea. She sighed, utterly content.

"When's the last time you did this?"

"Did what?" Megan tilted her head to look at him. Their faces were close, but she felt no danger now, only satisfaction.

"Enjoyed this park." Katch had caught the confusion on her face. "Just enjoyed it, Megan, for the fun."

"I…" The Ferris wheel slowed, then stopped. The carts rocked gently as old passengers were exchanged for new. She remembered times when she had been very young. When had they stopped? "I don't know." Megan rose when the attendant lifted the safety bar.

This time, as she walked with Katch, she looked around

thoughtfully. She saw several people she knew; locals out for an evening's entertainment mixed with tourists taking a preseason vacation.

"You need to do this more often," Katch commented, steering her toward the east end of the park. "Laugh," he continued as she turned her head to him. "Unbend, relax those restrictions you put on yourself."

Megan's spine stiffened. "For somebody who barely knows me, you seem remarkably certain of what's good for me."

"It isn't difficult." He stopped at a concession wagon and ordered two ice-cream cones. "You haven't any mysteries, Meg."

"Thank you very much."

With a laugh, Katch handed her a cone. "Don't get huffy, I meant that as a compliment."

"I suppose you've known a lot of sophisticated women."

Katch smiled, then his arm came around her as they began to walk again. "There's one, her name's Jessica. She's one of the most beautiful women I know."

"Really?" Megan licked at the soft swirl of vanilla.

"That blond, classical look. You know, fair skin, finely chiseled features, blue eyes. Terrific blue eyes."

"How interesting."

"Oh, she's all of that," he continued. "And more: intelligent, a sense of humor."

"You sound very fond of her." Megan gave the ice cream her undivided attention.

"A bit more than that actually. Jessica and I lived together for a number of years." He dropped the bomb matter-offactly. "She's married now and has a couple of kids, but we still manage to see each other now and again. Maybe she can make it down for a few days, then you can meet her."

"Oh, really!" Megan stopped, incensed. "Flaunt your relationship somewhere else. If you think I want to meet your—your…"

"Sister," Katch supplied, then crunched into his cone. "You'd like her. Your ice cream's dripping, Meg."

They walked to the entrance gates of the park.

"It's a very nice park," Katch murmured. "Small but well set up. No bored-faced attendants." He reached absently in his pocket and pulled out a slip of paper.

"I forgot to give you your check."

Megan stuffed it into her pocket without even glancing at it. Her eyes were on Katch's face. She was all too aware of the direction his thoughts had taken. "My grandfather's devoted his life to this park," she reminded him.

"So have you," Katch said.

"Why do you want to buy it?" she asked. "To make money?"

Katch was silent for a long moment. By mutual consent, they cut across the boardwalk and moved down the sloping sand toward the water. "Is that such a bad reason, Megan? Do you object to making money?"

"No, of course not. That would be ridiculous."

"I wondered if that was why you haven't done anything with your sculpting."

"No. I do what I'm capable of doing, and what I have time for. There are priorities."

"Perhaps you have them wrong." Before she could comment, he spoke again. "How would it affect the park's business if it had some updated rides and an expanded arcade?"

"We can't afford…"

"That wasn't my question." He took her by the shoulders and his eyes were serious.

"Business would improve, naturally," Megan answered. "People come here to be entertained. The more entertainment provided, the slicker, the faster the entertainment, the happier they are. And the more money they spend."

Katch nodded as he searched her face. "Those were my thoughts."

"It's academic because we simply haven't the sort of money necessary for an overhaul."

"Hmm?" Though he was looking directly at her, Megan saw that his attention had wandered. She watched it refocus.

"What are you thinking?" she demanded.

The grip on her shoulder altered to a caress. "That you're extraordinarily beautiful."

Megan pulled away. "No, you weren't."

"It's what I'm thinking now." The gleam was back in his eyes as he put his hands to her waist. "It's what I was thinking the first time I saw you."

"You're ridiculous." She made an attempt to pull away, but he caught her closer.

"I've never denied that. But you can't call me ridiculous for finding you beautiful." The wind blew her hair back, leaving her face unframed. He laid a soft, unexpected kiss on her forehead. Megan felt her knees turn to water. She placed her hands on his chest both for support and in protest. "You're an artist." He drew her fractionally closer, and his voice lowered. "You recognize beauty when you see it."

"Don't!" The protest was feeble as she made no attempt to struggle out of his gentle hold.

"Don't what? Don't kiss you?" Slowly, luxuriously, his mouth journeyed over her skin. "But I have to, Meg." His lips touched hers softly, then withdrew, and her heart seemed to stop. The flavor of his lips as they brushed against hers overwhelmed her. They tempted, then ruled. With a moan of pleasure, Megan drew him close against her.

Something seemed to explode inside her as the kiss deepened. She clung to him a moment, dazed, then terrified by the power of it. Needs, emotions and new sensations tumbled together too quickly for her to control them. As panic swamped her, Megan struggled in his arms. She would have run, blindly, without direction, but Katch took her arms and held her still.

"What is it? You're trembling." Gently, he tilted her chin until their eyes met. Hers were wide, his serious. "I didn't mean to frighten you. I'm sorry."

The gentleness was nearly her undoing. Love, so newly discovered, hammered for release. She shook her head, knowing her voice would be thick with tears if she spoke. Swallowing, Megan prayed she could steady it.

"No, it's...I have to get back. They're closing." Behind him, she could see the lights flickering off.

"Meg." The tone halted her. It was not a demand this time, but a request. "Have dinner with me."

"No—"

"I haven't even suggested an evening," he pointed out mildly. "How about Monday?"

Megan stood firm. "No."

"Please."

Her resolution dissolved on a sigh. "You don't play fair," she murmured.

"Never. How about seven?"

"No picnics on the beach," she compromised.

"We'll eat inside, I promise."

"All right, but just dinner." She stepped away from him. "Now, I have to go."

"I'll walk you back." Katch took her hand and kissed it before she could stop him. "I have to get my elephant."

chapter six

Megan held Katch's face in her hands. With totally focused absorption, she formed his cheekbones. She had thought when she had first begun to work on this bust that morning that it would be good therapy. To an extent, she'd been right. The hours had passed peacefully, without the restless worry of the past two nights. Her mind was centered on her work, leaving no spaces for the disturbing thoughts that had plagued her all weekend.

She opened and closed her hands slowly, using the muscles until the cramping was a dull ache. A glance at her watch told her she had worked for longer than she'd intended. Late afternoon sun poured through the windows. Critically, as she pulled on each finger to soothe it, Megan studied her work.

The model was good, she decided, with just the proper touches of roughness and intelligence she had aimed for. The mouth was strong and sensuous, the eyes perceptive and far too aware. The mobility of the face which Megan found fascinating could only be suggested. It was a face that urged one to trust against better judgment and common sense.

Narrowing her eyes, she studied the clay replica of Katch's face. There are certain men, she thought, who make a career out of women—winning them, making love to them, leaving them. There are other men who settle down and marry, raise families. How could she doubt what category Katch fell into?

Megan rose to wash her hands. Infatuation, she reflected. It's simply infatuation. He's different, and I can't deny he's exciting. I wouldn't be human if I weren't flattered that he's attracted to me. I've overreacted, that's all. She dried her hands on a towel and tried to convince herself. A person doesn't fall in love this quickly. And if they do, it's just a surface thing, nothing lasting. Megan's eyes were drawn to the clay model. Katch's smile seemed to mock all her sensible arguments. She hurled the towel to the floor.

"It can't happen this fast!" she told him furiously. "Not this way. Not to me." She swung away from his assured expression. "I won't let it."

It's only the park he wants, she reminded herself. Once he's finally convinced he can't have it, he'll go away. The ache was unexpected, and unwelcome. That's what I want, she thought. For him to go away and leave us alone. She tried not to remember the new frontiers she had glimpsed while being held in his arms.

With a brisk shake of her head, Megan pulled the tie from her hair so that it tumbled back to brush her shoulders. I'll start in wood tomorrow, she decided, and covered the clay model. Tonight, I'll simply enjoy a dinner date with an attractive man. It's that simple.

With a great deal more ease than she was feeling, Megan took off her work smock and left her studio.

"Hi, sweetheart." Pop pulled the truck into the driveway just as Megan reached the bottom step.

She noticed the weariness the moment he climbed from the cab. Knowing he hated fussing, she said nothing, but walked over and slipped an arm around his waist.

"Hi, yourself. You've been gone a long time."

"A problem or two at the park," he told her as they moved together toward the house.

That explained the weariness, Megan thought as she pushed open the back door. "What sort of problem?" Megan waited for him to settle himself at the kitchen table before she walked to the stove to brew tea.

"Repairs, Megan, just repairs. The coaster and the Octopus and a few of the smaller rides." He leaned back in his chair as Megan turned to face him.

"How bad?"

Pop sighed, knowing it was better to tell her outright than to hedge. "Ten thousand, maybe fifteen."

Megan let out a long, steady breath. "Ten thousand dollars." She ran a hand under her bangs to rub her brow. There was no purpose in asking if he was sure. If he'd had any doubt, he'd have kept the matter to himself.

"Well, we can come up with five," she began, lumping the check she had just received from Katch into their savings.

"We'll have to have a more exact amount so we can decide how big a loan we'll need."

"Banks take a dim view of lending great lumps of money to people my age," Pop murmured.

Because she saw he was tired and discouraged, she spoke briskly. "Don't be silly." She walked back to the stove to set on the kettle. "In any case, they'd be lending it to the park, wouldn't they?" She tried not to think of tight money and high interest rates.

"I'll go see a few people tomorrow," he promised, reaching for his pipe as if to indicate their business talk was over. "You're having dinner with Katch tonight?"

"Yes." Megan took out cups and saucers.

"Fine young man." He puffed pleasantly on his pipe. "I like him. Has style."

"He has style all right," she grumbled as the kettle began to sing. Carefully, she poured boiling water into cups.

"Knows how to fish," Pop pointed out.

"Which, of course, makes him a paragon of virtue."

"Well, it doesn't make me think any less of him." He spoke genially, smiling into Megan's face. "I couldn't help noticing the two of you on the wheel the other night. You looked real pretty together."

"Pop, really." Feeling her cheeks warm, Megan walked back to fiddle with the dishes in the sink.

"You seemed to like him well enough then," he pointed out before he tested his tea. "I didn't notice any objections when he kissed you." Pop sipped, enjoying. "In fact, you seemed to like it."

"Pop!" Megan turned back, astonished.

"Now, Meg, I wasn't spying," he said soothingly, and coughed to mask a chuckle. "You were right out in public, you know. I'd wager a lot of people noticed. Like I said, you looked real pretty together."

Megan came back to sit at the table without any idea of what she should say. "It was just a kiss," she managed at length. "It didn't mean anything."

Pop nodded twice and drank his tea.

"It didn't," Megan insisted.

He gave her one of his angelic smiles. "But you do like him, don't you?"

Megan dropped her eyes. "Sometimes," she murmured. "Sometimes I do."

Pop covered her hand with his and waited until she looked at him again. "Caring for someone is the easiest thing in the world if you let it be."

"I hardly know him," she said quickly.

"I trust him," Pop said simply.

Megan searched his face. "Why?"

After a shrug, Pop drew on his pipe again. "A feeling I have, a look in his eyes. In a people business like mine, you get to be a good judge of character. He has integrity. He wants his way, all right, but he doesn't cheat. That's important."

Megan sat silently for a moment, not touching her cooling tea. "He wants the park," she said quietly.

Pop looked at her through a nimbus of pipe smoke. "Yes, I know. He said so up front. He doesn't sneak around either."

Pop's expression softened a bit as he looked into Megan's eyes. "Things don't always stay the same in life, Megan. That's what makes it work."

"I don't know what you mean. Do you…are you thinking of selling him the park?"

Pop heard the underlying hint of panic and patted her hand again. "Let's not worry about that now. The first problem is getting the rides repaired for the Easter break. Why don't you wear the yellow dress I like tonight, Meg? The one with the little jacket. It makes me think of spring."

Megan considered questioning him further, then subsided. There was no harder nut to crack than her grandfather when he had made up his mind to close a subject. "All right. I think I'll go up and have a bath."

"Megan." She turned at the door and looked back at him. "Enjoy yourself. Sometimes it's best to roll with the punches."

When she walked away, he looked at the empty doorway and thoughtfully stroked his beard.

An hour later, Megan looked at herself in the yellow dress. The shade hinted at apricot and warmed against her skin. The lines were simple, suiting her willow-slim figure and height. Without the jacket, her arms and shoulders were bare but for wispy straps. She ran a brush through her hair in long, steady strokes. The tiny gold hoops in her ears were her only jewelry.

"Hey, Megan!"

The brush paused in midair as she watched her own

eyes widen in the mirror. He wasn't really standing outside shouting for her!

"Meg!"

Shaking her head in disbelief, Megan went to the window. Katch stood two stories down. He lifted a hand in salute when she appeared in the window.

"What are you doing?" she demanded.

"Open the screen."

"Why?"

"Open it," he repeated.

"If you expect me to jump, you can forget it." Out of curiosity, she leaned out the window.

"Catch!"

Her reflexes responded before she could think. Megan reached for the bundle he tossed up to her, and found her hands full of daffodils. She buried her face in the bouquet.

"They're beautiful." Her eyes smiled over the blooms and down at him. "Thank you."

"You're welcome," he returned. "Are you coming down?"

"Yes." She tossed her hair behind her shoulder. "Yes, yes, in a minute."

Katch drove quickly and competently, but not toward Restaurant Row as Megan had anticipated. He turned toward the ocean and headed north. She relaxed, enjoying the quieting light of dusk and his effortless driving.

She recognized the area. The houses there were larger, more elaborate than those in and on the very outskirts of town. There were tall hedges to assure privacy both from other houses and the public beaches. There were neatly trimmed lawns, willows, blossoming crepe myrtle, and asphalt drives. Katch pulled into one set well away from the other homes and bordered by purplish shrubbery.

The house was small by the neighborhood standards, and done in the weathered wood Megan invariably found attractive. It was a split-level building, with an observation deck crowning the upper story.

"What's this?" she asked, liking the house immediately.

"This is where I live." Katch leaned across her to unlatch her door, then slid out his own side.

"You live here?"

Katch smiled at the surprised doubt in her voice. "I have to live somewhere, Meg."

She wandered farther along the stone path that led to the house. "I suppose I really didn't think about you buying a house here. It suggests roots."

"I have them," he told her. "I just transplant them easily."

She looked at the house, the widespread yard. "You've picked the perfect spot."

Katch took her hand, interlocking fingers. "Come inside," he invited.

"When did you buy this?" she asked as they climbed the front steps.

"Oh, a few months ago when I came through. I moved in last week and haven't had a lot of time to look for furniture." The key shot into the lock. "I've picked up a few things here and there, and had others sent down from my apartment in New York."

It was scantily furnished, but with style. There was a low, sectional sofa in biscuit with a hodgepodge of colored pillows and a wicker throne chair coupled with a large hanging ivy in a pottery dish. A pair of étagères in brass and glass held a collection of shells; on the oak planked floor lay a large sisal rug.

The room was open, with stairs to the right leading to the second level, and a stone fireplace on the left wall. The quick survey showed Megan he had not placed her sculptures in the main room. She wondered fleetingly what he had done with them.

"It's wonderful, Katch." She wandered to a window. The lawn sloped downward and ended in tall hedges that gave the house comfortable privacy. "Can you see the ocean from the top level?"

When he didn't answer, she turned back to him. Her smile faded against the intensity of his gaze. Her heart beat faster. This was the part of him she had to fear, not the amiable gallant who had tossed her daffodils.

She tilted her head back, afraid, but wanting to meet him equally. He brought his hands to her face, and she felt the hardness of his palms on her skin. He brushed her hair back from her face as he brought her closer. He lowered his mouth, pausing only briefly before it claimed hers, as if to ascertain the need mirrored in her eyes. The kiss was instantly deep, instantly seeking.

She had been a fool—a fool to believe she could talk herself out of being in love with him. A fool to think that reason had anything to do with the heart.

When Katch drew her away, Megan pressed her cheek against his chest, letting her arms wind their way around his waist. His hesitation was almost too brief to measure before he gathered her close. She felt his lips in her hair and sighed from the sheer joy of it. His heartbeat was quick and steady in her ear.

"Did you say something?" he murmured.

"Hmm? When?"

"Before." His fingers came up to massage the back of her neck. Megan shivered with pleasure as she tried to remember the world before she had been in his arms.

"I think I asked if I could see the ocean from the top level."

"Yes." Again he took his hands to her face to tilt it back for one long, searing kiss. "You can."

"Will you show me?"

The grip on her skin tightened and her eyes closed in anticipation of the next kiss. But he drew her away until only their hands were touching. "After dinner."

Megan, content with looking at him, smiled. "Are we eating here?"

"I hate restaurants," Katch said, leading her toward the kitchen.

"An odd sentiment from a man who owns one."

"Let's say there are times when I prefer more intimate surroundings."

"I see." He pushed open the door to the kitchen and

Megan glanced around at efficiency in wood and stainless steel. "And who's doing the cooking this time?"

"We are," he said easily, and grinned at her. "How do you like your steak?"

There was a rich, red wine to accompany the meal they ate at a smoked-glass table. A dozen candles flickered on a sideboard behind them, held in small brass holders. Megan's mood was as mellow as the wine that waltzed in her head. The man across from her held her in the palm of his hand. When she rose to stack the dishes, he took her hand. "Not now. There's a moon tonight."

Without hesitation, she went with him.

They climbed the stairs together, wide, uncarpeted stairs which were split into two sections by a landing. He led her through the main bedroom, a room dominated by a large bed with brass head- and footboards. There were long glass doors which led to a walkway. From there, stairs ascended to the observation deck.

Megan could hear the breakers before she moved to the rail. Beyond the hedgerow, the surf was turbulent. White water frothed against the dark. The moon's light was thin, but was aided by the power of uncountable stars.

She took a long breath and leaned on the rail. "It's lovely here. I never tire of looking at the ocean." There was a click from his lighter, then tobacco mixed pleasantly with the scent of the sea.

"Do you ever think about traveling?"

Megan moved her shoulders, a sudden, restless gesture. "Of course, sometimes. It isn't possible right now."

Katch drew on the thin cigar. "Where would you go?"

"Where would I go?" she repeated.

"Yes, where would you go if you could?" The smoke from his cigar wafted upward and vanished. "Pretend, Meg. You like to pretend, don't you?"

She closed her eyes a moment, letting the wine swim with her thoughts. "New Orleans," she murmured. "I've always wanted to see New Orleans. And Paris. When I was young I used to dream about studying in Paris like the great artists." She opened her eyes again. "You've been there, I suppose. To New Orleans and to Paris?"

"Yes, I've been there."

"What are they like?"

Katch traced the line of her jaw with a fingertip before answering. "New Orleans smells of the river and swelters in the summer. There's music at all hours from open nightclubs and street musicians. It moves constantly, like New York, but at a more civilized pace."

"And Paris?" Megan insisted, wanting to see her wishes through his eyes. "Tell me about Paris."

"It's ancient and elegant, like a grand old woman. It's not very clean, but it never seems to matter. It's best in the spring; nothing smells like Paris in the spring. I'd like to take you there." Unexpectedly he took her hair in his hand. His eyes were intense again and direct on hers. "I'd like to see the emotions you control break loose. You'd never restrict them in Paris."

"I don't do that." Something more than wine began to swim in her head.

He tossed the cigar over the rail, then his free hand came to her waist to press her body against his. "Don't you?" There was a hint of impatience in his voice as he began to slide the jacket from her shoulders. "You've passion, but you bank it down. It escapes into your work, but even that's kept closed up in a studio. When I kiss you, I can taste it struggling to the surface."

He freed her arms from the confines of the jacket and laid it over the rail. Slowly, deliberately, he ran his fingers over the naked skin, feeling the warmth of response. "One day it's going to break loose. I intend to be there when it does."

Katch pushed the straps from her shoulders and replaced them with his lips. Megan made no protest as the kisses trailed to her throat. His tongue played lightly with the pulse as his hand came up to cup her breast. But when his mouth came to hers, the gentleness fled, and with it her passivity. Hunger incited hunger.

When he nipped her bottom lip, she gasped with pleasure. His tongue was avid, searching while his hands began a quest of their own. He slipped the bodice of her dress to her waist, murmuring with approval as he found her naked breasts taut with desire. Megan allowed him his freedom, riding on the crest of the wave that rose inside her. She had no knowledge to guide her, no experience. Desire ruled and instinct followed.

She trailed her fingers along the back of his neck, kneading the warm skin, thrilling to the response she felt to her touch. Here was a power she had never explored. She slipped her hands under the back of his sweater. Their journey was slow, exploring. She felt the muscles of his shoulders tense as her hands played over them.

The quality of the kiss changed from demanding to urgent. His passion swamped her, mixing with her own until the combined power was more than she could bear. The ache came from nowhere and spread through her with impossible rapidity. She hurt for him. Desire was a pain as sharp as it was irresistible. In surrender, in anticipation, Megan swayed against him.

"Katch." Her voice was husky. "I want to stay with you tonight."

She was crushed against him for a moment, held so tightly, so strongly, there was no room for breath. Then, slowly, she felt him loosen his hold. Taking her by the shoulders, Katch looked down at her, his eyes dark, spearing into hers. Her breath was uneven; shivers raced along her skin. Slowly, with hands that barely touched her skin, he slipped her dress back into place.

"I'll take you home now."

The shock of rejection struck her like a blow. Her mouth trembled open, then shut again. Quickly, fighting against the tears that were pressing for release, she fumbled for her jacket.

"Meg." He reached out to touch her shoulders, but she backed away.

"No. No, don't touch me." The tears were thickening her voice. She swallowed. "I won't be patted on the head. It appears I misunderstood."

"You didn't misunderstand anything," he tossed back. "And don't cry, damn it."

"I have no intention of crying," she said. "I'd like to go home." The hurt was in her eyes, shimmering behind the tears she denied.

"We'll talk." Katch took her hand, but she jerked it away.

"Oh, no. No, we won't." Megan straightened her shoulders and looked at him squarely. "We had dinner—things got a bit beyond what they should have. It's as simple as that, and it's over."

"It's not simple or over, Meg." Katch took another long look into her eyes. "But we'll drop it for now."

Megan turned away and walked back down the stairs.

chapter seven

Amusement parks lose their mystique in the light of day. Dirt, scratched paint and dents show up. What is shiny and bright under artificial light is ordinary in the sunshine. Only the very young or the very young hearted can believe in magic when faced with reality.

Megan knew her grandfather was perennially young. She loved him for it. Fondly, she watched him supervising repairs on the Haunted Castle. His ghosts, she thought with a smile, are important to him. She walked beside the track, avoiding her own ghost along the way. It had been ten days since Pop had told her of the repair problems. Ten days since she had seen Katch. Megan pushed thoughts of him from her mind and concentrated on her own reality—her grandfather and their park. She was old enough to know what was real and what was fantasy.

"Hi," she called out from behind him. "How are things going?"

Pop turned at the sound of her voice, and his grin was expansive. "Just fine, Megan." The sound of repairs echoed around his words. "Quicker than I thought they would. We'll be rolling before the Easter rush." He swung an arm around her shoulder and squeezed. "The smaller rides are already back in order. How about you?"

She made no objection when he began to steer her outside. The noise made it difficult to hear. "What about me?" she replied. The sudden flash of sunlight made her blink. The spring day had all the heat of midsummer.

"You've that unhappy look in your eyes. Have had, for more than a week." Pop rubbed his palm against her shoulder as if to warm her despite the strength of the sun. "You know you don't hide things from me, Megan. I know you too well."

She was silent a moment, wanting to choose her words carefully. "I wasn't trying to hide anything, Pop." Megan shrugged, turning to watch the crew working on the roller coaster. "It's just not important enough to talk about, that's all. How long before the coaster's fixed?"

"Important enough to make you unhappy," he countered, ignoring her evasion. "That's plenty important to me. You haven't gotten too old to talk to me about your problems now, have you?"

She turned dark apologetic eyes on him. "Oh no, Pop, I can always talk to you."

"Well," he said simply, "I'm listening."

"I made a mistake, that's all." She shook her head and would have walked closer to inspect the work crew had he not held her to him with a firm hand.

"Megan." Pop placed both hands on her shoulders and

looked into her eyes. As they were nearly the same height, their eyes were level. "I'm going to ask you straight," he continued. "Are you in love with him?"

"No," she denied quickly.

Pop raised an eyebrow. "I didn't have to mention any names, I see."

Megan paused a moment. She had forgotten how shrewd her grandfather could be. "I thought I was," she said more carefully. "I was wrong."

"Then why are you so unhappy?"

"Pop, please." She tried to back away, but again his broad hands held her steady.

"You've always given me straight answers, Meg, even when I've had to drag them out of you."

She sighed, knowing evasions and half-truths were useless when he was in this mood. "All right. Yes, I'm in love with him, but it doesn't matter."

"Not a very bright statement from a bright girl like you," he said with a gentle hint of disapproval. Megan shrugged. "Why don't you explain why being in love doesn't matter," he invited.

"Well, it certainly doesn't work if you're not loved back," Megan murmured.

"Who says you're not?" Pop wanted to know. His voice was so indignant, she felt some of the ache subside.

"Pop." Her expression softened. "Just because you love me doesn't mean everyone else does."

"What makes you so sure he doesn't?" her grandfather argued. "Did you ask him?"

"No!" Megan was so astonished, she nearly laughed at the thought.

"Why not? Things are simpler that way."

Megan took a deep breath, hoping to make him understand. "David Katcherton isn't a man who falls in love with a woman, not seriously. And certainly not with someone like me." The broad gesture she made was an attempt to enhance an explanation she knew was far from adequate. "He's been to Paris, he lives in New York. He has a sister named Jessica."

"That clears things up," Pop agreed, and Megan made a quick sound of frustration.

"I've never been anywhere." She dragged a hand through her hair. "In the summer I see millions, literally millions of people, but they're all transient. I don't know who they are. The only people I really know are ones who live right here. The farthest I've been away from the beach is Charleston."

Pop brushed a hand over her hair to smooth it. "I've kept you too close," he murmured. "I always told myself there'd be other times."

"Oh no, Pop, I didn't mean it that way." She threw her arms around him, burying her face in his shoulder. "I didn't mean to sound that way. I love you, I love it here. I wouldn't change anything. That was hateful of me."

He laughed and patted her back. The subtle scent of her perfume reminded him forcefully that she was no longer a girl but a woman. The years had been incredibly quick. "You've never done a hateful thing in your life. We both know you've wanted to see a bit of the world, and I know you've stuck close to keep an eye on me. Oh yes," he said, anticipating her objection. "And I was selfish enough to let you."

"You've never done anything selfish," she retorted and drew away. "I only meant that Katch and I have so little common ground. He's bound to see things differently than I do. I'm out of my depth with him."

"You're a strong swimmer, as I recall." Pop shook his head at her expression and sighed. "All right, we'll let it lie awhile. You're also stubborn."

"Adamant," she corrected, smiling again. "It's a nicer word."

"Just a fancy way of saying pigheaded," Pop said bluntly, but his eyes smiled back at her. "Why aren't you back in your studio instead of hanging around an amusement park in the middle of the day?"

"It wasn't going very well," she confessed, thinking of the half-carved face that haunted her. "Besides, I've always had a thing for amusement parks." She tucked her arm in his as they began to walk again.

"Well, this one'll be in apple-pie order in another week," Pop said, looking around in satisfaction. "With luck, we'll have a good season and be able to pay back a healthy chunk of that ten thousand."

"Maybe the bank will send us some customers so they'll get their money faster," Megan suggested, half listening to the sound of hammer against wood as they drew closer to the roller coaster.

"Oh, I didn't get the money from the bank, I got it from—"

Pop cut himself off abruptly. With a cough and a wheeze, he bent down to tie his shoe.

"You didn't get the money from the bank?" Megan frowned at the snowy white head in puzzlement. "Well, where in the world did you get it then?"

His answer was an unintelligible grunt.

"You don't know anybody with that kind of money," she began with a half-smile. "Where..." The smile flew away. "No. No, you didn't." Even as she denied it, Megan knew it had to be the truth. "You didn't get it from him?"

"Oh now, Megan, you weren't to know." Distress showed in his eyes and seemed to weaken his voice. "He especially didn't want you to know."

"Why?" she demanded. "Why did you do it?"

"It just sort of happened, Meg." Pop reached out to pat her hand in his old, soothing fashion. "He was here, I was telling him about the repairs and getting a loan, and he of-fered. It seemed like the perfect solution." He fiddled with his shoestrings. "Banks poke around and take all that time for paperwork, and he isn't charging me nearly as much interest. I thought you'd be happy about that..." He trailed off.

"Is everything in writing?" she asked, deadly calm.

"Of course." Pop assumed a vaguely injured air. "Katch said it didn't matter, but I know how fussy you are, so I had papers drawn up, nice and legal."

"Didn't matter," she repeated softly. "And what did you use as collateral?"

"The park, naturally."

"Naturally," she repeated. Fury bubbled in the single word. "I bet he loved that."

"Now, don't you worry, Megan. Everything's coming along just fine. The repairs are going well, and we'll be opening right on schedule. Besides," he added with a sigh, "you weren't even supposed to know. Katch wanted it that way."

"Oh, I'm sure he did," she said bitterly. "I'm sure he did."

Turning, she darted away. Pop watched her streak out of sight, then hauled himself to his feet. She had the devil's own temper when she cut loose, that girl. Brushing his hands together, he grinned. That, he decided, pleased with his own maneuvering, should stir up something.

Megan brought the bike to a halt at the crest of Katch's drive, then killed the engine. She took off her helmet and clipped it on the seat. He was not, she determined, going to get away with it.

Cutting across the lawn, she marched to the front door. The knock was closer to a pound but still brought no response. Megan stuffed her hands into her pockets and scowled. Her bike sat behind his black Porsche. Ignoring amenities, she tried the knob. When it turned, she didn't hesitate. She opened the door and walked inside.

The house was quiet. Instinct told her immediately that no one was inside. Still, she walked through the living room looking for signs of him.

A watch, wafer-thin and gold, was tossed on the glass

shelves of the étagère. A Nikon camera sat on the coffee table, its back open and empty of film. A pair of disreputable tennis shoes were half under the couch. A volume of John Cheever lay beside them.

Abruptly, she realized what she had done. She'd intruded where she had no right. She was both uncomfortable and fascinated. An ashtray held the short stub of a thin cigar. After a brief struggle with her conscience, she walked toward the kitchen. She wasn't prying, she told herself, only making certain he wasn't home. After all, his car was here and the door had been unlocked.

There was a cup in the sink and a half pot of cold coffee on the stove. He had spilled some on the counter and neglected to wipe it up. Megan curtailed the instinctive move to reach for a dish towel. As she turned to leave, a low mechanical hum from outside caught her attention. She walked to the window and saw him.

He was coming from the south side of the lawn, striding behind a power mower. He was naked to the waist, with jeans low and snug at his hips. He was tanned, a deep honey gold that glistened now with the effort of manual labor. She admired the play of muscles rippling down his arms and across his back.

Stepping back from the window with a jerk, she stormed through the side kitchen door and raced across the lawn.

The flurry of movement and a flash of crimson caught his eye. Katch glanced over as Megan moved toward him in a red tailored shirt and white jeans. Squinting against the sun, he wiped the back of his hand across his brow. He reached down and shut off the mower as she came to him.

"Hello, Meg," he said lightly, but his eyes weren't as casual.

"You have nerve, Katcherton," she began. "But even I didn't think you'd take advantage of a trusting old man."

He lifted a brow and leaned against the mower's handle. "Once more," he requested, "with clarity."

"You're the type who has to poke your fingers into other people's business," she continued. "You just had to be at the park, you just had to make a magnanimous offer with your tidy little pile of money."

"Ah, a glimmer of light." He stretched his back. "I didn't think you'd be thrilled the money came from me. It seems I was right."

"You knew I'd never allow it," she declared.

"I don't believe I considered that." He leaned on the mower again, but there was nothing restful in the gesture. "You don't run Pop's life from what I've seen, Meg, and you certainly don't run mine."

She did her best to keep her tone even. "I have a great deal of interest in the park and everything that pertains to it."

"Fine, then you should be pleased that you have the money for the repairs quickly, and at a low rate of interest." His tone was cool and businesslike.

"Why?" she demanded. "Why did you lend us the money?"

"I don't," Katch said after a long, silent moment, "owe you any explanation."

"Then I'll give you one," Megan tossed back. There was passion in her voice. "You saw an opportunity and grabbed it. I suppose that's what people do in your sort of world. Take, without the least thought of the people involved."

"Perhaps I'm confused." His eyes were slate, opaque and unreadable. His voice matched them. "I was under the impression that I gave something."

"*Lent* something," Megan corrected. "With the park as collateral."

"If that's your problem, take it up with your grandfather." Katch bent down, reaching for the cord to restart the mower.

"You had no right to take advantage of him. He trusts everyone."

Katch released the cord again with a snap. "A shame it's not an inherited quality."

"I've no reason to trust you."

"And every reason, it appears, to mistrust me since the first moment." His eyes had narrowed as if in speculation. "Is it just me or a general antipathy to men?"

She refused to dignify the question with an answer. "You want the park," she began.

"Yes, and I made that clear from the beginning." Katch shoved the mower aside so that there was no obstacle between them. "I still intend to have it, but I don't need to be devious to get it. I still intend to have you." She stepped back but he was too quick. His fingers curled tightly around her upper arm. "Maybe I made a mistake by letting you go the other night."

"You didn't want me. It's just a game."

"Didn't want you?" She made another quick attempt to pull away and failed. "No, that's right, I didn't want you." He pulled her against him and her mouth was crushed and conquered. Her mind whirled with the shock of it. "I don't want you now." Before she could speak, his mouth savaged hers again. There was a taste of brutality he had never shown her. "Like I haven't wanted you for days." He pulled her to the ground.

"No," she said, frightened, "don't." But his lips were silencing hers again.

There was none of the teasing persuasion he had shown her before, no light arrogance. These were primordial demands, eliciting primordial responses from her. He would take what he wanted, his way. He plundered, dragging her with him as he raced for more. Then his lips left hers, journeying to her throat before traveling downward. Megan felt she was suffocating, suffused with heat. Her breath caught in her lungs, emerging in quick gasps or moans. His fingers ran a bruising trail over her quivering flesh. He ran his thumb over the point of her breast, back and forth, until she was beyond fear, beyond thought. His mouth came back to hers, fever hot, desperate. She murmured mindlessly, clinging to him as her body shuddered with waves of need.

Katch lifted his head, and his breath was warm and erratic on her face. Megan's lids fluttered open, revealing eyes dazed with passion, heavy with desire. Silently, she trembled. If words had been hers, she would have told him that she loved him. There was no pride in her, no shame, only soaring need and a love that was painful in its strength.

"This isn't the place for you." His voice was rough as he rolled over on his back. They lay there a moment, side by side, without touching. "And this isn't the way."

Her mind was fogged, and her blood surging. "Katch," Megan managed his name and struggled to sit up. His eyes lingered on her form, then slid up slowly to brood on her face. It was flushed and aware. She wanted to touch him but was afraid.

For a moment their eyes met. "Did I hurt you?"

She shook her head in denial. Her body ached with longing.

"Go home then." He rose, giving her a last, brief glance. "Before I do." He turned and left her.

Megan heard the slam of the kitchen door.

chapter eight

It was difficult for Megan to cope with the two-week influx of tourists and sun seekers. They came, as they did every Easter, in droves. It was a preview of what the summer would hold. They came to bake on the beach and impress those left at home with a spring tan. They came to be battered and bounced around by the waves. They came to have fun. And what better place to find it than on white sand beaches or in an ocean with a gentle undertow and cresting waves? They came to laugh and sought their entertainment on spiraling water slides, in noisy arcades or crowded amusement parks.

For the first time in her life, Megan found herself resenting the intrusion. She wanted the quiet, the solitude that went with a resort town in its off-season. She wanted to be alone, to work, to heal. It seemed her art was the only thing she could turn to for true comfort. She was unwilling to speak of her feelings to her grandfather. There was still too much to be sorted out in her own mind. Knowing her, and her need for privacy, Pop didn't question.

The hours she spent at the park were passed mechanically.

The faces she saw were all strangers. Megan resented it. She resented their enjoyment when her own life was in such turmoil. She found solace in her studio. If the light in her studio burned long past midnight, she never noticed the time. Her energy was boundless, a nervous, trembling energy that kept her going.

It was afternoon at the amusement park. At the kiddie cars Megan was taking tickets and doing her best to keep the more aggressive youngsters from trampling others. Each time the fire engines, race cars, police cruisers and ambulances were loaded, she pushed the lever which sent the caravan around in its clanging, roaring circle. Children grinned fiercely and gripped steering wheels.

One toddler rode as fire chief with eyes wide with stunned pleasure. Even though she'd been on duty nearly four hours, Megan smiled.

"Excuse me." Megan glanced over at the voice, prepared to answer a parental question. The woman was an exquisite blonde, with a mane of hair tied back from a delicately molded face. "You're Megan, aren't you? Megan Miller?"

"Yes. May I help you?"

"I'm Jessica Delaney."

Megan wondered that she hadn't seen it instantly. "Katch's sister."

"Yes." Jessica smiled. "How clever of you—but Katch told me you were. There is a family resemblance, of course, but so few people notice it unless we're standing together."

Megan's artist eyes could see the similar bone structure

beneath the surface differences. Jessica's eyes were blue, as Katch had said, and the brows above them more delicate than his, but there were the same thick lashes and long lids.

"I'm glad to meet you." Megan reached for something to say. "Are you visiting Katch?" She didn't look like a woman who would patronize amusement parks, more likely country clubs or theaters.

"For a day or so." Jessica gestured to the adjoining ride where children flew miniature piper cubs in the inevitable circle. "My family's with me. Rob, my husband." Megan smiled at a tall man with a straight shock of dark hair and an attractive, angular face. "And my girls, Erin and Laura." She nodded to the two caramel-haired girls of approximately four and six riding double in a plane.

"They're beautiful."

"We like them," Jessica said comfortably. "Katch didn't know where I might find you in the park, but he described you very accurately."

"Is he here?" Megan asked, trying without much success to sound offhanded even as her eyes scanned the crowd.

"No, he had some business to attend to."

The timer rang, signaling the ride's end. "Excuse me a moment," Megan murmured. Grateful for the interruption, she supervised the unloading and loading of children. It gave her the time she needed to steady herself. Her two final customers were Katch's nieces. Erin, the elder, smiled at her with eyes the identical shade of her uncle's.

"I'm driving," she said positively as her sister settled beside her. "She only rides."

"I do not." Laura gripped the twin steering wheel passionately.

"It runs in the family," Jessica stated from behind her. "Stubbornness." Megan hooked the last safety belt and returned to the controls. "You've probably noticed it."

Megan smiled at her. "Yes, once or twice." The lights and noise spun and circled behind her.

"I know you're busy," Jessica stated, glancing at the packed vehicles.

Megan gave a small shrug as she followed her gaze. "It's mostly a matter of making certain everyone stays strapped in and no one's unhappy."

"My little angels," Jessica said, "will insist on dashing off to the next adventure the moment the ride's over." She paused. "Could we talk after you're finished here?"

Megan frowned. "Well, yes, I suppose…I'm due relief in an hour."

"Wonderful." Jessica's smile was as charming as her brother's. "I'd like to go to your studio, if that suits you. I could meet you in an hour and a half."

"At my studio?"

"Wonderful!" Jessica said again and patted Megan's hand. "Katch gave me directions."

The timer rang again, recalling Megan to duty. As she started yet another round of junior rides she wondered why Jessica had insisted on a date in her studio.

With a furrowed brow, Megan studied herself in the bedroom mirror. Would a man who admired Jessica's soft, delicate beauty be attracted to someone who seemed to be all planes and angles? Megan shrugged her shoulders as if it didn't matter. She twirled the stem of the brush idly between her fingers. She supposed that he, like the majority of people who came here, was looking for some passing entertainment

"You are," she said softly to the woman in the glass, "such a fool." She closed her eyes, not wanting to see the reflected accusation. Because you can't let go, her mind continued ruthlessly. Because it doesn't really matter to you why he wanted you with him, just that he wanted you. And you wish, you wish with all your heart that he still did.

She shook her head, disturbing the work she had done with the brush. It was time to stop thinking of it. Jessica Delaney would be arriving any moment.

Why? Megan set down her brush and frowned into middle distance. Why was she coming? What could she possibly want? Megan still had no sensible answer. I haven't heard from Katch in two weeks, she reflected. Why should his sister suddenly want to see me?

The sound of a car pulling into the drive below interrupted her thoughts. Megan walked to the window in time to see Jessica get out of Katch's Porsche.

Megan reached the back stoop before Jessica, as she had been taking a long, leisurely look at the yard. "Hello." Megan felt awkward and rustic. She hesitated briefly before stepping away from the door.

"What a lovely place." Jessica's smile was so like Katch's

that Megan's heart lurched. "How I wish my azaleas looked like yours."

"Pop—my grandfather babies them."

"Yes." The blue eyes were warm and personal. "I've heard wonderful things about your grandfather. I'd love to meet him."

"He's still at the park." Her sense of awkwardness was fading. Charm definitely ran in the Katcherton family. "Would you like some coffee? Tea?"

"Maybe later. Let's go up to the studio, shall we?"

"If you don't mind my asking, Mrs. Delaney—"

"Jessica," she interrupted cheerfully and began to climb the open back stairs.

"Jessica," Megan agreed, "how did you know I had a studio, and that it was over the garage?"

"Oh, Katch told me," Jessica said breezily. "He tells me a great many things." She stood to the side of the door and waited for Megan to open it. "I'm very anxious to see your work. I dabble in oil from time to time."

"Do you?" Jessica's interest now made more sense. Artistic kinship.

"Badly, I'm afraid, which is a constant source of frustration to me." Again the Katcherton smile bloomed on her face.

Megan's reaction was unexpectedly sharp and swift. She fumbled for the doorknob. "I've never had much luck on canvas," she said quickly. She needed words, lots of words to cover what she feared was much too noticeable. "Nothing seems to come out the way I intend," she continued as they entered the studio. "It's maddening not to be able to express yourself properly. I do some airbrushing during the summer rush, but…"

Jessica wasn't listening. She moved around the room much the same way her brother had—intently, gracefully, silently. She fingered a piece here, lifted a piece there. Once, she studied a small ivory unicorn for so long, Megan fidgeted with nerves.

What was she doing? she wondered. *And why?*

Sunlight stippled the floor. Dust motes danced in the early evening light. Too late, Megan recalled the bust of Katch. One slanted beam of sun fell on it, highlighting the planes the chisel had already defined. Though it was still rough hewn and far from finished, it was unmistakably Katch. Feeling foolish, Megan walked over to stand in front of it, hoping to conceal it from Jessica's view.

"Katch was right," Jessica murmured. She still held the unicorn, stroking it with her fingertips. "He invariably is. Normally that annoys me to distraction, but not this time." The resemblance to Katch was startling now. Megan's fingers itched to make a quick sketch even as she tried to follow the twisting roads in Jessica's conversation.

"Right about what?"

"Your extraordinary talent."

"What?" Meg's eyes widened.

"Katch told me your work was remarkable," she went on, giving the unicorn a final study before setting it down. "I agreed when I received the two pieces he sent up to me, but they were only two, after all." She picked up a chisel and tapped it absently against her palm while her eyes continued to wander. "This is astonishing."

"He sent you the sculptures he bought from me?"

"Yes, a few weeks ago. I was very impressed." Jessica set down the chisel with a clatter and moved to a nearly completed study in limestone of a woman rising from the sea. It was the piece Megan had been working on before she had set it aside to begin Katch's bust. "This is fabulous!" Jessica declared. "I'm going to have to have it as well as the unicorn. The response to the two pieces Katch sent me has been very favorable."

"I don't understand what you're talking about." Try as she might, Megan couldn't keep up with Jessica's conversation. "Whose response?"

"My clients'," said Jessica. "At my gallery in New York." She gave Megan a brilliant smile. "Didn't I tell you I run my own gallery?"

"No," Megan answered. "No, you didn't."

"I suppose I thought Katch did. I'd better start at the beginning then."

"I'd really appreciate it if you would," Megan told her, and waited until she had settled herself in the small wooden chair beside her.

"Katch sent me two of your pieces a few weeks ago," Jessica began briskly. "He wanted a professional opinion. I may only be able to dabble in oil, but I know art." She spoke with a confidence that Megan recognized. "Since I knew I'd never make it as a working artist, I put all the years of study to good use. I opened a gallery in Manhattan. *Jessica's*. Over the past six years, I've developed a rather nice clientele." She smiled.

"So naturally, when my wandering brother saw your work, he sent it off to me. He always has his instincts verified by an expert, then plunges along his own way notwithstanding." She sighed indulgently. "I happen to know he was advised against building that hospital in Central Africa last year but he did it anyway. He does what he wants to."

"Hospital." Megan barely made the jump to Jessica's new train of thought.

"Yes, a children's hospital. He has a soft spot for kids." Jessica tried to speak teasingly, but the love came through. "He did some astonishing things for orphaned refugees after Vietnam. And there was the really fabulous little park he built in New South Wales."

Megan sat dumbly. Could they possibly be speaking about the same David Katcherton? Was this the man who had brashly approached her in the local market?

She remembered with uncomfortable clarity that she had accused him of trying to cheat her grandfather. She had told herself that he was an opportunist, a man spoiled by wealth and good looks. She'd tried to tell herself he was irresponsible, undependable, a man in search of his own pleasure.

"I didn't know," she murmured. "I didn't know anything about it."

"Oh, Katch keeps a low profile when he chooses," Jessica told her. "And he chooses to have no publicity when he's doing that sort of thing. He has incredible energy and outrageous self-confidence, but he's also very warm." Her gaze slipped beyond Megan's shoulder. "But then, you appear to know him well."

For a moment, Megan regarded Jessica blankly. Then she twisted her head and saw Katch's bust. In her confusion, she had forgotten her desire to conceal it. Slowly, she turned her head back, trying to keep her voice and face passive.

"No. No, really I don't think I know him at all. He has a fascinating face. I couldn't resist sculpting it."

She noted a glint of understanding in Jessica's eyes. "He's a fascinating man," Jessica murmured.

Megan's gaze faltered.

"I'm sorry," Jessica said immediately. "I've intruded, a bad habit of mine. We won't talk about Katch. Let's talk about your showing."

Megan lifted her eyes again. "My what?"

"Your showing," Jessica repeated, dashing swiftly up a new path. "When do you think you'll have enough pieces ready? You certainly have a tremendous start here, and Katch mentioned something about a gallery in town having some of your pieces. I think we can shoot for the fall."

"Please, Jessica, I don't know what you're talking about." A note of panic slipped into Megan's voice. It was faint, almost buried, but Jessica detected it. She reached over and took both of Megan's hands. The grip was surprisingly firm.

"Megan, you have something special, something powerful. It's time to share it." She rose then, urging Megan up with her. "Let's have that coffee now, shall we? And we'll talk about it."

An hour later, Megan sat alone in the kitchen. Darkness was encroaching, but she didn't rise from the table to switch on the light. Two cups sat, her own half-filled with now cold coffee,

Jessica's empty but for dregs. She tried to take her mind methodically over what had happened in the last sixty minutes.

A showing at Jessica's, an art gallery in Manhattan. New York. A public show. Of her work.

It didn't happen, she thought. I imagined it. Then she looked down at the empty cup across from her. The air still smelled faintly of Jessica's light, sophisticated scent.

Half-dazed, Megan took both cups to the sink and automatically began rinsing them. How did she talk me into it? she wondered. I was agreeing to dates and details before I had agreed to do the showing. Does anyone ever say no to a Katcherton? She sighed and looked down at her wet hands. I have to call him. The knowledge increased the sense of panic. *I have to.*

Carefully, she placed the washed cups and saucers in the drainboard. I have to thank him. Nerves fluttered in her throat, but she made a pretense, for herself, of casually drying her damp hands on the hips of her jeans. She walked to the wall phone beside the stove.

"It's simple," she whispered, then bit her lip. She cleared her throat. "All I have to do is thank him, that's all. It'll only take a minute." Megan reached for the phone, then drew her hand away. Her mind raced on with her heartbeat.

She lifted the receiver. She knew the number. Hadn't she started to dial it a dozen times during the past two weeks? She took a long breath before pushing the first digit. It would take five minutes, and then, in all probability, she'd have no reason to contact him again. It would be better if they erased the remnants of their last meeting. It would be easier if their relationship ended on a calmer, more civilized note. Megan pressed the last button and waited for the click of connection, the whisper of transmitters and the ring.

It took four rings—four long, endless rings before he picked up the phone.

"Katch." His name was barely audible. She closed her eyes.

"Meg?"

"Yes, I…" She fought herself to speak. "I hope I'm not calling you at a bad time." How trite, she thought desperately. How ordinary.

"Are you all right?" There was concern in the question.

"Yes, yes, of course." Her mind fretted for the simple, casual words she had planned to speak. "Katch, I wanted to talk to you. Your sister was here—"

"I know, she got back a few minutes ago." There was a trace of impatience in his tone. "Is anything wrong?"

"No, nothing's wrong." Her voice refused to level. Megan searched for a quick way to end the conversation.

"Are you alone?"

"Yes, I…"

"I'll be there in ten minutes."

"No." Megan ran a frustrated hand through her hair. "No, please—"

"Ten minutes," he repeated and broke the connection.

chapter nine

Megan stared at the dead receiver for several silent moments. How had she, in a few uncompleted sentences, managed to make such a mess of things? She didn't want him to come. She never wanted to see him again. *That is a lie.*

Carefully, Megan replaced the receiver. I do want to see him, she admitted, have wanted to see him for days. It's just that I'm afraid to see him. Turning, she gazed blindly around the kitchen. The room was almost in complete darkness now. The table and chairs were dark shadows. She walked to the switch, avoiding obstacles with the knowledge of years. The room flooded with brightness. That's better, she thought, more secure in the artificial light. Coffee, she decided, needing something, anything, to occupy her hands. I'll make fresh coffee.

Megan went to the percolator and began a step-by-step preparation, but her nerves continued to jump. In a few moments, she hoped, she'd be calm again. When he arrived, she would say what she needed to say, and then they would part.

The phone rang, and she jolted, juggling the cup she held

and nearly dropping it. Chiding herself, Megan set it down and answered the call.

"Hello, Megan." Pop's voice crackled jovially across the wire.

"Pop…are you still at the park?" What time is it? she wondered distractedly and glanced down at her watch.

"That's why I called. George stopped by. We're going to have dinner in town. I didn't want you to worry."

"I won't." She smiled as the band of tension around her head loosened. "I suppose you and George have a lot of fish stories to exchange."

"His have gotten bigger since he retired," Pop claimed. "Hey, why don't you run into town, sweetheart? We'll treat you."

"You two just want an audience," she accused and her smile deepened with Pop's chuckle. "But I'll pass tonight, thanks. As I recall, there's some leftover spaghetti in the fridge."

"I'll bring you back dessert." It was an old custom. For as long as Megan could remember, if Pop had dinner without her, he'd bring her back some treat. "What do you want?"

"Rainbow sherbet," she decided instantly. "Have a good time."

"I will, darling. Don't work too late."

As she hung up the phone, Megan asked herself why she hadn't told her grandfather of Katch's impending visit. Why hadn't she mentioned Jessica or the incredible plans that had been made? It has to wait until we can talk, she told herself.

Really talk. It's the only way I'll be certain how he really feels—and how everything will affect him.

It's probably a bad idea. Megan began to fret, pushing a hand through her hair in agitation. It's a crazy idea. How can I go to New York and—

Her thoughts were interrupted by the glaring sweep of headlights against the kitchen window. She struggled to compose herself, going deliberately to the cupboard to close it before heading to the screen door.

Katch stepped onto the stoop as she reached for the handle. For a moment, in silence, they studied each other through the mesh. She heard the soft flutter of moths' wings on the outside light.

Finally he turned the knob and opened the door. After he had shut it quietly behind him, he reached up to touch her cheek. His hand lingered there while his eyes traveled her face.

"You sounded upset."

Megan moistened her lips. "No, no, I'm fine." She stepped back so that his palm no longer touched her skin. Slowly, his eyes on hers, Katch lowered his hand. "I'm sorry I bothered you—"

"Megan, stop it." His voice was quiet and controlled. Her eyes came back to his, a little puzzled, a little desperate. "Stop backing away from me. Stop apologizing."

Her hands fluttered once before she could control the movement. "I'm making coffee," she began. "It should be ready in a minute." She would have turned to arrange the cups and saucers, but he took her arm.

"I didn't come for coffee." His hand slid down until it encircled her wrist. Her pulse vibrated against his fingers.

"Katch, please, don't make this difficult."

Something flared in his eyes while she watched. Then it was gone, and her hand was released. "I'm sorry. I've had some difficulty the past couple of weeks dealing with what happened the last time I saw you." He noted the color that shot into her cheeks, but she kept her eyes steady. He slipped his hands into his pockets. "Megan, I'd like to make it up to you."

Megan shook her head, disturbed by the gentleness in his voice, and turned to the coffee pot.

"Don't you want to forgive me?"

The question had her turning back, her eyes darkened with distressed confusion. "No...that is, yes, of course."

"Of course you don't want to forgive me?" There was a faint glimmer of a smile in his eyes and the charm was around his mouth. She could feel herself sinking.

"Yes, of course I forgive you," she corrected and this time did turn to the coffee. "It's forgotten." He laid his hands on her shoulders, and she jumped.

"Is it?" Katch turned her until they were again face-to-face. The glimpse of humor in his eyes was gone. "You can't seem to abide my touching you. I don't much like thinking I frighten you."

She made a conscious effort to relax under his hands. "You don't frighten me, Katch," Megan murmured. "You confuse me. Constantly."

She watched his brow lift in consideration. "I don't have any intention of confusing you. I am sorry, Megan."

"Yes." She smiled, recognizing the simple sincerity. "I know you are."

He drew her closer. "Can we kiss and make up then?"

Megan started to protest, but his mouth was already on hers, light and gentle. Her heart began to hammer in her throat. He made no attempt to deepen the kiss. His hands were easy on her shoulders. Against all the warnings of her mind, she relaxed against him, inviting him to take whatever he chose. But he took no more.

Katch drew her away, waiting until her heavy lids fluttered open before he touched her hair. Without speaking, he turned and paced to the window. Megan struggled to fill the new gap.

"I wanted to talk to you about your sister." She busied her hands with the now noisy percolator. "Or, more accurately, about what Jessica came to see me about."

Katch turned his head, watching her pour the coffee into the waiting cups. He walked to the refrigerator and took out the milk.

"All right." Standing beside her now, he poured milk into one cup and, at her nod, into the second.

"Why didn't you tell me you were sending my work to your sister?"

"I thought it best to wait until I had her opinion." Katch sat beside Megan and cradled the cup in both hands. "I trust her.... And I thought you'd trust her opinion more than mine. Are you going to do the showing? Jessica and I didn't have time to talk before you called."

She shifted in her chair, studied her coffee, then looked directly at him. "She's very persuasive. I was agreeing before I realized it."

"Good," Katch said simply and drank.

"I want to thank you," Meg continued in a stronger voice, "for arranging things."

"I didn't arrange anything," he responded. "Jessica makes her own decisions, personal and professional. I simply sent her your sculptures for an opinion."

"Then I'll thank you for that, for making a move I might never have made for the hundreds of reasons which occurred to me five minutes after she'd left."

Katch shrugged. "All right, if you're determined to be grateful."

"I am," she said. "And I'm scared," she continued, "really terrified at the thought of putting my work on public display." Megan let out a shaky breath at the admission. "I may despise you when all this is over and art critics stomp all over my ego, so you'd better take the gratitude now."

Katch crossed to her, and her heart lifted dizzily, so sure was she that he would take her into his arms. He merely stroked her cheek with the back of his hand. "When you're a smashing success, you can give it to me again." He smiled at her, and the world snapped into sharp focus. Until that moment, she hadn't realized how dull everything had been without him.

"I'm so glad you came," she whispered and, unable to

resist, slipped her arms around him, pressing her face into his shoulder. After a moment, he rested his hands lightly at her waist. "I'm sorry for the things I said…about the loan. I didn't mean any of it really, but I say horrible things when I lose my temper."

"Is this your turn to be penitent?"

He made her laugh. "Yes." She smiled and tilted back her head. Her arms stayed around him. He kissed her and drew away. Reluctantly, she let him slip out of her arms. Then he stood silently, staring down at her.

"What are you doing?" she asked with a quick, self-conscious smile.

"Memorizing your face. Have you eaten?"

She shook her head, wondering why it should come as a surprise that he continued to baffle her. "No, I was going to heat up some leftovers."

"Unacceptable. Want a pizza?"

"*Mmm,* I'd love it, but you have company."

"Jessica and Rob took the kids to play miniature golf. I won't be missed." Katch held out his hands. "Come on."

His eyes were smiling, and her heart was lost. "Oh wait," she began even as she put her hand into his. Quickly, Megan scrawled a message on the chalkboard by the screen door.

OUT WITH KATCH

It was enough.

chapter ten

Katch drove along Ocean Boulevard so they could creep along in the traffic filled with tourists and beachers. Car radios were turned up high and windows rolled down low. Laughter and music poured out everywhere. The lights from a twin Ferris wheel glittered red and blue in the distance. People sat out on their hotel balconies, with colorful beach towels flapping over the railings, as they watched the sluggish flow of cars and pedestrians. To the left, there were glimpses of the sea in between buildings.

Sleepily content after pizza and Chianti, Megan snuggled deeper into the soft leather seat. "Things'll quiet down after this weekend," she commented. "Until Memorial Day."

"Do you ever feel as though you're being invaded?" Katch asked her with a gesture at the clogged traffic.

"I like the crowds," she said immediately, then laughed. "And I like the winter when the beaches are deserted. I suppose there's something about the honky-tonk that appeals to me, especially since I know I'm going to have a few isolated months in the winter."

"That's your time," Katch murmured, glancing back at her. "The time you give yourself for sculpting."

She shrugged, a bit uncomfortable with the intense look. "I do some in the summer, too—when I can. Time's something I forgot when Jessica was talking about a showing and making all those plans…" Megan trailed off, frowning. "I don't know how I can possibly get things ready."

"Not backing out, are you?"

"No, but—" The look in his eyes had her swallowing excuses. "No," she said more firmly. "I'm not backing out."

"What're you working on now?"

"I, ah…" Megan looked fixedly out the window, thinking of the half-formed bust of Katch's head. "It's just…" She shrugged and began to fiddle with the dial of the radio. "It's just a wood carving."

"Of what?"

Megan made a few inarticulate mumbles until Katch turned to grin at her. "A pirate," she decided as the light from a street lamp slanted over his face, throwing it into planes and shadows. "It's the head of a pirate."

His brow lifted at the sudden, narrow-eyed concentration with which she was studying him. "I'd like to see it."

"It's not finished," she said quickly. "I've barely got the clay model done. In any case, I might have to put it off if I'm going to get the rest of my pieces organized for your sister."

"Meg, why don't you stop worrying and just enjoy it?"

Confused, she shook her head and stared at him. "Enjoy it?"

"The show," he said, ruffling her hair.

"Oh, yes." She fought to get her thoughts back into some kind of order. "I will...after it's over," she added with a smile. "Do you think you'll be in New York, then?"

As the rhythm of the traffic picked up, he shifted into third. "I'm considering it."

"I'd like you to be there if you could arrange it." When he laughed, shaking his head, she continued, "It's just that I'm going to need all the friendly faces I can get."

"You're not going to need anything but your sculptures," Katch corrected, but the amusement was still in his eyes. "Don't you think I'd want to be around the night of your opening so that I can brag I discovered you?"

"Let's just hope we both don't live to regret it," Megan muttered, but he only laughed again. "You just can't consider the possibility that you might have made a mistake," she accused testily.

"You can't consider the possibility that you might be successful," he countered.

Megan opened her mouth, then shut it again. "Well," she said after a moment, "we're both right." Waiting until they were stopped in traffic again, Megan touched his shoulder. "Katch?"

"Hmm?"

"Why did you build a hospital in Central Africa?"

He turned to her then, a faint frown between his brows. "It was needed," he said simply.

"Just that?" she persisted, though she could see he wasn't pleased with her question. "I mean, Jessica said you were advised against it, and—"

"As it happens, I have a comfortable amount of money." He cut her off with an annoyed movement of his shoulder. "I do what I choose with it." Seeing her expression, Katch shook his head. "There are things I want to do, that's all. Don't canonize me, Meg."

She relaxed again and found herself brushing at the curls over his ear. "I wouldn't dream of it." He'd rather be thought of as eccentric than benevolent, she mused. And how much simpler it was to love him, knowing that one small secret. "You're much easier to like than I thought you'd be when you made a nuisance of yourself in the market."

"I tried to tell you," he pointed out. "You were too busy pretending you weren't interested."

"I wasn't interested," Megan insisted, "in the least." He turned to grin at her and she found herself laughing. "Well, not very much anyway." When he swung the car onto a side street, she looked back at him in question. "What are you doing?"

"Let's go out on the boardwalk." Expertly, he slid the Porsche into a parking space. "Maybe I'll buy you a souvenir." He was already out of the car—primed, impatient.

"Oh, I love rash promises," Megan crowed as she joined him.

"I said maybe."

"I didn't hear that part. And," she added as she laced her fingers with his, "I want something extravagant."

"Such as?" They jaywalked, maneuvering around stopped cars.

"I'll know when I see it."

The boardwalk was crowded, full of people and light and noise. The breeze off the ocean carried the scent of salt to compete with the aroma of grilling meat from concessions. Instead of going into one of the little shops, Katch pulled Megan into an arcade.

"Big talk about presents and no delivery," Megan said in disgust as Katch exchanged bills for tokens.

"It's early yet. Here." He poured a few tokens into her hand. "Why don't you try your luck at saving the galaxy from invaders?"

With a smirk, Megan chose a machine, then slipped two tokens into the slot. "I'll go first." Pressing the start button, she took the control stick in hand and began systematically to vaporize the enemy. Brows knit, she swung her ship right and left while the machine exploded with color and noise with each hit. Amused, Katch dipped his hands into his pockets and watched her face. It was a more interesting show than the sophisticated graphics.

She chewed her bottom lip while maneuvering into position, narrowing her eyes when a laser blast headed her way. Her breath hissed through her teeth at a narrow escape. But all the while, her face held that composed, almost serious expression that was so much a part of her. Fighting gamely to avoid being blown up in cross fire, Megan's ship at last succumbed.

"Well," Katch murmured, glancing at her score as she wiped her hands on the back of her jeans. "You're pretty good."

"You have to be," Megan returned soberly, "when you're the planet's last hope."

With a chuckle, he nudged her out of the way and took the control.

Megan acknowledged his skill as Katch began to blast away the invaders with as much regularity as she had, and a bit more dash. He likes to take chances, she mused as he narrowly missed being blown apart by laser fire in order to zap three ships in quick succession. As his score mounted, she stepped a bit closer to watch his technique.

At the brush of her arm against his, Megan noticed a quick, almost imperceptible break in his rhythm. Now, that was interesting, she reflected. Feeling an irrepressible surge of mischief, she edged slightly closer. There was another brief fluctuation in his timing. Softly, she touched her lips to his shoulder, then smiled up into his face. She heard rather than saw the explosion that marked his ship's untimely end.

Katch wasn't looking at the screen either, but at her. She saw something flash into his eyes—something hot, barely suppressed, before his hand released the control to dive into her hair.

"Cheat," he murmured.

For a moment, Megan forgot the cacophony of sound, forgot the crowds of people that milled around them. She was lost somewhere in those smoky gray eyes and her own giddy sense of power.

"Cheat?" she repeated, and her lips stayed slightly parted. "I don't know what you mean."

The hand on her hair tightened. He was struggling, she realized, surprised and excited. "I think you do," Katch said quietly. "And I think I'm going to have to be very careful now that you know just what you can do to me."

"Katch." Her gaze lowered to his mouth as the longings built. "Maybe I don't want you to be careful anymore."

Slowly, his hand slid out of her hair, over her cheek, then dropped. "All the more reason I have to be," he muttered. "Come on." He took her arm and propelled her away from the machine. "Let's play something else."

Megan flowed with his mood, content just to be with him. They pumped tokens into machines and competed fiercely—as much with each other as with the computers. Megan felt the same lighthearted ease with him that she'd experienced that night at the carnival. Spending time with him was much like a trip on one of the wild, breathless rides at the park. Quick curves, fast hills, unexpected starts and stops. No one liked the windy power of a roller coaster better than Megan.

Hands on hips, she stood back as he consistently won coupons at Skee Ball. She watched another click off on the already lengthy strip as he tossed the ball neatly into the center hole.

"Don't you ever lose?" she demanded.

Katch tossed the next ball for another forty points. "I try not to make a habit of it. Wanna toss the last two?"

"No." She brushed imaginary lint from her shirt. "You're having such a good time showing off."

With a laugh, Katch dumped the last two balls for ninety points, then leaned over to tear off his stream of coupons. "Just for that, I might not turn these in for your souvenir."

"These?" Megan gave the ream of thin cardboard an arched-brow look. "You were supposed to *buy* me a souvenir."

"I did." He grinned, rolling them up. "Indirectly." Slipping an arm companionably around her shoulder, he walked to the center counter where prizes were displayed. "Let's see... I've got two dozen. How about one of those six-function penknives?"

"Just who's this souvenir for?" Megan asked dryly as she scanned the shelves. "I like that little silk rose." She tapped the glass counter to indicate a small lapel pin. "I have all the tools I need," she added with an impish grin.

"Okay." Katch nodded to the woman behind the counter, then tore off all but four of the tickets. "That leaves us these. Ah..." With a quick scan of the shelves, he pointed. "That."

Thoughtfully, Megan studied the tiny shell figure the woman lifted down. It seemed to be a cross between a duck and a penguin. "What're you going to do with that?"

"Give it to you." Katch handed over the rest of the tickets. "I'm a very generous man."

"I'm overwhelmed," she murmured. Megan turned it over in the palm of her hand as Katch pinned the rose to the collar of her shirt. "But what is it?"

"It's a mallard." Draping his arm over her shoulder again, he led her out of the arcade. "I'm surprised at your attitude. I figured, as an artist, you'd recognize its aesthetic value."

"Hmm." Megan took another study, then slipped it into her pocket. "Well, I do recognize a certain winsome charm. And," she added, rising on her toes to kiss his cheek, "it was sweet of you to spend all your winnings on me."

Smiling, Katch ran a finger down her nose. "Is a kiss on the cheek the best you can do?"

"For a shell penguin it is."

"It's a mallard," he reminded her.

"Whatever." Laughing, Megan slipped an arm around his waist as they crossed the boardwalk and walked down the slope to the beach.

The moon was only a thin slice of white, but the stars were brilliant and mirrored in the water. There was a quiet swish of waves flowing and ebbing over the sand. Lovers walked here and there, arm in arm, talking quietly or not speaking at all. Children dashed along with flashlights bobbing, searching the sand and the surf for treasures.

Bending, Megan slipped out of her shoes and rolled up the hem of her jeans. In silent agreement, Katch followed suit. The water lapped cool over their ankles as they began to walk north, until the laughter and music from the boardwalk was only a background echo.

"Your sister's lovely," Megan said at length. "Just as you said."

"Jessica was always a beauty," he agreed absently. "A little hardheaded, but always a beauty."

"I saw your nieces at the park." Megan lifted her head so that the ocean breeze caught at her hair. "They had chocolate all over their faces."

"Typical." He laughed, running a hand up and down her arm as they walked. Megan felt the blood begin to hum beneath her flesh. "Before they left tonight, they were out digging for worms. I've been drafted to take them fishing tomorrow."

"You like children."

He twisted his head to glance down at her, but Megan was looking out to sea. "Yes. They're a constant adventure, aren't they?"

"I see so many of them in the park every summer, yet they never cease to amaze me." She turned back then with her slow, serious smile hovering on her lips. "And I see a fair number of harassed or long-suffering parents."

"When did you lose yours?"

He saw the flicker of surprise in her eyes before she looked down the stretch of beach again. "I was five."

"It's difficult for you to remember them."

"Yes. I have some vague memories—impressions really, I suppose. Pop has pictures, of course. When I see them, it always surprises me how young they were."

"It must have been hard on you," Katch murmured. "Growing up without them."

The gentleness in his voice had her turning back to him. They'd walked far down the beach so that the only light now came from the stars. His eyes caught the glitter of reflection as they held hers. "It would have been," Megan told him, "without Pop. He did much more than fill in." She stopped to take a step farther into the surf. The water frothed and bubbled over her skin. "One of my best memories is of him struggling to iron this pink organdy party dress. I was eight or nine, I think." With a shake of her head, she laughed and kicked the water. "I can still see him."

Katch's arms came around her waist, drawing her back against him. "So can I."

"He was standing there, struggling with frills and

flounces—and swearing like a sailor because he didn't know I was there. I still love him for that," she murmured. "For just that."

Katch brushed his lips over the top of her hair. "And I imagine you told him not long afterward that you didn't care much for party dresses."

Surprised, Megan turned around. "How did you know that?"

"I know you." Slowly, he traced the shape of her face with his fingertip.

Frowning, she looked beyond his shoulder. "Am I so simple?"

"No." With his fingertip still on her jaw, he turned her face back to his. "You might say I've made a study of you."

She felt her blood begin to churn. "Why?"

Katch shook his head and combed his fingers through her hair. "No questions tonight," he said quietly. "I don't have the answers yet."

"No questions," she agreed, then rose on her toes to meet his mouth with hers.

It was a soft, exploring kiss—a kiss of renewal. Megan could taste the gentleness. For the moment, he seemed to prize her, to find her precious and rare. He held her lightly, as though she would break at the slightest pressure. Her lips parted, and it was she who entered his mouth first, teasing his tongue with hers. His sound of pleasure warmed her. The water swayed, soft and cool, on her calves.

She ran her hands up his back, letting her strong, artist's fingers trail under his hair to caress the nape of his neck. There was tension there, and she murmured against his lips as if to soothe it. Megan felt both his resistance and the tightening of his fingers against her skin. Her body pressed more demandingly into his.

Passion began to smolder quietly. Megan knew she was drawing it from him without his complete consent. The wonder of her own power struck her like a flash. He was holding back, letting her set the pace, but she could feel the near-violence of need in him. It tempted her. She wanted to undermine his control as he had undermined hers. She wanted to make him need as blindly as she needed. It wasn't possible to make him love her, but she could make him want. If it was all she could have from him, then she would be satisfied with his desire.

Megan felt his control slipping. His arms tightened around her, drawing her close so they were silhouetted as one. The kiss grew harder, more urgent. He lifted a hand to her hair, gripping it, pulling her head back as if now he would take command. There was fire now, burning brightly. Heat rose in her, smoking through her blood. She caught his bottom lip between her teeth and heard his quiet moan. Abruptly, he drew her away.

"Meg."

She waited, having no idea what she wanted him to say. Her head was tossed back, her face open to his, her hair free to the breeze. She felt incredibly strong. His eyes were nearly black, searching her face deeply. She could feel his breath feather, warm and uneven, on her lips.

"Meg." He repeated her name, bringing his hands back to her shoulders slowly. "I have to go now."

Daring more than she would have believed possible, Megan pressed her lips to his again. Hers were soft and hungry and drew instant response from him. "Is that what you want?" she murmured. "Do you want to leave me now?"

His fingers tightened on her arms convulsively, then he pulled her away again. "You know the answer to that," he said roughly. "What are you trying to do, make me crazy?"

"Maybe." Desire still churned in her. It smoldered in her eyes as they met his. "Maybe I am."

He caught her against him, close and tight. She could feel the furious race of his heart against hers. His control, she knew, balanced on a razor's edge. Their lips were only a whisper apart.

"There'll be a time," he said softly, "I swear it, when it'll just be you and me. Next time, the very next time, Meg. Remember it."

It took no effort to keep her eyes level with his. The power was still flowing through her. "Is that a warning?"

"Yes," he told her. "That's just what it is."

chapter eleven

It took two more days for Megan to finish the bust of Katch. She tried, when it was time, to divorce herself from emotion and judge it objectively.

She'd been right to choose wood. It was warmer than stone. With her tongue caught between her teeth, she searched for flaws in her workmanship. Megan knew without conceit it was one of her better pieces. Perhaps the best.

The face wasn't stylishly handsome, but strong and compelling. Humor was expressed in the tilt of the brows and mouth. She ran her fingertips over his lips. An incredibly expressive mouth, she mused, remembering the taste and texture. I know just how it looks when he's amused or angry or aroused. And his eyes. Hers drifted up to linger. I know how they look, how they change shades and expression with a mood. Light for pleasure, turning smoky in anger, darker in passion.

I know his face as well as my own…but I still don't know his mind. That's still a stranger. With a sigh she folded her arms on the table and lowered her chin to them.

Would he ever permit me to know him? she wondered. Tenderly, she touched a lock of the disordered hair. Jessica knows him, probably better than anyone else. If he loved someone…

What would happen if I drew up the courage to tell him that I love him? What would happen if I simply walked up to him and said *I love you?* Demanding nothing, expecting nothing. Doesn't he perhaps have the right to know? Isn't love too special, too rare to be closed up? Then Megan imagined his eyes with pity in them.

"I couldn't bear it," she murmured, lowering her forehead to Katch's wooden one. "I just couldn't bear it." A knock interrupted her soul-searching. Quickly, Megan composed her features and swiveled in her chair. "Come in."

Her grandfather entered, his fishing cap perched jauntily on his mane of white hair. "How do you feel about fresh fish for supper?" His grin told her that his early morning expedition had been a success. Megan cocked her head.

"I could probably choke down a few bites." She smiled, pleased to see his eyes sparkling and color in his cheeks. She sprang up and wound her arms around his neck as she had done as a child. "Oh, I love you, Pop!"

"Well, well." He patted her hair, both surprised and pleased. "I love you too, Megan. I guess I should bring you home trout more often."

She lifted her face from the warm curve of his neck and smiled at him. "It doesn't take much to make me happy."

His eyes sobered as he tucked her hair behind her ear. "No…. It never has." His wide, blunt hand touched her cheek. "You've given me so much pleasure over the years, Megan, so much joy. I'm going to miss you when you're in New York."

"Oh, Pop." She buried her face again and clung. "It'll only be for a month or two, then I'll be home." She could smell the cherry-flavored scent of the tobacco he carried in his breast pocket. "You could even come with me—the season'll be over."

"Meg." He stopped her rambling and drew her up so that their eyes met. "This is a start for you. Don't put restrictions on it."

Shaking her head, Megan rose to pace nervously. "I'm not. I don't know what you mean…"

"You're going to make something of yourself, something important. You have talent." Pop glanced around the room at her work until his eyes rested on the bust of Katch. "You've got a life to start. I want you to go after it at full speed."

"You make it sound as if I'm not coming home." Megan turned and, seeing where his eyes rested, clasped her hands together. "I've just finished that." She moistened her lips and struggled to keep her voice casual. "It's rather good, don't you think?"

"Yes, I think it's very good." He looked at her then. "Sit down, Megan, I need to talk to you."

She recognized the tone and tensed. Without a word, she obeyed, going to the chair across from him. Pop waited until she was settled, then studied her face carefully.

"Awhile back," he began, "I told you things change. Most of your life, it's been just the two of us. We needed each other, depended on each other. We had the park to keep a roof over our heads and to give us something to work for." His tone softened. "There hasn't been one minute in the eighteen years I've had you with me that you've been a burden. You've kept me young. I've watched you through all the stages of growing up, and each time, you've made me more proud of you. It's time for the next change."

Because her throat was dry as dust, Megan swallowed. "I don't understand what you're trying to tell me."

"It's time you moved out into the world, Megan, time I let you." Pop reached in the pocket of his shirt and took out carefully folded papers. After spreading them out, he handed them to Megan.

She hesitated before accepting them, her eyes clinging to his. The instant she saw the papers, she knew what they were. But when she read, she read each sentence, each word, until the finish. "So," she said, dry-eyed, dry-voiced. "You've sold it to him."

"When I sign the papers," Pop told her, "and you witness it." He saw the look of devastation in her eyes. "Megan, hear me out. I've given this a lot of thought." Pop took the papers and set them on the table, then gripped her hands. "Katch isn't the first to approach me about selling, and this isn't the first time I've considered it. Everything didn't fit the way I wanted before—this time it does."

"What fits?" she demanded, feeling her eyes fill.

"It's the right man, Meg, the right time." He soothed her hands, hating to watch her distress. "I knew it when all those repairs fell on me. I'm ready to let it go, to let someone younger take over so I can go fishing. That's what I want now,

Megan, a boat and a rod. And he's the man I want taking over." He paused, fumbling in his pocket for a handkerchief to wipe his eyes. "I told you I trusted him and that still holds. Managing the park for Katch won't keep me from my fishing, and I'll have the stimulation without the headaches. And you," he continued, brushing tears from her cheeks, "you need to cut the strings. You can't do what you're meant to do if you're struggling to balance books and make payroll."

"If it's what you want," Megan began, but Pop cut her off.

"No, it has to be what you want. That's why the last lines are still blank." He looked at her with his deep-set eyes sober and quiet. "I won't sign it, Megan, unless you agree. It has to be what's best for both of us."

Megan stood again, and he released her hands to let her walk to the window. At the moment, she was unable to understand her own feelings. She knew agreeing to do a show in New York was a giant step away from the life she had led. And the park was a major part of that life. She knew in order to pursue her own career, she couldn't continue to tie herself to the business end of Joyland.

The park had been security—her responsibility, her second home—as the man behind her had been both mother and father to her. She remembered the look of weariness on his face when he had come to tell her that the park needed money. Megan knew the hours and endless demands that summer would bring.

He was entitled to live his winter years as he chose, she decided. With less worry, less responsibility. He was entitled to fish, and to sleep late and putter around his azaleas. What right did she have to deny him that because she was afraid to cut the last tie with her childhood? He was right, it was time for the change.

Slowly, she walked to her workbox and searched out a pen. Going to Pop, Megan held it out to him. "Sign it. We'll have champagne with the trout."

Pop took the pen, but kept his eyes on her. "Are you sure, Meg?"

She nodded, as sure for him as she was uncertain for herself. "Positive." She smiled and watched the answering light in his eyes before he bent over the paper.

He signed his name with a flourish, then passed her the pen so that she could witness his signature. Megan wrote her name in clear, distinct letters, not allowing her hand to tremble.

"I suppose I should call Katch," Pop mused, sighing as though a weight had been lifted. "Or take the papers to him."

"I'll take them." Carefully, Megan folded them again. "I'd like to talk to him."

"That's a good idea. Take the pickup," he suggested as she headed for the door. "It looks like rain."

Megan was calm by the time she reached Katch's house. The papers were tucked securely in the back pocket of her cut-offs. She pulled the truck behind his car and climbed out.

The air was deadly still and heavy, nearly shimmering with restrained rain. The clouds overhead were black and bulging with it. She walked to the front door and knocked as she had many days before. As before, there was no answer. She walked back down the steps and skirted the house.

There was no sign of him in the yard, no sound but the voice of the sea muffled by the tall hedges. He'd planted a willow, a young, slender one near the slope which led to the beach. The earth was still dark around it, freshly turned. Unable to resist, Megan walked to it, wanting to touch the tender young leaves. It was no taller than she, but she knew one day it would be magnificent...sweeping, graceful, a haven of shade in the summer. Instinct made her continue down the slope to the beach.

Hands in his pockets, he stood, watching the swiftly incoming tide. As if sensing her, he turned.

"I was standing here thinking of you," he said. "Did I wish you here?"

She took the papers and held them out to him. "It's yours," she told him calmly. "Just as you wanted."

He didn't even glance down at the papers, but she saw the shift of expression in his eyes. "I'd like to talk to you, Meg. Let's go inside."

"No." She stepped back to emphasize her refusal. "There really isn't anything more to say."

"That might be true for you, but I have a great deal to say. And you're going to listen." Impatience intruded into his tone. Megan heard it as she felt the sudden gust of wind which broke the calm.

"I don't want to listen to you, Katch. This is what Pop wants, too." She thrust the papers into his hands as the first spear of lightning split the sky. "Take them, will you?"

"Megan, wait." He grabbed her arm as she turned to go. The thunder all but drowned out his words.

"I will not wait!" she tossed back, jerking her arm free. "And stop grabbing me. You have what you wanted—you don't need me anymore."

Katch swore, thrust the papers in his pocket and caught her again before she'd taken three steps. He whirled her back around. "You're not that big an idiot."

"Don't tell me how big an idiot I am." She tried to shake herself loose.

"We have to talk. I have things to say to you. It's important." A gust of wind whipped violently across Megan's face.

"Don't you understand a simple no?" she shouted at him, her voice competing with pounding surf and rising wind. She struggled against his hold. "I don't want to talk. I don't want to hear what you have to say. I don't *care* about what you have to say."

The rain burst from the clouds and poured over them. Instantly, they were drenched.

"Tough," he retorted, every bit as angry as she. "Because you're going to hear it. Now, let's go inside."

He started to pull her across the sand, but she swung violently away and freed herself. Rain gushed down in torrents, sheeting around them. "No!" she shouted. "I won't go inside with you."

"Oh yes you will," he corrected.

"What are you going to do?" she demanded. "Drag me by the hair?"

"Don't tempt me." Katch took her hand again only to have her pull away. "All right," he said. "Enough." In a swift move that caught her off guard, he swept her up into his arms.

"Put me down." Megan wriggled and kicked, blind with fury. He ignored her, dealing with her struggles by shifting her closer and climbing the slope without any apparent effort. Lightning and thunder warred around them. "Oh, I hate you!" she claimed as he walked briskly across the lawn.

"Good. That's a start." Katch pushed open the door with his hip, then continued through the kitchen and into the living room. A trail of rain streamed behind them. Without ceremony, he dumped her on the sofa. "Sit still," he ordered before she could regain her breath, "and just be quiet a minute." He walked to the hearth. Taking a long match, he set fire to the paper waiting beneath kindling and logs. Dry wood crackled and caught almost instantly.

Regaining her breath, Megan rose and bounded for the door. Katch stopped her before her fingers touched the knob. He held her by the shoulders with her back to the door. "I warn you, Meg, my tolerance is at a very low ebb. Don't push me."

"You don't frighten me," she told him, impatiently flipping her dripping hair from her eyes.

"I'm not trying to frighten you. I'm trying to reason with you. But you're too stubborn to shut up and listen."

Her eyes widened with fresh fury. "Don't you talk to me that way! I don't have to take that."

"Yes, you do." Deftly, he reached in her right front pocket and pulled out the truck keys. "As long as I have these."

"I can walk," she tossed back as he pocketed them himself.

"In this rain?"

Megan hugged her arms as she began to shiver. "Let me have my keys."

Instead of answering, he pulled her across the room in front of the fire. "You're freezing. You'll have to get out of those wet clothes."

"I will not. You're crazy if you think I'm going to take off my clothes in your house."

"Suit yourself." He stripped off his own sopping T-shirt and tossed it angrily aside. "You're the most hardheaded, single-minded, stubborn woman I know."

"Thanks." Barely, Megan controlled the urge to sneeze. "Is that all you wanted to say?"

"No." He walked to the fire again. "That's just the beginning—there's a lot more. Sit down."

"Then maybe I'll have my say first." Chills were running over her skin, and she struggled not to tremble. "I was wrong about you in a lot of ways. You're not lazy or careless or glory-seeking. And you were certainly honest with me." She wiped water from her eyes, a mixture of rain and tears. "You told me up front that you intended to have the park, and it seems perhaps for the best. What happened between then and now is my fault for being foolish enough to let you get to me." Megan swallowed, wanting to salvage a little pride. "But then you're a difficult man to ignore. Now you have what you wanted, and it's over and done."

"I only have part of what I wanted." Katch came to her

and gathered her streaming hair in his hand. "Only part, Meg."

She looked at him, too tired to argue. "Can't you just let me be?" she asked.

"Let you be? Do you know how many times I've walked that beach at three in the morning because wanting you kept me awake and aching? Do you know how hard it was for me to let you go every time I had you in my arms?" The fingers in her hair tightened, pulled her closer.

Her eyes were huge now while chills shivered over her skin. *What was he saying?* She couldn't risk asking, couldn't risk wondering. Abruptly, he cursed her and dragged her into his arms.

Thin wet clothes were no barrier to his hands. He molded her breasts even while his mouth ravished hers. She made no protest when he lowered her to the floor, as his fingers worked desperately at the buttons of her blouse. Her chilled wet skin turned to fire under his fingertips. His mouth was hungry, hot as it roamed to her throat and downward.

There was only the crackle of wood and the splash of rain on the windows to mix with their breathing. A log shifted in the grate.

Megan heard him take a long, deep breath. "I'm sorry. I wanted to talk—there are things I need to tell you. But I need you. I've kept it pent up a long time."

Need. Her mind centered on the word. Need was infinitely different from want. Need was more personal—still apart from love—but she let her heart grip the word.

"It's all right." Megan started to sit up, but he leaned over her. Sparks flicked inside her at the touch of naked flesh to naked flesh. "Katch…"

"Please, Meg. Listen to me."

She searched his face, noting the uncharacteristically grave eyes and mouth. Whatever he had to say was important to him. "All right," she said, quieter now, ready. "I'll listen."

"When I first saw you, the first minute, I wanted you. You know that." His voice was low, but without its usual calm. Something boiled just under the surface. "The first night we were together, you intrigued me as much as you attracted me. I thought it would be a simple matter to have you…a casual, pleasant affair for a few weeks."

"I know," she spoke softly, trying not to be wounded by the truth.

"No—shh." He lay a finger over her lips a moment. "You don't know. It stopped being simple almost immediately. When I had you here for dinner, and you asked to stay…" He paused, brushing wet strands of hair from her cheeks. "I couldn't let you, and I wasn't completely sure why. I wanted you—wanted you more than any woman I'd ever touched, any woman I'd ever dreamed about—but I couldn't take you."

"Katch…" Megan shook her head, not certain she was strong enough to hear the words.

"Please." She had closed her eyes, and Katch waited until she opened them again before he continued. "I tried to stay away from you, Meg. I tried to convince myself I was imagining what was happening to me. Then you were charging across the lawn, looking outraged and so beautiful I couldn't think of anything. Just looking at you took my breath away." While she lay motionless, he lifted her hand and pressed it to his lips. The gesture moved her unbearably.

"Don't," she murmured. "Please."

Katch stared into her eyes for a long moment, then released her hand. "I wanted you," he went on in a voice more calm than his eyes. "Needed you, was furious with you because of it." He rested his forehead on hers and shut his eyes. "I never wanted to hurt you, Meg—to frighten you."

Megan lay still, aware of the turmoil in him. Firelight played over the skin on his arms and back.

"It seemed impossible that I could be so involved I couldn't pull away," he continued. "But you were so tangled up in my thoughts, so wound up in my dreams. There wasn't any escape. The other night, after I'd taken you home, I finally admitted to myself I didn't want an escape. Not this time. Not from you." He lifted his head and looked down at her again. "I have something for you, but first I want you to know I'd decided against buying the park until your grandfather came to me last night. I didn't want that between us, but it was what he wanted. What he thought was best for you and for himself. But if it hurts you, I'll tear the papers up."

"No." Megan gave a weary sigh. "I know it's best. It's just like losing someone you love. Even when you know it's the best thing, it still hurts." The outburst seemed to have driven out the fears and the pain. "Please, I don't want you to apologize. I was wrong, coming here this way, shouting at you. Pop has every right to sell the park, and you have every right to buy it." She sighed, wanting explanations over. "I suppose I felt betrayed somehow and didn't want to think it all through."

"And now?"

"And now I'm ashamed of myself for acting like a fool." She managed a weak smile. "I'd like to get up and go home. Pop'll be worried."

"Not just yet." When Katch leaned back on his heels to take something from his pocket, Megan sat up, pushing her wet, tangled hair behind her. He held a box, small and thin. Briefly, he hesitated before offering it to her. Puzzled, both by the gift and by the tension she felt emanating from him, Megan opened it. Her breath caught.

It was a dark, smoky green emerald, square cut and exquisite in its simplicity. Stunned, Megan stared at it, then at Katch. She shook her head wordlessly.

"Katch." Megan shook her head again. "I don't understand...I can't accept this."

"Don't say no, Meg." Katch closed his hand over hers. "I don't handle rejection well." The words were light, but she recognized, and was puzzled by, the strain in the tone. A thought trembled in her brain, and her heart leaped with it.

She tried to be calm and keep her eyes steady on his. "I don't know what you're asking me."

His fingers tightened on hers. "Marry me. I love you."

Emotions ran riot through her. He must be joking, she thought quickly, though no hint of amusement showed in his eyes. His face was so serious, she reflected, and the words so simple. Where were the carelessly witty phrases, the glib charm? Shaken, Megan rose with the box held tightly in her hand. She needed to think.

Marriage. Never had she expected him to ask her to share a lifetime. What would life be like with him? *Like the roller coaster.* She knew it instantly. It would be a fast, furious ride, full of unexpected curves and indescribable thrills. And quiet moments too, she reflected. Precious, solitary moments which would make each new twist and turn more exciting.

Perhaps he had asked her this way, so simply, without any of the frills he could so easily provide because he was as vulnerable as she. What a thought that was! She lifted her fingers to her temple. David Katcherton vulnerable. And yet…Megan remembered what she had seen in his eyes.

I love you. The three simple words, words spoken every day by people everywhere, had changed her life forever. Megan turned, then walking back, knelt beside him. Her eyes were as grave, as searching as his. She held the box out, then spoke quickly as she saw the flicker of desperation.

"It belongs on the third finger of my left hand."

Then she was caught against him, her mouth silenced bruisingly. "Oh, Meg," he murmured her name as he rained kisses on her face. "I thought you were turning me down."

"How could I?" She wound her arms around his neck and tried to stop his roaming mouth with her own. "I love you, Katch." The words were against his lips. "Desperately, completely. I'd prepared myself for a slow death when you were ready to walk away."

"No one's going to walk away now." They lay on the floor

again, and he buried his face in her rain-scented hair. "We'll go to New Orleans. A quick honeymoon before you have to come back and work on the show. In the spring, we'll go to Paris." He lifted his face and looked down on her. "I've thought about you and me in Paris, making love. I want to see your face in the morning when the light's soft."

She touched his cheek. "Soon," she whispered. "Marry me soon. I want to be with you."

He picked up the box that had fallen beside them. Drawing out the ring, he slipped it on her finger. Then, gripping her hand with his, he looked down at her.

"Consider it binding, Meg," he told her huskily. "You can't get away now."

"I'm not going anywhere." She lifted her mouth to meet his kiss.

epilogue

Nervously, Megan twisted the emerald on her finger and tried to drink the champagne Jessica had pushed into her hand. She felt as though the smile had frozen onto her face. People, she thought. She'd never expected so many people. What was she doing, standing in a Manhattan gallery pretending she was an artist? What she wanted to do was creep into the back room and be very, very sick.

"Here now, Meg." Pop strolled over beside her, looking oddly distinguished in his best—and only—black suit. "You should try one of these—tasty little things." He held out a canapé.

"No." Megan felt her stomach roll and shook her head. "No, thanks. I'm so glad you flew up for the weekend."

"Think I'd miss my granddaughter's big night?" He ate the canapé and grinned. "How about this turnout?"

"I feel like an impostor," Megan murmured, smiling gamely as a man in a flowing cape moved past her to study one of her marble pieces.

"Never seen you look prettier." Pop plucked at the sleeve

of her dress, a swirl of watercolored silk. "'Cept maybe at your wedding."

"I wasn't nearly as scared then." She made a quick scan of the crowd and found only strangers. "Where's Katch?"

"Last time I saw him he was cornered by a couple of ritzy-looking people. Didn't I hear Jessica say you were supposed to mingle?"

"Yes." Megan made a small, frustrated sound. "I don't think I can move."

"Now, Meg, I've never known you to be chicken-hearted."

With her mouth half-opened in protest, she watched him walk away. *Chicken-hearted,* she repeated silently. Straightening her shoulders, she drank some champagne. All right then, she decided, she wouldn't stand there cowering in the corner. If she was going to be shot down, she'd face it head on. Moving slowly, and with determined confidence, Megan walked toward the buffet.

"You're the artist, aren't you?"

Megan turned to face a striking old woman in diamonds and black silk. "Yes," she said with a fractional lift of her chin. "I am."

"Hmmm." The woman took Megan in with a long, sweeping glance. "I noticed the study of the girl with the sand castle isn't for sale."

"No, it's my husband's." After two months, the words still brought the familiar warmth to her blood. *Katch, my husband.* Megan's eyes darted around the room to find him.

"A pity," the woman in black commented.

"I beg your pardon?"

"I said it's a pity—I wanted it."

"You—" Stunned, Megan stared at her. "You wanted it?"

"I've purchased 'The Lovers,'" she went on as Megan only gaped. "An excellent piece, but I want to commission you to do another sand castle. I'll contact you through Jessica."

"Yes, of course." *Commission?* Megan thought numbly as she automatically offered her hand. "Thank you," she added as the woman swept away.

"Miriam Tailor Marcus," a voice whispered beside her ear. "A tough nut to crack."

Megan half turned and grabbed Katch's arm. "Katch, that woman, she—"

"Miriam Tailor Marcus," he repeated and bent down to kiss her astonished mouth. "And I heard. I've just been modestly accepting compliments on my contribution to the art world." He touched the rim of his glass to hers. "Congratulations, love."

"They like my work?" she whispered.

"If you hadn't been so busy trying to be invisible, you'd know you're a smashing success. Walk around with me," he told her as he took her hand. "And look at all the little blue dots under your sculptures that mean SOLD."

"They're buying?" Megan gave a wondering laugh as she spotted sale after sale. "They're really buying them?"

"Jessica's frantically trying to keep up. Three people've tried to buy the alabaster piece she bought from you herself— at twice what you charged her. And if you don't talk to a couple of the art critics soon, she's going to go crazy."

"I can't believe it."

"Believe it." He brought Megan's hand to his lips. "I'm very proud of you, Meg."

Tears welled up, threatening to brim over. "I have to get out of here for a minute," she whispered. "Please."

Without a word, Katch maneuvered his way through the crowd, taking Megan into the storage room and shutting the door behind them.

"This is silly," she said immediately as the tears rolled freely down her cheeks. "I'm an idiot. I have everything I've ever dreamed of and I'm crying in the back room. I'd have handled failure better than this."

"Megan." With a soft laugh, he gathered her close. "I love you."

"It doesn't seem real," she said with a quaver in her voice. "Not just the showing…it's everything. I see your ring on my finger and I keep wondering when I'm going to wake up. I can't believe that—"

His mouth silenced her. With a low, melting sigh, she dissolved against him. Even after all the days of her marriage, and all the intimate nights, he could still turn her to putty with only his mouth. The tears vanished as her blood began to swim. Pulling him closer, she let her hands run up the sides of his face and into his hair.

"It's real," he murmured against her mouth. "Believe it." Tilting his head, he changed the angle of the kiss and took her deeper. "It's real every night when you're in my arms, and every morning when you wake there." Katch drew her away slowly, then kissed both her damp cheeks until her lashes fluttered up. "Tonight," he said with a smile, "I'm going to make love to the newest star in the New York art world. And when she's still riding high over the reviews in the morning papers, I'm going to make love to her all over again."

"How soon can we slip away?"

Laughing, he caught her close for a hard kiss. "Don't tempt me. Jessica'd skin us both if we didn't stay until the gallery closes tonight. Now, fix your face and go bask in the admiration for a while. It's good for the soul."

"Katch." Megan stopped him before he could open the door. "There's one piece I didn't put out tonight."

Curious, he lifted a brow. "Oh?"

"Yes, well..." A faint color rose to her cheeks. "I was afraid things might not go well, and I thought I could handle the criticism. But this piece—I knew I couldn't bear to have anyone say it was a poor attempt or amateurish."

Puzzled, he slipped his hands into his pockets. "Have I seen it?"

"No." She shook her head, tossing her bangs out of her eyes. "I'd wanted to give it to you as a wedding present, but everything happened so fast and it wasn't finished. After all," she added with a grin, "we were only engaged for three days."

"Two days longer than if you'd agreed to fly to Vegas," he pointed out. "All in all, I was very patient."

"Be that as it may, I didn't have time until later to finish it. Then I was so nervous about the showing that I couldn't give it to you." She took a deep breath. "I'd like you to have it now, tonight, while I'm feeling—really feeling like an artist."

"Is it here?"

Turning around, Megan reached up on the shelf where the bust was carefully covered in cloth. Wordlessly, she handed it to him. Katch removed the cloth, then stared down into his own face.

Megan had polished the wood very lightly, wanting it to carry that not-quite-civilized aura she perceived in the model. It had his cockiness, his confidence and the warmth the artist had sensed in him before the woman had. He stared at it for so long, she felt the nerves begin to play in her stomach again. Then he looked up, eyes dark, intense.

"Meg."

"I don't want to put it out on display," she said hurriedly. "It's too personal to me. There were times," she began as she took the bust from him and ran a thumb down a cheekbone, "when I was working on the clay model, that I wanted to smash it." With a half-laugh, she set it down on a small table. "I couldn't. When I started it, I told myself the only reason I kept thinking about you was because you had the sort of face I'd like to sculpt." She lifted her eyes then to find his fixed on hers. "I fell in love with you sitting in my studio, while my hands were forming your face." Stepping forward, Megan lifted her hands and traced her fingers over the planes and bones under his flesh. "I thought I couldn't love you more than I did then. I was wrong."

"Meg." Katch brought his hands to hers, pressing her palms to his lips. "You leave me speechless."

"Just love me."

"Always."

"That just might be long enough." Megan sighed as she rested her head against his shoulder. "And I think I'll be able to handle success knowing it."

Katch slipped an arm around her waist as he opened the door. "Let's go have some more champagne. It's a night for celebrations."

★ ★ ★ ★ ★

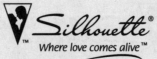

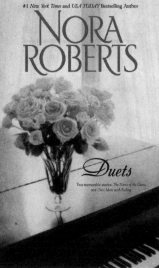